Praise for T

A story about forgiveness and the healing that is achieve[illegible] inside out, The Journal of Hidden Truths is an emotionally hard-hitting novel that deftly tackles many sensitive subjects. Star's character might be unique in the setting of Aspen Creek Junior High, but her outlook and experiences are relevant to contemporary audiences. Vital thematic elements including LGBTQ issues, bullying, mental health, and the way we cope with loss are woven into the novel. Skillfully writing a story with alternating perspectives can be tricky, but Mary Avery Kabrich does an impeccable job of giving Star and Mariah their own distinct voices so that readers are always confident about where they are in the story... Psychological dimension and nuanced sophistication are elegantly revealed in The Journal of Hidden Truths.

—JENNIFER JACKSON, INDIES TODAY

The Journal of Hidden Truths by Mary Avery Kabrich elegantly bridges the realms of coming-of-age and speculative fiction, appealing to a broad audience spanning adults, teens, and young adults... Kabrich showcases her adept writing skills, seamlessly drawing readers into the narrative and cultivating a plot that beckons one to eagerly anticipate the unfolding events... For those seeking a narrative intertwined with mystery, introspection, and a touch of the metaphysical, *The Journal of Hidden Truths* is a commendable choice. Kabrich's narrative talents breathe life into the captivating journey of an enigmatic girl and her pragmatic mother.

—LITERARY TITANS

I haven't read anything by this author before, and what a hidden gem. I enjoyed it so much that I have now followed the author and looked for more books to read. This author has a grand imagination, and talent for showing the story. Mary Avery Kabrich not only tells the story but shows it with words as well. This is an embraceable story. The Journal of Hidden Truths is a definite recommendation by Amy's Bookshelf Reviews.

THE JOURNAL OF HIDDEN TRUTHS

A NOVEL

MARY AVERY KABRICH

OPEN
WINGS
PRESS

The Journal of Hidden Truths

ISBN 978-0-9972332-1-6

Library of Congress Control Number: 2023917823

Designed by *the*BookDesigners

Author may be contacted at mary@maryaverykabrich.com

For Janis. The wind beneath my wings.

THE JOURNAL OF HIDDEN TRUTHS

Prologue

Beneath the mounds of loose cotton blanket lay Star, sprawled on her back like a carefree sunbather. With her fingers spread out and palms open, her lips parted and slightly turned up, she had a look of tender openheartedness.

To Mariah, Star lived in her own galaxy, far away. She leaned forward to smooth the blanket around the mattress edge, gently tucking it in, attempting to secure Star to this universe.

She brought her lips to the exposed forehead, free from the loose curls that typically shielded her round high-cheek-boned face, and stopped short of contact. Her legs gave way, and she was on her knees, her fourteen-year-old self praying for forgiveness.

Except it was from Star, not God, she needed forgiveness. Mariah no longer believed in God.

Chapter 1

My Journal of Hidden Truths
September 12, 2012

Hello, new Journal. Welcome to my crazy world. Guess what? You are special, so I've given you a name—My Journal of Hidden Truths.

Where should I start? You've entered my life during the onslaught of seventh grade. I wasn't the only one nervous about going to junior high. Each time Mom mentioned or even thought of Aspen Creek, I suffered her fear oozing out in shades of blue and gray.

When you arrived for my thirteenth birthday wrapped in my favorite color, purple, I knew Mom planned for you to be special. And you are. An ecological pinnacle—a sign Mom's finally starting to get me. Your cover is made from recycled cork; your pages, also recycled. When I opened you, Mom couldn't hide her grin, and I threw my arms around her.

Now that I'm a teenager, it's time I get serious about life. After all, I'm one year closer to being considered a grown-up. If there was a pill I could swallow making growing up happen faster, I'd take it now. I know what I want to do with my life. Of course I plan to be a scientist, like David Bohm, and specialize in the nature of reality and consciousness. Who wouldn't choose to spend their life uncovering the secrets of the universe?

I'm sitting on the floor leaning against my bed, using my knees as my desk. Forgive me for my sloppy writing.

You're special for reasons more serious than your cool looks and green source. You may be my last journal. I know this sounds creepy. But I have this aching sense that I may not survive this year. Which means you will be around longer than me. So, Journal, I'm writing to more than you. I'm writing to whoever *You* are who may someday read this.

I need to be honest. You are the only one I trust. It's possible I'll meet someone my age who sees and understands the craziness of this world the way I do. But for now, you are all I have. Mom being Mom would freak at the very hint of me being unsettled. Leaving Mountain View and entering Aspen Creek has been a horrifying experience. More later.

Given this potentially ill-fated reality, I'll introduce myself to whoever You are. You probably won't get me, most people don't, but since I'll never meet You, that's okay. My name is Star, like the self-luminous celestial bodies, those twinkling points of light. I named myself when I was two years old. I love hearing the story of how this happened.

My "real" name is Mildred. Can you imagine having such an old-lady name! Mom said she planned on calling me Milly for short. But I'm not a Milly. How is Milly related to Mildred anyway? Weird.

Okay. I must admit, it's cool that Mom took my lead. I don't remember naming myself. But for sure this is not something Mom would make up.

At the time, Jeffrey was only a puppy, and as night set in, Mom took him out for one last potty trip before bedtime. I came along. The sky was a pincushion of stars. More stars than even Mom was used to seeing. The crisp night air had Jeffrey racing in circles around the deck.

Even so, my eyes were glued to the sky, my finger pointing upward. "Mommy, look!" She picked me up so I could be closer, and then as she bounced me on her hip, she began chanting: "Star light, star bright, first star I see tonight, I wish I may, I wish I might, have this wish I wish tonight."

By the time Mom put me to bed, I was chanting this to my stuffed raven. The next day, I insisted she call me Star and had a fit whenever she didn't. Mom was amazed by my determination. Hum. I guess I've always had certain strong feelings. Now I wonder. How could I have known then that my teenaged self would absolutely die of embarrassment to be called Mildred?

Though I don't remember any of this, I can imagine it. Little me, looking at stars and yearning to see the universe from the perspective of a star. Or maybe I simply wanted to be a bright point in the universe. I love how Jeffrey was also little at the time. We both felt the awesome energy of a sky filled with stars.

Here is an interesting fact: In tarot, the star card predicts the future—the card offers hope and possibilities. I've read that it's the most beautiful card. Maybe because hope is beautiful. But since I've never held and examined a real tarot deck, I wouldn't know.

In Ash Grove, they don't sell tarot cards. But they do in Boulder, and someday I'm going to hitch a ride there. It's only five miles away, given enough time I can probably walk it. But this would mean not getting home by the time Mom comes home, and she wouldn't believe me if suddenly I said I stayed after for schoolwork or some stupid school project. And if I said to meet with friends, I'd never hear the end. She'd want to know who and would pester me every day until I told her.

I'm sure she knows kids think I'm weird, she just doesn't want to admit it. Whatever. I'm used to it. Except I can tell it bothers her.

A year ago, I'd have had no reason to take tarot seriously. Since I'm now reading David Bohm's ideas about the implicate order, I think there might be something to tarot. Something that has to do with a favorite word of mine—*synchronicity*! A word I love for more reasons than its beautiful five syllables. A word Mom is clueless about. Case in point:

"Mom, I saw this way cool unusual butterfly while walking to school."

She replied in her stern-mom voice, "You weren't in the forest, were you?"

"Of course not." I crossed my fingers because how could I see any kind of amazing anything *outside* the forest? "It was so rad I had to google it—orange wings, small black patches with a green tinge, and light silver streaks. I found it online, it's called a Mormon Fritillary. Odd name, right?"

"Hum. Yes, odd name. Your description sounds like a monarch. I've never heard of a Mormon Fritillary."

"Me neither. This is the amazing part." And then I lowered my voice and said, "As in, synchronicity."

Mom gave a partial smile that more or less said, "Oh, this nonsense again." She might have grasped the significance of it if I told her that I seldom choose to eat my lunch in the stupid cafeteria. Yet that day something came over me and I actually felt like hanging out. Which I also didn't want to share with Mom. I mean, likely she knows I rarely hang out with others. But I'm sure she doesn't know I *never* hang out with anyone. That is, students. I mingle with birds and chipmunks in the forest.

"That *same* day, I sat next to a girl during lunch who started talking about Mormons!" I gave Mom my surprised look to cue her in. It didn't work. She merely raised her eyebrows as if waiting for the punch line. "Don't you get it? I see the most unusual butterfly ever, discover its name, which I'd never heard of, and what are the chances that I sit next to a girl who starts talking about Mormons?"

Mom's lame response: "Who was this girl? What did she say about Mormons?"

I had no idea who she was. I sat down, heard her talking about Mormons, and, like the butterfly who flew away upon a closer look, she gave me a "get lost" glare and took off with her friends.

"Mom, she was just some random girl I sat next to. You're missing the point. This was just one of many examples of synchronicity."

The day I met Mr. Seng, my only friend who understands me, this too was synchronicity. I had been thinking about how weird it was our school didn't recycle, and that same day, my teacher introduced me to Mr. Seng, who I sort of knew, our custodian at Mountain View. But I'm sure Ms. Caper didn't know I wanted to meet someone just like him. When we met and I learned he needed a helper to get recycling going, I blurted out, "This is synchronicity!" I'll never forget the exploding warmth of his smile—flooding my chest, making me want to dance, which of course I didn't do.

My favorite part of the school day was spending lunch recess with him. I'd help with sorting lunch compost and recycling, and he'd tell me about the mind-blowing ideas of David Bohm. Mr. Seng is the smartest man I know. A professor of physics in Cambodia before moving to California because he had to leave his country. Then, because he wanted to, he moved to Ash Grove. Before I graduated to junior high, he gave me David Bohm's book *Wholeness and the Implicate Order.*

On my way to school today, I was thinking about a conversation I had with Mr. Seng about *bardo*, the Tibetan word for an in-between state. This is the place souls go when they're not ready to move on to whatever is next. And this morning, Jeffrey showed up in my first class of the day, Mrs. Severson's class. She caught me talking to him. For sure, I freaked her out.

Poor Jeffrey, he's missing me and having a hard time. I somehow arrived fifteen minutes early and discovered Mrs. Severson's classroom was open. I'd much rather settle into my desk and read David Bohm than hang around the lockers. When I read *Wholeness and the Implicate Order*, I'll confess to you, Journal, there is a lot I don't get. I'm okay with this. I know someday I will understand. In the meantime, I can imagine Mr. Seng also reading David Bohm, and this makes me feel close, as if we're still having conversations.

Mr. Seng understood how important Jeffrey was to me. When Jeffrey died last spring, I missed an entire week of school. Mr. Seng wouldn't be at all surprised Jeffrey came back to visit; he understands about souls searching for what's next. And what David Bohm knows—the hidden truth of reality is that it's one big pulsing wave of connected particles.

I needed to let Jeffrey know he couldn't be my dog again. For his sake, even though I'm not sure I believe in reincarnation, I told him he could choose to come back in any form he wanted. Except I warned him, being a girl is not as fun as being a boy and being a human may not be as much fun as being a bird or a cat or even a dog—unless you end up in the wrong family. Mrs. Severson came in without me noticing. Jeffrey was listening, and I had to make sure he understood. He must have. I haven't seen him since.

Chapter 2

The call came ten minutes before her shift at Behavioral Health Professionals was officially over. The six-member hoarder/clutter support group had finished their final round of sharing, ending with Georgie's ritual bellowing in her throaty voice, "Messies, be gone!"

Amid the shuffling of chairs and bits of unfinished conversation, Mariah heard the ringtone chiming in her pocket. Across the cell's screen paraded "Aspen Creek Junior High." She took a deep breath; she had been bracing herself for a phone call ever since school started. Star's recent transition from elementary school to junior high was a change Mariah had dreaded a full year in advance.

"Hello?"

"Is this Ms. Palmer?"

"Yes."

"This is Chad Petersen," the voice said. "From the counseling office."

Her muscles tensed. Of course, the head counselor for seventh grade. She had sought him out during curriculum night, introducing herself as the mother of a bright, misunderstood child. He had worn a baby-blue dress shirt that stretched at the buttons, and his thin strands of russet hair were combed neatly, framing his full face. She had wondered if he had kids. He was certainly too young to have a child in junior high school.

"Are you available to meet?" The quiver in his voice made her stomach drop.

"One moment, please." She pulled the phone away from her face. *This is* not *unexpected. Stay calm.* She scanned the group of middle-aged women gathering their belongings and called out to them, "Good session."

They came to a stop and turned toward her. They must have sensed the adrenaline coursing through her.

"See you all back next week," she said. "Remember, before making any buying decisions, ask yourself the four key questions."

The women nodded, and she moved toward the conference room. She slowed her breathing and returned the phone to her ear. "Okay . . . are you saying meet now? Is . . . is this an emergency?"

"Well . . . no. Just a few concerns. But if you can come now, that would be ideal. Mr. Jiles and Mrs. Hadley can also be available." He sounded breathless. She had no recollection of Mr. Jiles or Mrs. Hadley. "We work as a team. The three of us. Counselors."

"I can be there in ten minutes." Mariah glanced at her watch. It was 3:20. Star was home by now, most likely online, chatting with various internet friends, or writing in her journal. She pulled up Star's number. But what could she say? She shoved the phone back into her purse, gathered her things, and headed to the parking lot.

Her hand trembled as she attempted to insert her key into the ignition. She steadied her focus and tried a second time.

Aspen Creek's parking lot stretched across an expanse of pavement vast enough to consume all of Mountain View Elementary. She recalled her own transition from a grade school of two hundred in Daphne to South Pasadena Junior High, with a thousand-plus students. In Daphne, all the girls dressed in variations of the same. But at South Pasadena, she encountered fresh, exciting styles. Her mother, under the influence of Reverend Eddie, made sure she stayed in tune with Daphne's dress code.

Entering the main office at Aspen Creek, she knew the drill—she had been a regular visitor at Mountain View Elementary. Once signed in, Mariah was escorted by a prim secretary down the hall into an office suite adorned with motivational posters.

The three-member counseling team rose to greet her: A woman with long coffee-colored hair peppered with streaks of gray, who might, like Mariah, be at least forty. Mr. Petersen, whom she recognized—not wearing the baby-blue shirt, but a different dress shirt that didn't quite button comfortably. And another rather young man—early twenties, with dark hair slicked back, like a younger version of Leonardo DiCaprio.

She settled into a cushioned chair beside the woman. A poster on the wall featured a quote from Einstein: "In the middle of difficulty lies opportunity." She stopped herself from rolling her eyes. With a neutral expression, she listened to introductions and pronouncements of how effectively they worked as a team, supporting all 634 seventh and eighth graders.

Abruptly, head counselor Mr. Petersen said, "Allow me to be direct, Ms. Palmer." Mrs. Hadley and Mr. Jiles trained their gaze in unison first toward Mr. Petersen and then back to her. "Mildred—"

"She goes by Star." Mariah straightened her back.

Star's father, Charlie, had insisted on naming their daughter Mildred (though Mariah had idly fantasized about Hannah, Jessica, or Kaitlin). Mildred was the name of Charlie's older sister who had died of a brain tumor when he was just ten years old. Mariah had ultimately agreed, taking comfort in learning from Charlie that the Old English origin of the name meant "gentle strength," and this was the role his sister had played in his life. With time, the name grew on Mariah. Combined with knowing that little Mildred would be Milly for short. She could still hear the cry of joy Charlie shouted as he first held his daughter, see his blue eyes spilling with tears and a grin so deep and wide the entire room radiated. The memory dwelt in a painful, sealed-off chamber of her heart.

It was after Mariah and her daughter had moved to Ash Grove that Milly insisted on a new name. And though Mariah had thought the chosen name would be temporary, her daughter's conviction never wavered, and she had been Star ever since.

"Excuse me," Mr. Petersen said. "Yes. *Star* has had several . . ." He seemed to be searching for the right word. "Incidents, which are concerning to us."

Her belly somersaulted. She kept her lips tight.

"Taken together, it suggests a child who is crying out for help. We wanted you to be aware. And, in all honesty, consider an evaluation and counseling."

"Wait a minute, Chad." She leaned forward. "Excuse me. Mr. Petersen. Do you remember me from curriculum night?"

"I'm afraid not. I'm sorry. I was introduced to so many parents."

"I'm the parent who explained that my daughter is easily mistaken as being imbalanced, when actually she's extremely sensitive and quite bright." Was her voice too shrill? No one made a peep. She met their eyes before continuing. "Okay, what has Star done to lead you to conclude she is mentally unstable?" Her face flushed; she cringed.

"Ms. Palmer, I'm sorry," Mrs. Hadley began. "Mr. Petersen didn't mean to be so abrupt."

"Mrs. Hadley's right. I apologize. Let me begin again." He leaned forward. "Several of Star's teachers have come to us with concerns. We wouldn't be doing our job if we didn't communicate this with you." He glanced at the other two counselors before continuing. "Mrs. Severson, Star's social studies teacher, came to us yesterday, clearly shaken by what she observed." He paused; the silence was tormenting. "She had left her classroom door open. When she returned, she heard Star talking and was surprised to find Star alone and distraught. Mrs. Severson said her name multiple times before Star turned and acknowledged her. Star appeared disoriented. Mrs. Severson was concerned Star may be using drugs."

Mariah's throat went dry; for a long moment she couldn't swallow. She heard herself sputtering. "No. No. Not Star. She's a health food nut—vegetarian, no additives, she doesn't even eat sugar. Believe me, I would know if my daughter had a drug problem." Then she thought to ask, "Did she call her Star?" Although Star would have answered to her birth name, Mildred, with a rash of correction.

"Um, I believe so," he said. "I observed Star and agree. She doesn't fit the profile of a youth experimenting with drugs." Mr. Petersen paused as if to expand his air of authority. "She said she was talking to her dog, and, well, she shut out Mrs. Severson because she wanted to make sure her dog understood what she was saying." Mr. Petersen molded his face into a less-than-sincere look of concern.

Of course. Star had mentioned that Jeffrey was visiting her. "Star's highly imaginative," Mariah said. "She had Jeffrey, our dog, most of her life, he died six months ago. Now she's in a new school and misses her dog. There's nothing *crazy* about this."

Mrs. Hadley reached out with a limp hand, perhaps to rest on Mariah's wrist, and then withdrew it. Instead, she spoke in a matronly tone. "This is not at all what we mean, we don't think your daughter's *crazy*."

"Star's a very bright girl," chimed in Mr. Petersen, "and we want to make sure she's getting all her needs met." Another heavy pause.

Mariah arched her shoulders back, stretched her spine upward, and sat at least an inch taller.

"This afternoon, Mr. Haze—her science teacher—approached us." Mr. Petersen turned to the young counselor, Mr. Jiles, who sported a blue-and-white-striped shirt and smiled as if he were on stage. Mariah's chest tightened.

"Yes," Mr. Jiles said, "Mr. Haze described Star as a quiet student who seems to easily grasp the concepts."

Mariah repositioned herself, preparing to hear the rest.

"Evidently, during a science experiment, all six of her test tubes shattered, creating quite the commotion. It's not unusual for a single test tube to drop to the floor or get bumped, but Mr. Haze said the only way this could have happened is if she had crashed into them. Star claimed she had nothing to do with it."

Mariah asked, "What did her classmates say? Did they see her break them?"

"No one saw her, she was the only one working at that station."

Mariah wanted to scream, *Why had Star been alone?* But an unease washed over her. Just last week a favorite glazed piece of pottery used as a serving bowl had fallen off the counter as Star walked by. Star claimed not to have touched it. But she must have bumped it—like the test tubes. She often got distracted.

Mariah turned to Mr. Petersen. "There's more?" Her voice, high pitched, revealed the distress she had tried to conceal. Her face reddened.

"This morning, during social studies, while Mrs. Severson reviewed the next assignment, Star had her head down. She was sobbing. Mrs. Severson asked Star if she'd like to come to our office. Star refused and pulled herself together. After class, Mrs. Severson tried to find out what was going on. Star reported having no idea why she had felt sad."

Mariah envisioned a class full of gawking seventh graders watching Star in disarray. Star had always cried easily over things most people hardly notice—a squirrel dead on the side of the road—but in school? This was new. Or perhaps *this* was what her teachers at Mountain View had meant each time they proclaimed how sensitive Star was.

Mariah said, "She's thirteen. And junior high is a big transition." She held back from adding that kindergarten had been a complete disaster, and first grade equally so. "Her teachers at Mountain View understood her, and she did well." The counselors' faces, expectant, pressed into her. Clearly waiting for some admission of tragedy or dysfunctional family dynamics to account for Star's behavior.

She glared at Mr. Petersen and, in a voice solid and unwavering, said, "I work in mental health. I would know if my daughter needed professional help. What I do know is that your concerns pose a serious risk for Star, and I will not let you label her." Her body trembled, inflaming her anger.

Mr. Petersen tightened his lips and said nothing. Mrs. Hadley's eyes grew watery—certainly not out of compassion for Star but for the parent in front of her refusing to believe there was a problem. And Mr. Jiles—she detected a smirk across his handsome young face.

She stood and stepped toward the door, only to turn back before walking out. "You have misjudged my daughter. You have no idea how bright and talented she is."

Chapter 3

Mariah strode across the parking lot toward her sedan. Orange berries from a nearby mountain ash pelted the ground with startling urgency. At least she had left the meeting on her own terms. She had been raised to fit in and follow rules, but the need to become her daughter's advocate had toughened a part of her that had lain dormant throughout most of her life.

Mariah had known from day one that Star was special. Star entered the world in a state of perpetual discomfort, as though she previously belonged to a realm without sensory intrusions. Noises too loud, lights too bright, and clothing that clung would prompt a spasm of wails. By age two, she seemed a fully formed adult, frustrated with the limitations of a child's body and mind. She would point and babble as if on a podium, and when the response didn't match her expectations, she'd collapse into a tantrum.

She struggled to adjust to preschool socially, preferring to play by herself, and since she had learned to read at age four, kindergarten bored her. Her refusal to participate in most activities and her lack of friends prompted the school to recommend she be assessed for special education. She would have qualified in social delays. But Mariah refused to consent to having her daughter evaluated and labeled.

In first grade, when the school counselor attributed Star's irritability and moodiness to childhood depression, Mariah advocated for a different view—Star was a bright child who expressed her boredom with irritation. Mariah's outward confidence belied a tormenting fear that she had played a role in creating the conditions that gave rise to her daughter's unusual behaviors.

Now, as Mariah slid into the silver Honda, she palmed her phone. There was no reason to call Star; this was the time Mariah would typically leave work. But she couldn't shake the image of Star sobbing in social studies class for no apparent reason. She put the phone down and started the car. From the forest at the edge of the parking lot, four kids Star's age emerged, several of them stomping out cigarette butts. *My God, they could be Star's classmates.*

Farland Park, as the forest was officially known, was a six-acre expanse of lush old-growth pine, aspen, and ash—a nature reserve for all kinds of fowl, deer, fox, and even coyotes—that had greeted Mariah as a welcome-home invitation, sealing her decision to move twelve years ago. But later, Mariah became aware of a more sinister reputation for the tangle of woods and ravines. Parents warned that beyond the perimeter, where one could hear the busy chatter of birds, lurked drug dealers, rapists, and the occasional gun-toting maniac. And now the forest lazed in daring allure between home and Star's new school. Mariah strictly forbade Star from roaming through its tempting tangles of greenery.

As she pulled out of the parking lot, Mariah wondered whether Star had any friends who smoked. Growing up, Mariah had been a model student and daughter, and cigarettes were repugnant to her. She had vowed at an early age never to smoke. Her mother reinforced this vow and eventually kicked her own habit, blamed squarely on Mariah's father. "I had no idea how addictive they were. He went from one compulsion to the next. Smoking was the only habit that rubbed off on me. Don't you ever try these." And later, "Quitting cigarettes was the hardest task I've ever faced. A whole lot harder than letting go of your father."

Thus, Mariah's foray into smoking as a teen had been innocent. Unexpected. The purchase of her first pack signified her most daring deed. She was fifteen. Upon inhaling a lungful of burning vapor, her head spun, euphoria enveloped her, and at once she understood why her mother had chosen to smoke. A lit cigarette casually resting between her fingers provided a needed slice of popularity with a tang of defiance.

She had hoped to impress Devin, a lanky boy with penetrating blue eyes, and made a point of revealing the cigarettes in her purse during social studies class. He had leaned over, whispered—by chance did she have an extra pen? He pointed to his paper of faded ink, and she seized the opportunity to counter the good-girl perception she was trying so hard to shed. She opened her bag, making sure he saw the pack of Marlboros as she pulled out the ballpoint pen. In return she caught his expression of surprise and disapproval—as if her mother had peered into her purse.

Once alone, she tried to dismiss him along with the half-used pack of cigarettes that she tossed into a wastebasket. Later, she would thank him for keeping her from developing the full-blown habit. Mariah's father, according to her mother, had struggled with all kinds of addictions. Which, in theory, put both her and Star at risk.

Mariah pulled into the driveway of their two-bedroom bungalow nestled among juniper and maples. She savored coming home to her little refuge, away from the world. The surrounding low hills gave way to the distant jutting peaks of the Rocky Mountains. The small square house with a miniature deck and a patch of grass easily trimmed with a push mower had met her criteria twelve years ago—simple and solitary. A fresh promise to a new beginning. Charlie had been her rock. Even with fate's brutality, Charlie's life insurance had provided.

"Be sensible." Her mother had harped and then pleaded, "You can't raise my only grandchild five thousand miles away." Mariah pointed out that Colorado was one thousand miles away, not five, and a mere sixteen-hour road trip. To no avail. Olivia could not grasp Mariah's need to take complete charge of her life. Even in the wake of disaster.

As she stepped inside, she half expected to encounter an enthusiastic

Jeffrey. His chubby cockapoo body wiggling like Jell-O, the stub of his tail propelling him in circles. He'd whimper a welcome, which, until this year, would send Star out from her room to join in. But the house was silent, the living room empty. Hanging up her coat failed to lighten the heaviness that had lodged within her.

She entered the galley kitchen and saw a peanut-butter-encrusted knife left on the counter, a breakfast cereal bowl with an inch of milk and soggy Cheerios, a half-empty glass of juice. Mariah had emptied the dishwasher that morning, making it easy for Star to clean up after herself. She sighed. But the image of Star sobbing in social studies softened her annoyance.

A small shaft of light streamed from the bottom of Star's bedroom door. Mariah knocked and entered. Star sat on the floor with her back propped against her bed, her long legs triangled up, her eco-friendly cork-covered journal resting on her thighs. Late-afternoon light filtered through the chiffon curtains behind her, casting shadows.

Mariah slipped out of her shoes, tiptoed to Star, and knelt to be at eye level with her daughter's pale face. Star closed her journal. Mariah allowed the silence to settle around them. She waited until Star turned toward her.

"Star," she began. "I'm worried. I met with Mr. Petersen and the other counselors."

Star's eyes widened and then turned downward. "What'd they tell you?"

"They're worried."

"Why is everyone worried? I'm getting good grades, isn't this what school's supposed to be about?"

"Yes . . . but they told me about how sad you were in Mrs. Severson's class."

"Mom, I just get sad about some things. I can't help it. Besides, this happened all the time at Mountain View, and everyone knew I needed to be left alone." She looked up with pleading eyes. Mariah tried to remember if any of Star's former teachers had discussed this with her.

"And the problem with breaking test tubes?"

Star stared wide-eyed into the vast space between them. Mariah forced a calming breath.

"No one understands!" Star's tense face collapsed, and she burst into tears. Her head tilted forward into her hands, thick wavy auburn hair cascading, shielding her wet face from Mariah.

Mariah leaned into Star's shoulder. "Sweetheart, we want to help. It's not normal to all at once be so sad in class. And the test tubes, well, I imagine that was an embarrassing accident."

"I didn't do it. They just broke. No one believes me."

Mariah extended her arm around Star's shoulders and pulled her in close. When Star's breathing returned to normal, she asked, "Sweetie, is there something bothering you? Would you like me to find someone you can talk to?"

"A shrink?" Star pulled away, looking startled, wounded.

"Not necessarily. It's just, I don't want you to be so alone. It can be helpful sharing feelings with someone other than your mother."

Star shifted her gaze to the journal sitting beside her. It had been a long time since she had disclosed anything personal with Mariah. They had gotten into a rhythm of coming, going, eating, and cleaning up, devoid of meaningful conversation. Growing up as the only child of a single parent, Mariah had loathed being in the never-ending spotlight. When she was Star's age, as other children raced home after getting off the school bus, Mariah would meander home, resisting her mother's effusive greeting followed by a barrage of questions. Now, Mariah deliberately gave Star space. Perhaps too much.

"I have my online friends."

"That's not what I mean."

Star sighed and pronounced with exasperation, "Mom, I'm okay." She flung her head away, leaving Mariah to face a wall of auburn curls and the unsettling silence that draped between them.

Chapter 4

The first glimmers of light silhouetted hills and trees as Mariah headed to work the next morning. She smiled inwardly at the note she had left next to the box of Cheerios: "Star light, Star bright, I love you with all my might. Have a nice day." This was not a morning to remind Star of chores.

How could she lure Star from her bedroom into an extended dinner hour that evening? And then what? A meal surrounded by silence and the pall of unasked questions: Do you still see Jeffrey? Did you get angry in science? And the question that pained her the most, the one she knew the answer to: Do you have any friends at school?

Mariah's heart ached. Star needed real friends, not unseen, unknown, virtual people who called themselves friends.

Once parked, she stared ahead at the sprawling seventies-style building that housed Behavioral Health Professionals. She sighed and glanced at her watch. By now Star would be out of the shower, perhaps discovering her note. She unbuckled her seat belt and caught sight of Gretchen Higgins's sturdy frame striding toward the entrance to BHP. Mariah stayed seated, waiting for Gretchen to pass through the front doors.

Mariah had met Gretchen when Star was in preschool, and it was thanks to her that Mariah was finally able, once Star entered first grade, to use her hard-earned psychology degree. Prior, she'd had no choice but to tend to Star's social-emotional needs. She worked half days at Star's day care, making little above minimum wage despite her master's degree.

Her relationship with Gretchen had started out on equal footing, navigating the explosive territory of their four-year-old girls. Except even then, Gretchen had an edge on Mariah. Tilly was her youngest—clearly Gretchen had learned a thing or two with her older daughter, Tamara.

Watching their girls playing in preschool one day, Gretchen said, referring to Star, "She seems incredibly creative. Look, all the other girls are trying to dress up as princesses, and your daughter—"

"Star."

"Wonderful name." Code for *unusual*; Mariah wouldn't dare venture into the fact that Star had named herself. "Star is dressing up as . . . it's hard to say, maybe a clown pretending to be a dog?"

"She loves animals. I bet if you asked, she'd say Jeffrey, our dog."

Later, relief had washed over Mariah when she discovered that the girls would attend different elementary schools. A series of unsuccessful playdates made it clear: the only thing Star and Tilly had in common was age. Now, the two of them were assigned to the only public junior high school in Ash Grove—a large, rambling complex, half of which wrapped around the forest.

It seemed eons ago she and Gretchen sat side by side in a huge auditorium filled with anxious parents whose children were slated to attend Aspen Creek. Did Star have any classes with Tilly? Could it be, after all these years, change had occurred in ways that an alliance could be possible?

Two days ago, Gretchen had been in hysterics over Tilly's failure to make the drill team. Mariah summoned an empathetic response to this perceived catastrophe. Now she found it amusing to imagine Gretchen's reaction to the reason why Mariah had raced off from work the day before. Yes, it was just yesterday she had faced three school counselors who believed her daughter needed a mental health evaluation. This would surely top Gretchen's notion of a family crisis.

Gretchen was a stout woman, about Mariah's height, with bleached-blond hair pulled neatly back in a ponytail. She radiated a confidence

Mariah herself could only imitate. Perhaps, unlike her daughter, Gretchen had made the drill team—or maybe she had been one of those popular cheerleaders. Gretchen's clients clearly had to sense her certainty about life and benefit from working with someone capable of joining them, illuminating a multitude of solutions to the torment of their lives.

Mariah rifled through her briefcase and pulled out her schedule, relieved to see one less support group today. The groups drained her, especially the hoarders. She herself loathed messiness. Tidy was her pathology—if such existed. The opposite of Star, who flung excess clothing off here and there as she made her way toward her bedroom sanctuary. Years ago, Mariah had learned simply to gather the errant clothes and toss them into Star's room rather than pick a battle.

Inside BHP, within striking distance of her office, Gretchen's cheery voice called out, "Good morning!" Mariah turned and greeted Gretchen's expectant round face. Mariah generated a smile. "Oops," Gretchen said, "didn't mean to startle you."

"Oh, it's nothing. Too much caffeine this morning. Makes me jumpy."

"I had to give that drug up a decade ago—I was jumping out of my skin."

Mariah nodded, forcing the smile to stay in place.

"I missed you yesterday at the safety committee. I heard you left early."

"Oh, I'm so sorry. I completely forgot." This was the truth. Yet remembering wouldn't have changed the outcome. Her mind raced. She hated lying—thanks to Reverend Eddie, even the mildest lie conjured the horror of bodies burning in hell. "By the time my group ended, it was all I could do to stay standing. Felt a migraine coming on."

"You didn't miss anything. Clarissa couldn't make it either, so we canceled. You're here, so clearly you did the right thing."

"I should've called." This, she was sincere about. "I've learned over the years to take the symptoms seriously." Guilt churned inside her as she took in Gretchen's sympathetic eyes. Steeling herself, Mariah asked her least favorite question, "How's Tilly doing?" She even managed to say it with a lilt to her voice.

"Well, she's gotten over it."

"Such a huge disappointment."

"The painful part is the girl who won her spot was her best friend, Chrystal."

"Ouch."

"A while back, that is."

Mariah nodded. Best-friend drama had sadly not entered her daughter's life.

"Yeah. They were as thick as thieves until last year when Chrystal's family joined the Unitarian church."

"Unitarian?" Mariah surprised herself with the inquiry. Early on, sensing Gretchen's traditional churchiness, she had made it clear she was not a churchgoing person and did not want to hear about church activities. She had tried to couch her preference in an air of professionalism, but Gretchen had seemed to distance herself after that. Which Mariah had taken comfort in.

"It's a one-size-fits-all sort of church." Gretchen rolled her eyes as she pronounced *church* in a surly way.

Mariah cocked her head, wordlessly asking, *Really?*

"They profess to believe in everything except God."

"That's odd," Mariah said, but she was intrigued. "I thought God and church were one and the same."

"Not to the Unitarians. They take acceptance to an extreme, welcoming atheists, pagans, you name it. And, I suppose, Christians. Poor Chrystal evidently tried the whole smorgasbord. Thankfully I have a close relationship with Tilly."

Mariah murmured a neutral "Hum," and stopped herself from stating that she too had a close relationship with her daughter.

"So how is Star doing?"

"You know, junior high is such a big change—"

"Oh my God, yes! As is turning thirteen. I'll admit, Tilly's become so hormonal. Dare I say histrionic?"

"Oh yeah. Star too."

"Well," Gretchen said. "I'm grateful to have the community of a *real* church. So is Tilly." Gretchen's pat smile and a nod assumed agreement. "I simply can't imagine how young people navigate the world of pulsing hormones and temptation without guidance."

Again, the specter of Reverend Eddie haunted Mariah. She had followed the guidance. That is, until she met Devin.

She yanked her cell phone out to check the time. And although she had plenty of time before settling in with her client, she reported, "Oops, my first client arrives in five minutes."

In her spartan office, as she opened the blinds, the word Unitarian echoed in her mind. Had she heard correctly? A church in which God was not necessary?

The morning passed slowly. Her first client spoke in his measured way about his loss—divorce—so different from her own. And then her next client aired her usual list of grievances against her husband. Once lunchtime came, it was a welcome relief.

She entered the bright cafeteria, a fluorescently lit rectangular box of a room with Formica countertops. Mariah grabbed the bottle of balsamic vinaigrette from the fridge for the salad she brought each day. If lunch represented her other meals, she'd be a good twenty pounds lighter. The evenings with the glass or two of wine and the noshing were what prevented her from losing the weight she'd fantasized releasing.

In the center of the room were two square tables pushed together with a copy of the *Boulder Weekly* splayed out in sections. Mariah pulled a piece of the newspaper toward her while ruminating on yesterday's meeting and Star's upset response to her inquiries. Several others sat at the opposite corner chatting in a sophomoric trill. She nibbled at the pile of greens, eyeing the paper as a ruse to hide her simmering discontent.

Halfway through her lunch, Richard Stevens swung through the cafeteria doors whistling. He had an annoying way of drawing attention to himself. Today the distraction was welcome. He plopped down across from her with a worn paper sack from which he drew out a sandwich. She met his eyes, and an undeterred smile claimed her face. She braced herself for his bid of engagement as he reached for the paper.

"Did you hear about the attempted teen suicide behind Boulder Junior High?"

Oh God, this was exactly why she avoided the news. She shook her head.

"A thirteen-year-old boy took his father's handgun to school; thank goodness another kid saw him and got help."

Mariah gasped and felt her face flush. Richard's eyes reflected her panic. She willed herself to stay calm.

"I'm sorry," he mumbled.

"I, I have a hard time with suicide. Children in particular." The breath she drew in was audible.

"Oh God, Star's now a teenager."

She looked up at Richard's troubled face, where lines lightly sketched turned to deep rivulets. She'd have burst into tears if she were alone. Yesterday's meeting was too much.

"Of course this is news you'd avoid," he said.

She nodded and dabbed the rim of her eyelids with a napkin.

"So . . . how's school going?"

Mariah considered. Was the answer *Terrible*? Or, *As well as expected*?

"It's a big change." The question continued to spool in her mind. Despite some of his annoying habits, Richard was the only one she trusted to share what had taken place yesterday. But she had yet to wrap her mind around it herself. "She's still grieving over Jeffrey. It's only been six months, not enough time to get a new dog. He's been with her most of her life. So, yes, she's finding her way—I mean, Aspen Creek is, what, five times the size of Mountain View? I'm sure she'll do fine academically. Otherwise, well, we're only at the end of the second week."

"It's too bad they can't break it into several smaller schools. Makes sense she would be missing Jeffrey and feeling lonely."

Star had never expressed being lonely. But how could she not be? A tear spilled down her cheek.

"I didn't realize Jeffrey had been so significant in her life," Richard said. "I had a special relationship with a cat named Tabatha when I was young. She was part of our family for twenty-two years. The stable part." He glanced wistfully off. "I'm so glad to be through adolescence. In some ways, it's so different today—phones in pockets, Facebook, new social pressures. And yet nothing has changed. Kids are still lonely. Seeking acceptance. It's just plain damn hard to live through the teen years, which now seem to stretch into, what, late twenties?"

Mariah nodded and took a bite of salad. A familiar morose state began to take hold of her.

"I was fourteen when my parents separated. I'm sure I told you about this." He had. Mariah met his eyes. "In the end, it didn't turn into a divorce, but my brother and I thought our world was ending. The hard part was keeping it to ourselves, withdrawing into our own isolated version of hell. We had no language to express what was happening to our family."

Her lips moved into a gentle smile. He was so earnest. A very sweet man. She wished he would meet someone special.

Richard had come to work as a therapist at BHP five years ago. They paired up, cofacilitating several young-adult anxiety support groups. Within the second month, it became clear that Richard was interested in a romantic relationship. Offhandedly, he referred to her as a "mystery woman." She found him wise and kind to his clients and could imagine someone, possibly even herself, being attracted to him.

Though he was not especially overweight, he lacked a certain lean, muscular body she had once been so drawn to. He was, however, the most sensitive, caring man she had ever met.

His flirtatious overtures flattered her. She surprised herself, smiling back and spontaneously flirting in return. It wasn't the prospect of sex that brought about her encouraging responses, it was the vision of cuddling on the couch late evenings, a movie on a Friday, or dinner in Boulder. She longed for companionship.

After their fourth date, she invited him to spend the night. In the candlelit bedroom, with a soft cool breeze lightly billowing her cotton lace curtains, Mariah did her best to appear mutually satisfied. She was truly grateful for the dates. Later, as they spooned in bed, his breath becoming heavy with intermittent snoring sounds, a profound emptiness encircled the middle of her chest, where his right hand had settled.

The next morning, as she scrambled eggs, he sat at the kitchen table watching her. When she sat down with her cup of coffee, he intently searched her face before saying, "I don't know you. Here you and your daughter are in Ash Grove, but—why? I've poured out my entire history—growing up, the separation, dropping out and returning to college, my brother's overdose—still, you remain a mystery to me. You, showing up here, of all places, with a beautiful daughter and no family."

She had peered into the dark coffee in a cup hardly touched. "All I can say is what I've already told you. I needed to start over." Her eyes darted past him down the hall leading to Star's room, and suddenly, all sounds were muted: the pulsing orb of blue that pressed on her forehead had silenced the hum of the refrigerator and the ticking clock. "My husband left me. Okay, he died. It's easier to say he left me." Her voice tensed. "It wasn't cancer or a heart attack—it was a tragic, violent event I prefer not to go over. He's gone. Coming here was the closest thing I could imagine to starting over. My God, Star was only four months old. I couldn't keep her in the same town that had witnessed my husband's death." She shook her head, shutting out the image of their mangled Ford Taurus spread across the front page of the *Daphne Daily*.

When she met his eyes, he held her gaze, pleading for more. He was a skilled therapist, the kind she avoided. Not at all like herself, who rarely veered from a cognitive behavioral approach. His piercing stare demanded more than the facts. He was mining for the emotional truth. But she could not have unraveled the pieces for him.

Her hands were clammy; she felt short of breath. The full magnitude of the loss was incomprehensible. Her voice shifted to the parental tone she'd use with Star when she meant business. "I won't spend time with you if you insist I share what I left behind."

She and Richard had dated for another two years. He had never again asked about her past.

Sitting across from her now, Richard looked soft and vulnerable, and Mariah could imagine him small and sad when his parents parted ways. Professionally, she knew how hard separation was on children—but at least in the end, he got his father and mother back as a unit.

Later that afternoon, Mariah's client who battled anxiety also mentioned the church Mariah had never heard of before—Unitarian—as she recounted pleasant memories of feeling safe and accepted. This revelation arrived as a thunderbolt. Other than Gretchen's thinly veiled evangelizing attempts, the topic of churches never surfaced at work. Such an odd fluke. Star would call it . . . a word Mariah could not recall. A word denoting cosmic coincidence.

Her heart swelled with warmth as she thought about Star forever seeking meaning in the simplest of chance events. A blue jay squawking endlessly at the very moment Star described an annoying classmate having a fit over nothing.

She decided to take the coincidence seriously. During a break between clients, she googled "Unitarian church" and found one in Boulder with a program for children and teens.

Chapter 5

My Journal of Hidden Truths
September 14, 2012

Mom thinks I need to see a shrink. This shouldn't surprise me. Okay, to be honest, her words were as painful as swallowing an ice cube. I held my breath so I wouldn't cry. I know she thinks I'm crazy.

Actually, she's the one who needs a shrink. She becomes upset because I don't share my entire life with her—but why should I if I know she can't handle it? Whenever I've brought up "the big question," which I now never bring up—I mean, *obviously* I have a father, we all do even if it's from a test tube—she gets all weird on me, shifting her eyes around and making up excuses to change the subject. I used to wonder if this is because I'm "an accident," and she's afraid I'll feel bad about this, and that's why she left her church. I have no idea. All I know is that Mom has secrets. Secrets she carries like solid squares of sadness that cram her insides.

It's the little boy who shows up in my dreams I want most to know about.

This is another whopping way Mom and I are different. I take my dreams seriously. She doesn't. Just because most dreams appear random doesn't mean they all are. Why would I conclude something is meaningless because I can't see the meaning at the moment?

I suspect he's been visiting on and off for years, but I'm only now taking notice. Maybe this has to do with my coming of age. Or maybe my premonition: this may be my last year in physical form.

When he appears, I'm never surprised. It's as if we've always been together. His three-year-old self, with loopy waves of blond hair and crimson cheeks, is so familiar—like someone who has been with me from the very beginning of my life. Like déjà vu. I wake up and reality shifts. Unmovable structures, colors no longer bleeding into one another, edges that are solid. A dimension he's not able to cross over to.

Whoever this child is, he's more than a dream. He knows me as deeply as Jeffrey did, like family. He's sad and needs help. He is also seeking a truth that is hidden. I wish I could talk with Mom about him.

In science today, Jasper said his mother was cured from cancer without medicine or surgery. She used alternative medicine because science doesn't have all the answers.

Shawn blurted out, "It's because she never had it to begin with." Mr. Haze crossed his arms, tapped his foot, and tried to say "Hum" in a way that didn't mean what he thought, that Shawn was right.

Jasper is brave and foolish for sharing this. I agree with him. Which makes me want to get to know him. Science doesn't have all the answers, especially the stupid textbooks used in our classes.

If I were the type of student who "actively" participated in class, I'd have announced, "David Bohm, a brilliant scientist, would try to learn more about how this happened. He understands that all matter is energy, and nothing we see and touch is what we think it is." This would for sure lead to all kinds of idiotic questions and arguing, which is why I keep my mouth shut and pretend to be as stupid as everyone else.

Mom's right. It was majorly mortifying a couple days ago when all those test tubes busted up on me. I didn't touch a single one. At least that's my memory.

During lunch break, like always, I slipped out to the forest. Unlike Tilly and her friends, I'm not doing it to sneak a smoke. I just want to visit with the crows and chipmunks. I was so pissed off with that scumbag Shawn for narking on me. It wouldn't have been a problem if it wasn't for him and his big mouth. He spied me leaving the forest and yelled out so the duty teacher could hear, "Mildred, what were you doing in the forest?" I hate it when kids call me that old-lady name. He had a fakey smile on his face I wanted to slap. To make it worse, the duty teacher threatened to call Mom and tell her, which would have freaked her out big-time. Mom's convinced the forest is full of perverts.

So, now I wonder . . . when I was at my station in science class cuz no one paired up with me, I thought of Shawn and his weasel-like face taunting me. Seeing the neatly placed test tubes all lined up, I imagined one swift whack and all of them clattering to the floor in shards of glass. That is what I *imagined.* I didn't do it. I know I didn't. It would have been way too embarrassing. But all at once they crashed to the floor, causing me to scream, and then I was freaked and almost ran out.

Maybe I'm imagining that I imagined it and I really did it, and the kids who call me psycho are right—I am a psycho.

Chapter 6

Mariah turned off the car. The early-morning chill of mid-September entered through the open spaces, overtaking the heat she had blasted moments before. Her hands intertwined, clamoring for warmth. More than twelve years had passed since she had set foot in a church.

She didn't have to enter today; she now knew the location in Boulder and could come back next week. Or the week after . . .

She took a deep breath and a searing truth assailed her: Star needed at least one real friend. Maybe this church could deliver. It had, after all, presented itself so unusually—a set of serendipitous events Star would surely approve of.

Had it not been for the sign, "Unitarian Universalist Church of Boulder," she would have driven past, looking for a structure with a steeple. The unassuming tan building stood in sharp contrast to her childhood church—a classic cloud-white rectangular frame, a spire gracing the entrance. Now, as she walked in step with a group of churchgoing strangers into a building that held no resemblance to a church, an incessant thumping hammered her chest. Stepping through the doorway, she reminded herself, *This is not a real church. Here, God is optional.*

The date she had last attended church remained etched in her mind: January 16, 2000. Jesus the Savior Church took center stage in hardening a loss that had altered her entire view of the world.

The details stayed liquid. Everyone she knew and grew up with was in attendance. Merciless bewilderment threatened to strangle her. How could they trust and give praise to a God who had allowed such a hideous tragedy? She had done her best, enveloped in a fog, to go through the motions of being gracious.

In the months following, she wondered where all the concerned people had gone. She saw the averted eyes and the loss for words when she encountered friends and colleagues. There was a particular look on the faces of those who knew of her tragedy—pitying yet guarded, as if her brand of victimhood could be contagious.

As the reality of her life descended on her, grief's heaviness stripped her of all acts of volition, plunging her into a bottomless vessel of anguish. Aware she was drowning, she felt powerless to swim to the surface. She invited the dark waters; fantasized burrowing deep into the sand, like a sea creature. Her mother, caring for Star, became an unwelcome buoy, forcing her to acknowledge the life that had not perished.

Rage rescued her from the alluring depths. Not the rage targeted at the drunk driver. Her unrepentant fury had little to do with the reckless twenty-year-old who also lost his life. Her wrath was directed at an irrational notion of God implanted within her. A God who paid attention to those who played by his rules, rewarding those who did and punishing those who didn't. There was nothing she, Charlie, or Markus had ever done to deserve this level of retribution.

Her outrage was beyond the understanding of her mother and friends. Even the girls she had spent long summers in church camp with would have viewed her anger as nothing less than blasphemy.

Now, stepping into this new concept of a church, she found comfort in the soft watercolor paintings hanging in the corridor that depicted the surrounding mountains and rivers. A doorway to her right led to a room with folding chairs arranged in a semicircle. A spacious room to her right, designated as "discussion room," was filling up with those who chose not to attend the service in the main sanctuary, an option she would keep in mind.

On the other side of the corridor, a group of teens with multicolored hair and piercings, dressed in ways that suggested Star would fit in, headed down a set of stairs for their own program. A spark of hope ignited. Mariah wavered between following the teens or proceeding forward with the crowd of adults. Her heart said teens; her head led her in the sanctuary's direction.

She entered the sanctuary with sweaty palms, a chill rippling through her arms. She would not bring Star if this church introduced the God of her youth—even a distant cousin to that God would be a deal breaker.

Most of the adults were clad in practical and stylish clothing, though a few went to extremes to be noticed: rainbow hair, colorful sixties skirts—perhaps they represented the pagan contingency. Mariah spent time each morning straightening out her curls, while Star ignored her inherited hair, allowing it to be as unruly as the passel of teens that Mariah had just encountered. She felt at ease blending into the polite crowd of Unitarians as they moved down the aisle and respectfully arranged themselves into pews.

From the sea of hatless men, she picked out three who kept their ball caps on their heads. When she spotted the third, it was as if a long-forgotten piece of herself had remembered something tender: the supple neck rising from broad shoulders, the unimaginably narrow waist, given the sturdiness of those shoulders. No one feature jumped out; it was the collection. Inexplicably familiar.

Her body quivered and she looked away, training her eyes on the watercolor images gracing the wall to her right. When the choir sang Haydn's *The Creation*, a calmness settled, drawing her into an unfamiliar state of peace.

The minister, someone about her age, wearing a celebratory purple stole around his neck but otherwise dressed in typical church clothes, stepped to the podium. Behind him was an austere wood carving of a chalice. He raised his arms, and a shift happened—organ music and a familiar melody from her childhood church. The congregation rose and sang in unison, "Holy, Holy, Holy," sweeping her to her feet along with an unwelcome rush of raw memories. She knew these lyrics by heart: "Lord God Almighty, early in the morning our song shall rise to Thee."

A moment later, my God! These were *not* the words the congregants were singing. Instead of "Lord God Almighty," it was "Author of creation," omitting the word God!

She muffled a giggle and listened to the last stanza: "God in three persons, blessed Trinity" turned into "Who was, and is, and evermore shall be." Maybe this *was* a church she could tolerate.

The sermon, which seemed more like a talk or presentation, was about taking a stand in one's own way when justice issues were at stake. Reverend Scott used the Occupy movement, which she had vaguely been aware of, to make his point.

Following the talk, another song, also omitting the word God. In her childhood church, next would be the Our Father, followed by shaking hands in peace. Here, after the so-called sermon, there was a comfortable secular chant about peace and a gentle invitation from Reverend Scott to greet one another.

She turned to her right and took the warm wrinkled hand of a silver-haired woman with an expansive smile. As she turned to her left, the baseball-capped man three rows up turned to his right. She caught his warm smile: a certain delicacy in its formation, slightly dimpled and intense. Every cell in her body knew this face, a visage as familiar as the angles of his back. This wasn't a case of some partial look-alike that fell apart when she had a more complete view. And yet, it was only a brief exposure. Shockwaves pulsed through her. She could barely remain seated. *What would Devin look like twenty years later?*

Politely, she excused herself and shimmied past the row of Unitarians and out of the sanctuary to head downstairs. After all, it was the youth program she had come for. At the base of the stairs was a long hall and an open door to the left with a sign: "Director of Religious Education." She peeked into the office and saw no one. The doors along the right side of the hall were closed. Of course, classes were still in session.

She paced anxiously while waiting for the director of religious education. Her thoughts cleaved to the baseball-capped man and his smile. Should she return to the sanctuary to take another look, possibly to counter what her body knew to be true? How preposterous. Devin had wanted nothing to do with church and religion. He was happily married and, last she heard, living in Manhattan.

Nevertheless, she climbed back up the stairs, moving down the hall to the sanctuary as a gush of members made their way toward her, the salmon swimming upstream on instinct. At once, she turned and beat it back downstairs. She had come for Star.

Entering the director's office, she faced a woman who looked close to her own age but wore her hair like someone who was in her twenties—that is, twenty years ago. She wore two ponytails, leggings, boots, and a rainbow-colored shirt. She greeted Mariah with a grin.

"Hello. I'm Trudi Reese. How can I help you?"

"Hi, I'm Mariah. I have a thirteen-year-old daughter, and I'm . . ." What were the questions she had in mind?

"Welcome. Are you new here?"

"Yes. My daughter has never been to church."

"Not a problem. We don't do church here." She made air quotes around the word *church.*

"To be honest, it was only a few days ago I heard about Unitarians." Trudi's green eyes had so much sincerity she almost went on to say it was the coincidence—two mentions in one day—that compelled her. "Thought I'd check it out."

"Glad you came." Trudi faced Mariah with the open expectancy of a teacher meeting her students on the first day of school.

"I understand, you don't . . ." Mariah searched for the right word. "Proselytize." The formality of this word made her blush.

Trudi laughed. "Oh my God, no. We encourage our youth to question beliefs and explore their own. A core principle we embrace is free and responsible search for truth and meaning."

Mariah cast her eyes about. Had she truly heard this? "Sounds like a match," Mariah said. "What are the next steps to getting Star involved?"

"Star. What a beautiful name."

Mariah nodded, and a pearl of delight lodged in her chest.

"Why not invite her to come join us next week? You might suggest it's just a trial, to see what she thinks."

"Nice idea, but I think I should first come . . . scout it out for her. That way, I can pitch it from firsthand experience."

Trudi agreed and arranged to have Mariah sit in on a class next week and then meet with a youth in private to find out what he or she thought about the program.

Outside, the church parking lot was thinning as Mariah slid into her car. She checked her cell. Of course, no word from Star. It was, after all, before noon on Sunday. She inched out of the narrow parking space and navigated toward Pearl Street, where she hesitated, her breath quickening, and then turned left instead of right, which would have pointed her home.

She trained her mind to the road with multiple crosswalks; even on a Sunday morning, this town was flooded with pedestrians, and they ruled the right-of-way. Her thoughts circled back to Star; she should head home. Yet she found herself driving to the place centered in her past—Shiva Lotta Latte. A place where, twenty years ago, love and possibility had found her.

Chapter 7

Stepping into Shiva Lotta Latte was like being transported back to the sixties, at least the way she and Devin had imagined the sixties to be. For twelve years running, she'd been drawn back to the café that still served granola and yogurt. She found comfort in the barista wearing a ponytail who was slow to get her order and the music of Bob Dylan filling the air. In this small universe, little had changed. Mariah ordered the drink she'd always had in what seemed like a past life—a double cappuccino.

In their senior year of high school, Devin and Mariah and ten others had been invited to the University of Colorado for a one-week journalism program. For him, the experience cemented his life calling. For her, it was a boost in self-esteem and confidence—the first time she had traveled outside of California. The surrounding mountain peaks and high-altitude air kept her on a continual high. Or maybe it had more to do with the late-afternoon and midnight trysts. She and Devin separated from the group, settling into lattes at this hip café with music their mothers had listened to. They indulged in conversations lapsing into half a day. Openly kissing in this other world, Mariah found it easy to imagine a future life together. By the end of the week, they became known by the baristas as the lovers from Pasadena.

Months prior, Devin had submitted his application to attend CU Boulder; he wanted to enroll in the very program where they were being mentored. He had a mother who stayed on top of the requirements demanded of the future. His acceptance letter came a week after they returned to Pasadena. Applying out of state was not something she could have envisioned for herself. Besides, her mother couldn't afford it—and needed her close. She was accepted at San Diego State, within driving distance from home.

That first year, living at home, she had imagined Devin leaving the bustle of the dorms to slip into Shiva, intent on writing articles for the college paper but finding himself lingering over the memory of them kissing in a booth. What childish foolishness. Devin had been busy discovering all kinds of possibilities, including Nicole.

A young barista with dreadlocks and a quarter-inch gauge in his ear slid her frothy drink in a wide-mouthed cup and saucer across the counter. In the meantime, the scent of pastries compelled her to order a blueberry-walnut scone to go with her cappuccino.

She settled into a dimly lit corner table and stirred the foam. Could it have been him, that baseball-capped man with the smile that sent shivers through her? *Absolutely not,* she told herself. It was easy to mistake someone for someone else when seen from a distance. Even at a distance of three church pews. She licked the milk from her spoon, and pangs of guilt beckoned her to go home.

In the storefront window, propped up against a large potted comfrey plant, was a statue of Shiva. She found an unexpected calm in the deity that graced this café. It communicated a thousand-plus words of peace and equanimity, all in one glance. As a teen, when she had known nothing of religion outside the brand of Christianity she had grown up with, she thought the statue was Buddha, but Devin set her straight. It was the café's namesake.

Devin had openly mocked her religious upbringing. Not initially, but eventually it seeped out. *How can you believe in a God that oversees everything but allows so much of the world to fall apart? Why would you believe innocent babies are born with sin? Do you honestly believe God will punish you for expressing love?* These were questions she too had struggled to resolve but would never dare bring up.

Their mothers might as well have come from different planets. Mariah's worked as a dental hygienist. Devin's mother, Dr. Candice Quinn, was a physicist at UCLA. Mariah didn't even know what a physicist was when he first mentioned it. When she met his mother, she realized the distance between Dr. Quinn and her own mother was immeasurable.

The day Devin invited Mariah over to work on a piece for the school newspaper, she had been surprised by the spaciousness inside his home. The lack of knickknacks, as her mother would call them—ceramic figurines, artificial flowers, crocheted doilies—that made her own house feel like home. Even their sleek stainless-steel refrigerator—so modern compared to the yellow squat fridge in her kitchen—was devoid of clutter. Her Sunday school art projects, school photos, the to-do lists, endless coupons, and other scraps were plastered across her fridge.

Beyond the kitchen, in the living room, a mobile of planets and stars dangled from the ceiling. She could hear her mother's dismay at this odd exhibition, and this made her squelch a giggle. Peeking down the hall, she spotted a framed picture she recognized as Einstein. She wondered if there might also be one of Devin when he was young, the way her mother had collected and hung pictures of her from kindergarten into high school.

Mariah experienced a giddy sense of freedom that afternoon, without a mother hovering over. Her own mother greeted her as soon as she arrived home from school.

Later, as they sat close enough for her to feel his breath on her bare arm, a tall, slender woman walked in. She had to have been her mother's age, but she didn't look it. In fact, there was nothing about Dr. Quinn that looked "motherly." Her cream-colored hair was pulled tight into a bun, and she sported a tailored charcoal-gray suit that made her look like an official of some sort—or perhaps the professor she was—but not a mother. She reminded Mariah of her biology teacher, who dressed in a suit and went by Dr. Finch, which she presumed meant he was highly intelligent.

Dr. Quinn placed a takeout container on the kitchen counter and gazed at Mariah. "Hello. I'm Candice. And you?"

Mariah's mind raced. Devin evidently had not told his mother that she was going to come over. She began to rise to attention, but he placed a firm hand on her thigh. She had lost her voice. Devin answered.

She had never met a grown woman who introduced herself by her first name. Mariah would have preferred to call her Dr. Quinn, but Candice insisted that her first name was fine. In fact, that is what Devin called her. It was odd to hear Devin call his mother Candice. Yet, in a strange way, it began to make sense. Mariah's own experience of a "mother" was entirely different: her own mother suggested, and then pouted, and at last, demanded. Candice merely announced her expectations.

Unlike Mariah's own mother, Candice didn't shower them with questions. She simply asked Devin if he had made the revisions on his English essay, said nothing about the breakfast dishes in the sink—something her mother always commented about in a derogatory way—and then announced that she had picked up Thai food, and if they were interested, there was plenty. Mariah had never had Thai food before. Pizza from Pizza Hut was the extent of her experience eating "ethnic food."

Candice placed the food on the table with small plates and chopsticks (declared optional—although both Devin and his mother used them). Mariah wasn't sure how to proceed. The only people she had ever had dinner with outside her home were church friends, and they never ate food without first saying grace.

The contrast between herself and Devin was alluring. Her first friend outside her church community. The friends she did have were all girls. Girls who flirted with the church boys. Boys she viewed as shallow containers of disdainful righteousness—acting all holy in front of Reverend Eddie only to disparage him for a laugh with certain willing girls.

Devin was honest in a way she had never encountered. Her fascination shifted to dismay when she heard he had never been to church. She wondered, Was he saved? And then, more menacing questions began. How could a God not see his beauty? He was more sensitive and loving than the church boys she was practically raised with. And Dr. Quinn, his mother, both intimidating and . . . well, intriguing. So unmotherly. Direct. As if her job was solely to impart information. Not to badger and insist on certain conventions.

The one and only time she had allowed her mother to meet Devin, he had liked her. Had found it amusing that she called him honey and sweetie. Mariah tried to explain this was just how her mother talked. Evidently, he had craved that kind of endearment.

But the person she had seen in church today couldn't have been Devin. Even if it was, her relationship with him resided in the unreachable past. Like this café. Upon entering, she'd been comforted by the coffee grinder's whirr and the rising chatter as locals spilled in, but as she finished her scone and coffee, Shiva felt dated. This retro café no longer served her life. She stood up and decided this was the last time she would ever step into Shiva Lotta Latte.

Chapter 8

My Journal of Hidden Truths
September 18, 2012

The little boy showed up again last night! His small aqua-blue eyes pleading with me to take him to his mother. His sadness formed a dark cloud I couldn't escape. I wept dry tears. My shoulders heaved up and down. I hadn't a clue where his mother was. I scanned the dreamscape and spotted in the distance a woman running. Seeing only her departing self, I recognized Mom. Her stiff blond hair swishing side to side. I tried to follow, but in that nightmarish way, my legs refused to lift. I woke up with damp eyes. A deep sorrow bubbled up. I sobbed for what seemed like hours before falling back to sleep.

Later I crazily thought I'd tell Mom about my dream. But then I got real. Mom thinks dreams are nothing more than a bunch of brain farts. I get this. I also have senseless dreams. But this was *not* a random misfiring of synapses. For sure, he wants my help. He's trying to reach Mom.

I wondered how he might be connected to Mom. And then it came to me. Maybe Mom had a miscarriage. If she did, this would have been a traumatic experience, and Mom, being Mom, would have tried to forget about it as soon as it happened. She would never consider that the child who expected to be in her life may need her help. Like reassurance. The way I let Jeffrey know it's okay to move on.

After dinner, while rinsing plates and cramming silverware into the dishwasher, I popped the question.

"Mom, I'm wondering. Did you ever have a miscarriage?"

"Star, why would you ask that?"

"Because I've been having dreams in which a small boy keeps showing up and . . ." My heart sped up as if I were making some kind of profound confession. Trying to ignore this, I grabbed a couple of glasses and shoved them into the dishwasher. I could feel Mom staring at me. When I shot her a look, she had stopped handwashing the fry pan she had been cleaning. It was her crazy energy that had stirred me up. "I'm just wondering why he shows up and seems to know me."

"Star. You know what I think about dreams. This is ridiculous. No, I did not have a miscarriage." She then said she needed to check the laundry, which was totally lame, and walked away.

If he is from a miscarriage, it would have been a long time ago. Maybe while Mom was trying to have me. It's odd how I get this sense of knowing him from my beginning.

Time is such a tricky concept. David Bohm agrees: Time is the ultimate mystery in the universe. The true nature of the universe is wholeness, but time is a necessary concept to keep our thoughts ordered. Now, and then now, and then now.

Okay, here's my way of understanding David Bohm's concept of time. In the end, it all comes back to wholeness being the truth of reality and us chopping our experience into segments because of our limited equipment for seeing all the connections. This makes us think events are isolated episodes. Our experience of life is the opposite of old movies, where we are fooled into thinking it is something whole moving before us even though it is really one separate scene after another flipping by fast. Reverse this, and that's how we experience life. We see and think in pieces, but life is not a flip-book or a movie, time is an eternity that we slice into sections.

Today, I got my period. I sort of wanted to tell Mom about it, but I didn't want to deal with her reaction. I'll wait until next month and act all surprised and tell her then. From what I've read, this first one will only create a little blood for a few days. From here on out, it'll be a good excuse to skip a day of school. I'm sure I'll have major cramps.

I'm excited to know that I am now officially considered a grown-up by ancient cultures. It's sort of weird and amazing. My body knows what to do to prepare me for having kids and what to do since I'm not allowing any sperm into my uterus. I'll never have a human child! There are way too many people on Earth. I plan on adopting dogs, cats, and other creatures in need of a home.

I read about periods messing up hormones. This must be why whenever I'm around Angel, Jasper, or Audrey, I get super sad and I get this huge lump in my throat. I can barely keep myself from crying. Sometimes I can't. I don't know these kids. I just can tell they are majorly unhappy. No one else seems to notice. I try not to glance their way to avoid their sadness. But even so, I feel their heaviness press against me even without seeing and knowing they are in the room.

This only happened a few times last year. I'm almost freaked out by it. Mom would be majorly upset if she knew. She already thinks I'm crazy. Boys are lucky not to have periods. This is why I told Jeffrey not to come back as a girl.

Chapter 9

The phone rang as Mariah finished her second cup of coffee. Of course. Her mother. Who else called the landline at ten on a Saturday morning? Three weeks had lapsed since hearing from Olivia.

"Hi, Mom."

"Hi, sweetie. How are things going?"

"Just fine. Star and I are planning on a shopping date in Boulder this afternoon, we'll probably end up at her favorite pizzeria."

"Sounds lovely." And then a pause. "I'm wondering, did Star get my birthday present?"

"Of course."

"I didn't hear back, so I wasn't sure. I have no idea if she even liked it."

Damn. Why hadn't she made time to pressure Star into sending a simple thank-you note? Or better still, a phone call.

"Sorry, Mom. I meant to let you know. It's a little loose, but yes, she likes it."

"Well, if you lived near a J. C. Penney's, I'd send something that could be exchanged. Since you don't, I found this in a charming boutique five miles from Daphne, and the saleswoman went on and on about how popular these fringed jean jackets are. Maybe I can get you to send me a picture. It's been a long time since I've seen my only grandchild."

Two years, in fact. They had last visited Olivia when Star was eleven, leaving the winter weather in Colorado for something more like early fall, disorienting all on its own. They had arrived two days before Christmas, and Star had taken an interest in the various knickknacks her mother had on display.

Though Olivia had agreed that Mariah would be the one—when the time was right—to share with Star the family tragedy, Mariah had to race to stay ahead of Star's vigilant eyes, nabbing the eight-by-ten silver-framed wedding picture sitting on the mantel. And the family photo of their last Thanksgiving. How dare her mother keep these on display? When she nabbed the family portrait, her eyes caught and hung painfully on the grinning faces of Charlie and Markus.

Following a strained dinner of small talk, Mariah trailed her mother upstairs to her childhood bedroom. Five strides up the staircase, there was the familiar creak that had never let her slip by unnoticed. In the bedroom, she breathed in the smell of dust bunnies huddled in corners and the ever-present scent of emptiness. At age twenty-eight, she'd had to return home, unable to care for her baby daughter. It was this memory that tormented her, generating a deep and drenching pain.

Olivia tossed half of the beige fitted sheet across the bed to Mariah, who stood wedged between anguish and grief. Mariah tucked her end around the mattress corner. With a firm jerk from her mother, off it slipped. Her mother fixed her side and Mariah jerked back, stretching the fitted sheet into place, provoking an anger she could no longer contain.

"Mom!" She recognized the tone at once—her fifteen-year-old self had slipped in somewhere between the creaky stair and the wrangling of bedsheets. "I told you I'm not ready. How dare you sprinkle pieces of my shattered past in front of my daughter."

Her mother, wearing an outdated, flowery house dress, stared back wide-eyed.

Mariah's teen self charged forward. "We had an agreement. I never would have come if I had known you'd do this."

Her mother's head dropped and, with a jitteriness Mariah hadn't seen before, she tossed the cover sheet onto the bed and folded her corner. Mariah stood waiting. Finally, Olivia made eye contact.

"You're forgetting. This is my house, and I have fond memories of Markus and Charlie."

Hearing their names snapped her to the present—the thirty-eight-year-old who had lost her husband and son a decade earlier. And a daughter unprepared to hear the truth of her past.

"Mom. You're not honoring our agreement. Or respecting me as a parent." She fisted her hands, turned away, and then again faced her mother. "You chose not to tell me about my father."

Her mother stepped back; closed her eyes.

Mariah pressed on. "I have a right to raise Star in the manner I see fit—just as you raised me the way you thought best." Olivia started to say something but faltered. Fleetingly, she appeared defenseless. "You can't be parading my past in front of her. I need to be the one to share it."

Olivia stiffened and then drove her eyes deep into Mariah. No different from when Mariah had chosen not to follow rules as a child. "She's eleven years old and deserves to know the truth. I can't hide with you."

"Mom. You are good at hiding." Her mother flinched, but Mariah pushed on. "Please. Trust me. I promise I'll tell her. I need more time."

Mariah had never intended to conceal from Star that she had had a loving father and an older brother. How could she gaze into the innocent face of a two-, three-, or four-year-old and disclose a horrific event no one would want to hear?

Preschool was the first time Star had asked, "Who's my daddy?" Mariah had expected this and responded as if it were well rehearsed, but it wasn't: "Some people have only a mommy, some have only a daddy, and some have both. You have me. I don't have a daddy either, that's why you only have one grandma."

Age five seemed like the right time to tell Star. She had promised her mother that would be the year. But she had been unprepared for Star's issues in kindergarten. Learning about the tragic event on top of her difficult transition to kindergarten would have made life unbearable. That year, Star told her, "Everyone has a daddy, it's just that they don't always live with you." It was a statement. All Mariah needed to do was nod and say, "You're right."

When Star turned nine, she point-blank asked, "Do you know my father?"

"I only knew him for a short time. He went away."

By fourth grade Star either stopped having emotional meltdowns, or the school learned to manage them. Mountain View Elementary made accommodations, and Star found the teachers who accepted her. This might have been the year to bring up the past tragedy. But who was she, Mariah, to rain on a somewhat successful school year?

And now, Star was thirteen and still didn't know the truth.

"It's hard to believe she's a teenager," Olivia said, "that it's been twelve years since . . ."

Mariah gripped the phone and held her breath while Olivia finished the sentence.

"You left."

And Mariah filled in what her mother omitted: *Since Charlie and Markus were taken.*

"Yes, it is." A long moment passed, a silence that lay between them like a welt.

"Mariah." The tenor of her mother's voice made Mariah purse her lips, willing patience. "Star has a right to know who her father was, and that she had a brother."

"Mom, I'm going to tell her. It's just, she's so sensitive. She's still grieving over losing Jeffrey." Mariah's chest tightened—her mother had to have noticed the trill in her voice as it rose—she had a point to make. Olivia didn't understand—in fact, did not know—this grandchild of hers. But then, how could she? Star remained a mystery to Mariah as well.

"Jeffrey?"

"Mom. Our dog. We had him for ten years."

"Oh yes, Jeffrey. The way you said his name, I thought this was a classmate or—"

"I know. It's been six months. But that's my point. She's still grieving his death. And now I'm supposed to explain to her she had a brother and a father that were killed? It's too much. Junior high is a big change." A silence welled. She was done, ready to hang up. But she imagined her mother clutching the phone to her ear a thousand miles away, waiting to hear an answer. She lowered her voice. "I will tell her. But you must trust me. Now is not the right time."

"Sweetheart, I miss you."

Mariah wiped a tear from the corner of her eye. She could not imagine a visit—here or there. It was all too much. Everything, too heavy. Including the phone pressed against her ear.

"Mom, I need to get Star up and going if we're to have our big Boulder date. Thanks for calling." She must have been too abrupt. "Mom, are you there?"

"I'm here." Her voice was laced with fatigue.

"We'll talk next week."

Chapter 10

As Mariah pulled onto the two-lane highway between Ash Grove and Boulder, her thoughts returned to her mother. Not seeing her wasn't an option. To be honest, nor was it her choice. Her mother was right. If a client were in a similar situation, she would advise them to share the truth at once. Except Star was anything but typical. She became bereft upon discovering a dead crow. Something Mariah would never reveal to her mother, who could not conceive of Star's sensitivity. Olivia had no patience for this level of sentimentality.

Mariah glanced at Star in the passenger seat, transfixed by the palm-sized phone in her hand. The competition to nab her daughter's attention irritated her. She was eager to talk about her experience of attending the Sunday school class—nothing could have been further from her own experience.

But then, she had never attempted to disclose to Star the suffocating nature of her childhood church school. In fact, she shared little of her past. Which, come to think of it, rang true regarding her own mother as well. Mariah never heard the full story of why her father had left them.

The previous Sunday, Mariah had met Trudi prior to class. "So students get to have complete say in the ways they choose to define their God—or not?" Choosing beliefs in religion was foreign to Mariah. *Obedience* was the word she associated with church.

"It all gets down to respect," Trudi had said. "Learning who we are in relation to our earthly community can take a lifetime, and we value the process. Our youth have a right to be given the space to explore. Since all of life is an exploration, it makes little sense to mold them into rigid ways of believing. We have principles instead of dogma."

Principles instead of dogma? Mariah had been raised on dogma. The opportunities these youths had available to them shone like glints of sun illuminating a lake.

The classroom comprised a motley group of fifteen adolescents, grades six through eight, pimply faced, pierced, colored in shocking ways, and wearing clothes her own mother never would have allowed. They engaged in a lively discussion that veered toward unwieldy. Chaos would have reigned were it not for the sage teacher, Don—an older gentleman with proud square shoulders and graying hair that didn't require a comb to fix in place—who functioned more as a facilitator than an instructor. His own two sons had taken part in the church from grade school on.

These teens discussed with passion how saving raccoons, birds, or cats in a shelter, or raising awareness of homelessness, racism, or transgender issues qualified as projects that would improve their world. It was an open-ended, free-for-all decision-making class aimed at settling the next service project.

Toward the end of class, Trudi stepped into the room and invited Caleb, an outspoken youth with a colorful mohawk tinted in purple and orange, to join her and Mariah. He had soft cheeks tinged with crimson and a jawline not yet firmly defined; together the picture of a youngster poised for adulthood, unable to conceal an endearing quality of youth. His eyes were an aqua blue, and she knew if his milky-blond hair had not been waxed, it would curl, just as Star's did. An unexpected ripple of affection poured out of her. *My God,* she realized, *he's the same age Markus would be.*

Caleb reported having attended the Unitarian church his entire life. He appeared fully indoctrinated, an evangelist. She found herself in favor of this brand of proselytizing—here was a place that acknowledged the messy dimensions of humanity. Talking with this confident teen, she wished she had discovered this church eight years earlier, when Star had begun her journey in public school.

"Would a thirteen-year-old who has never set foot in a church mix in?"

Caleb grinned and nodded. "It's not really a church, it's a community."

As they neared Boulder, Mariah glanced again at Star, who continued to focus on the small screen held in front of her. Mariah censored the urge to launch into testimonials about the church.

"Star."

"Yeah."

"What are you reading?"

"A blog."

"About?"

"Stuff you'd find boring."

"Such as?"

Star sighed, brushed her hair back. "How the big bang theory fits into Einstein's theory of relativity and Bohm's ideas about . . ."

Star was right. Science was not Mariah's forte. She wasn't totally tuned in to what Star was saying anyway because suddenly, as if her body had its own curriculum, her palms started to sweat. The damn four-way stop prior to entering Boulder. Even being the furthest thing from her mind, that four-way got her heart pumping. It was the stopping and knowing about the not-stopping of a derelict drunk driver in a two-ton truck that had irrevocably altered the course of her life.

Approaching the intersection, she refrained from additional glances at Star, who always turned away, and kept her focus on whose turn it was to move ahead. Once the sedan cruised forward, she relaxed into the drive, dismissing the nonsense of her reaction.

She found a parking spot ten blocks from the church and another five from the main street. She had made a mental map of the route they'd take, beginning first with a tour of the church. She hoped Trudi would be there, but it was Saturday. For Star to at least see the space prior to attending would be helpful.

She breathed in the early-fall air of damp leaves and buttoned her sweater as she stepped out onto the street. Mariah couldn't recall when she and Star had last strolled through Boulder together. Star's agreement to come with a flat statement of "Whatever" had fetched a rush of relief. She waved for Star to follow and together they strode down the root-buckled sidewalk lined with aging elm and oak trees.

"Mom, can we look at tarot cards?"

"At what?"

"Tarot cards. They sell them at Soothsayers, just a few blocks off Pearl Street. I don't need to buy any, but I want to see what a real deck looks like."

"Is this something you've been reading about on the internet?"

"I can't remember. You know what a tarot deck is, don't you?"

"Of course." Mariah had at least heard of it. Was it used to predict the future? Ouija boards had been popular when she was in school, but she could never get near one. Her church referred to Ouija boards and anything else that attempted to reveal a manner of truth outside Christianity as the work of the devil.

"Have you ever seen one?"

"Hmm. No."

"Me neither. But I might want a deck someday, and I want to see what they look like. I heard they're pretty cool."

"Oh. Who says?"

"I don't remember. I probably read it somewhere." And then she turned to her phone and tapped on it while walking, as if something urgent demanded her attention.

Mariah gazed with envy at one gorgeous Craftsman after another. Painted in cheery yellows or showy mauves, some with daring violet-colored window trim. Their inviting porches suggested a leisurely pace. She envisioned evenings spent reading the paper in the fading light, gazing at the sunset as it descended behind the Rockies. She turned back to wait for Star to catch up.

"I thought we'd start by taking a quick look at the church. That way it won't feel so new when you come tomorrow."

Star shoved her cell phone back into her front pocket before responding with "Mmm." Her thick waves of hair combined with the unnecessary sunglasses hid whatever expression was on her face.

"When I sat in on one class, they were brainstorming ways to make a difference in their community." She turned toward Star, taking in the lanky awkwardness of her thirteen-year-old body.

Star had inherited Mariah's curly hair with Charlie's auburn color and his tall, slender lines. Her gait was anything but smooth. Her longish neck leaned forward, as if the weight of her hair slung frontward left her no choice. Given her growth spurt, at five foot eight, she had reached the height of many adults. Her polyester-blend navy-blue pants could have been mistaken as something a middle-aged woman would wear. The psychedelic cotton shirt under a sleeveless black quilted vest most likely threw her back into the camp of preteen or teen. Although there was no trendy purse dangling from her shoulder, and she wore no jewelry, she did have the requisite electronics poking out of her pocket.

"Remember when you decided in fifth grade that recycling was important and got the janitor to help?"

"Mom. He's not a janitor. He's a custodian."

"Okay. Custodian."

"His name is Mr. Seng."

"The point I'm making is that getting recycling going in your school was an example of an activist project."

"Oh."

Mariah waited, expecting more, but Star did not reply. "One student at UUCB . . ." Mariah glanced over to see if Star understood before continuing. "That stands for Unitarian Universalist Church of Boulder."

"I know, Mom."

"Well, this student, like you, was concerned about wildlife." Mariah waited and Star returned her gaze. Star loved animals. An ache swelled in Mariah's chest; she needed to consider getting another dog. "This young woman—"

"Do you mean my age?"

"Yes, I mean your age. Okay—youth."

"No one says *youth.*"

"What do they say?"

"Kid."

"So, this *kid* was concerned about the impact of recent housing developments on wildlife. Trees being cut down, birds and other animals losing their habitat." She glanced over at Star but failed to penetrate the sunglasses. "She reminded me of you, when you decided to be a vegetarian."

Mariah dismissed the impulse to tell her about a student who wanted to create toys for cats waiting in a shelter and the many other novel ideas Star would surely appreciate. Instead, she matched Star's pace and reminded herself that she had despised the way her own mother would go on and on about some event or church matter. The wisest information her mother had ever imparted was that there were no instruction manuals that came with children. If only. Mariah would follow it religiously. In place of religion.

"Maybe." Star said, with a tone of surliness. There was no denying it; Star was now officially a teenager. "You got to admit, Mom, there are lots of trees surrounding Boulder. Most animals are adaptable. It's the warblers I'd be most concerned about because they only nest in alder and cottonwood."

"That was just one example of a project. Someone else suggested bringing greater awareness about discrimination of sexual minorities."

"Cool," Star said in a flat tone.

The church parking lot was empty, but the door that led to the classrooms was unlocked. The steps leading into the classrooms had a hollow resonance. Mariah directed her attention to the student artwork displayed on the hallway walls, hoping something might speak to her daughter, but she was disappointed, and Star was busy looking at her phone. Mariah had fantasized about running into Trudi, imagining that her captivating smile would draw Star right in, and then encountering Caleb, who would impress Star with the possibility of community and friends. Being Saturday afternoon, though, only a few people were passing through. No one Mariah recognized.

After showing Star the classroom, vacant of the vibrancy Mariah had experienced, and sharing again how amazingly different and welcoming both Trudi and the teacher named Don were, they left and continued to walk south toward Pearl Street.

"How about we get a bite to eat at Poppy's?" Mariah asked.

"Mmm. Our favorite."

Stepping inside, the smell of garlic, the lively rhythm of Bob Marley, and the brisk hum of conversation were welcome changes from the serious, austere church. Multicolored blown-glass light fixtures hung above the gleaming Formica tables that lined the tall windows fronting Pearl Street. Deeper into the center, the kitchen staff demonstrated the acrobatic art of pizza tossing.

A bright-eyed young man with slicked-back hair and a pierced ear seated them next to a window where they could look out on the Pearl Street Mall, a four-block pedestrian-only section of downtown Boulder.

The menu offerings were familiar from the last time. Was it a year ago, or perhaps two? Even though they'd eaten at Poppy's Pizzeria only about three times in the past five years, Mariah thought of it as a tradition. She and Star always ordered the same dishes. Watching her daughter studying the menu amid the other families in the pizzeria buoyed her sense of normalcy. Anyone passing by the window would see mother and daughter eating at the popular pizza joint. How much more normal could this be?

Star turned toward the window. What might capture her daughter's attention—the occasional teenage boy? The stylish girls? The street artists? Or perhaps her gaze was disguised to avert conversation.

"I love that the menu is the same," Mariah said. "Seems like so much is changing these days."

Star ignored this and said, "I'll take the veggie pizza." She turned to Mariah and added, "You're going to have the Greek salad, and we'll share cheese sticks, right?"

"That's exactly what I was thinking. And should we order a root beer?"

"Too sweet. I'll have the mango Izze."

And then, before she could hold Star's attention, a minor commotion outside the window—a clown passing out animal-shaped balloons—pulled her daughter away again.

Once the swell of onlookers passed, Mariah said, "Grandma called this morning. She asked if you liked the jacket she sent for your birthday. I told her it's a little loose—"

"And nothing I'd ever wear."

"Maybe when she calls next weekend, you should also talk with her and let her know what you like to wear." A loud silence. Ugh. She knew better than to be so direct. Besides, Star would not be up when her mother called late on Saturday morning.

Halfway through their meal, the high-pitched melodic trill of a young child seized Mariah's attention. She tried to shift her focus to

Star, but Star too was captivated, holding her piece of pizza midway to her mouth while gazing beyond Mariah, toward the front entrance.

Although she'd already had more than her share, Mariah impulsively grabbed another cheese stick. She bit into the buttery, chewy, garlic-laden bread, longing to experience its comfort. But her throat constricted. For a moment, she wasn't sure if she'd swallow or choke.

Clearing her throat for a second time, she heard the unmistakable banter of a child who had just mastered simple sentences. The lilting tone of a toddler—a soft and warm voice she would never again hold next to her. She drew a quick breath as Star stared wide-eyed.

The toddler came into view then, from behind Mariah, parading in front of them with newfound confidence in striped overalls, a sunny red shirt, and with wavy blond hair. His soft pink cheeks puffing out in exuberance sent a swift slice of pain from her heart to her gut. Nausea crept up, and her mouth filled with an unwelcome surge of saliva. Mariah drew her napkin to her face.

Star had dropped her piece of pizza and gazed with indifference at the rest. Finally, Mariah took a long sip of water.

"Star," Mariah said, forcing a partial smile. "Let's go find Soothsayers."

Chapter 11

My Journal of Hidden Truths
September 29, 2012

Well, Journal, today was one of the weirdest days I've had in a while. For starters, I spent most of it with Mom. A rarity. Actually, she's the only person I might spend a day with since I don't have friends. Which is why I miss Jeffrey so much.

Okay, the truth. When she suggested we go to Boulder, I knew something was up. Because you are my journal of hidden truths, I'll be honest. I was hoping somehow Mom and I could have a real conversation. Maybe even have fun. Instead, time with Mom started out intense and ended even more intense.

I'm going to start with the end of our mother-daughter outing, where things got totally wacky, and then go to the beginning, which deserves its own prize for being bizarre.

Mom cheerfully suggested we eat at our favorite pizzeria—favorite being theoretical. Poppy's is our favorite by default since we've never tried any of the other four pizzerias in Boulder. The beginning of this crazy end to our outing started out totally awesome. Mom finally let go of all the pushing and agitating about this new church.

Hum. I'm changing my mind here. I'll start with the beginning, which was also weird but nothing like the ending.

This church business was Mom's whole reason for suggesting a day together in Boulder. She was all about trying to get me interested in a new church she discovered—UUCB. Except Mom is totally not the church type! Way back when Mom was trying to match me up with Tilly to be my friend, Tilly's mom, who's now Mom's boss, suggested we check out her church. Mom was quick to shoot that idea down. One evening after her second glass of wine, she let it slip that she thinks church is a bunch of crock.

Having looked up Mom's childhood church online, I don't blame her. I completely get why she's not into churches. Especially hers. Digging in, anyone with a brain could see it smacks of falsehood. Think wicked club using rules and scare tactics to make the uninitiated feel guilty about themselves. It's clear to me they push the creepy idea of a devil to children to scare them into following a bunch of insane rules. I'm so glad Mom didn't make me go to church to get brainwashed.

Once we parked, Mom started telling me all about her discovery of UUCB—as if out of the blue she suddenly got in the mood to go church shopping. Totally turned off by the word *church*, I had a nasty attitude. But honestly, what she said was pretty cool. Like, unbelievable. Too bad UUCB has to be called a church.

The classes are held in a dreary basement. To its credit, even though the art on the walls was dreadful, at least there wasn't a single visible cross. Like the devil, displaying a cross is another tactic to stir up guilt and make people think God made them full of evil and their only salvation is church. Poor Mom. She had no choice but to suffer through this as a child. Even as a teenager. She rarely talks about it. There's lots Mom doesn't talk about.

When Mom brought up my recycling project with Mr. Seng, all I could say was: "Mom. He's not a janitor. He's a custodian, and his name is Mr. Seng."

I'm now smiling as I remember Mr. Seng laughing. I had told him I didn't understand why girls all want to dress one way and boys another and I just want to wear what I feel like wearing without thinking about stupid unspoken rules. His laughing made me laugh even though I wasn't in the mood to laugh. Truth is, Mom thinks it's weird that I don't take an interest in "fashion." Which gets back to why I didn't like Grandma's birthday present and then had to make up excuses why I don't like it.

Mom totally doesn't get my relationship with Mr. Seng, even with him being the most important person in my life all of fifth and sixth grade. I wanted to tell her I miss him almost as much as Jeffrey. He was the only one who understood the painful loneliness of school boredom. And he is the smartest person I've ever met. When he gave me David Bohm's book, he knew I wouldn't understand it all. But he knew David's radical concepts were ideas I'd eventually get. David writes, "If we are not aware that our theories are ever-changing forms of insight, giving shape and form to experience in general, our vision will be limited." This is profound! But still, I work to wrap my mind around it.

I wish Mom understood how challenging it is every day going to school without a friend like Mr. Seng. Someone who understands the importance of seeking the truth about reality.

Once at Poppy's, Mom and I knew what each other wanted to order, which was totally rad. I snagged a window view. My favorite. To be shielded by a plate of glass while observing the goings-on outside is awesome. Boulder is way different from Ash Grove, and I love to let myself get lost in amusement. Like seeing this crazy clown person blowing up balloons and gleefully handing them out. Never in Ash Grove.

When the food showed up, the smell of garlic and cheese primed our appetite. I had mentally prepared for Mom's grilling, making it easy to shrug off her questions. Even the bit about Grandma's birthday present. I could tell right away she was aiming to guilt-trip me.

Now for the truly bizarre part. Whoever You are who may be reading this, know that I don't use the word *bizarre* lightly.

Imagine this. We're hungry. The food arrives as wonderful as expected. Our eyes meet and we smile because I know "the grilling" is over; it's time to enjoy Poppy's. And to anticipate going to Soothsayers.

I glance out the window, content in viewing what Mom would call "odd-balls." I'm one. And I delight in knowing I'm not alone.

A swelling and a warming to the possibility of a real conversation with Mom emerges. There's so much about junior high I haven't shared. Tons of new kids I can't avoid, having to pass them in the halls, and multiple teachers. I'm not sure where to begin. I notice the familiar tickly sensation inside me that comes just before I'm about to invite Mom into a piece of my world.

And then, at once, I flash on the little boy who last night showed up in my dreams. I shake my head thinking this is a blip. Except, moments later, coming towards us, behind Mom, I see a child who looks to be the same age and with the same wavy blond hair as the boy in my dreams! *Wow, big display of synchronicity.*

Of course, I took a long pause with my eating. My hand stopped midway between the table and my mouth while holding a slice of pizza, which Mom being Mom obviously noticed. And then she heard what I heard—high-pitched squeals of delight and a string of ill-formed words colliding together. Mom's half-eaten breadstick hovered in the air between her trembling thumb and fingers. I glanced up, thinking this is *my* synchronicity experience. This has nothing to do with Mom.

And then, the little boy paraded in front of us. Mom's eyes widened, her quick pain sliced through me. Unlike the boy in my dreams, who can no longer be in this world, this child was happy and solid—but Mom completely lost it.

I worried she'd lose her entire lunch and be all embarrassed. Thankfully, that didn't happen. Neither of us finished eating. She tried to recover by offering to go to Soothsayers to look at tarot cards. It was a weak request. And too late. Her upset had already spilled on me the same way I get hit by the sadness of Angel or Audrey when they walk by my desk in Mrs. Severson's class. All I wanted was to go home. I could tell this was true for Mom as well.

Here is my hidden truth—the boy in my dreams belongs to her. And to me. Mom hasn't finished saying goodbye. I want to know his name.

Chapter 12

Squinting at her bedside clock, Mariah made out 3:00 a.m. She pinched the bridge of her nose to dull the headache. This rarely worked. Her nemesis came in the package of a booming clash of twisting metal and screams of terror. The dream, visiting monthly, awakened her to a drenched nightgown and a racing heart, and left her in a state of exhaustion, unable to sleep. Tonight was the exception. Within an hour she briefly slipped into a tranquil emptiness. She woke again, wide-eyed, at 5:20, only two hours before planned.

Mariah adjusted to the glimmer of the early-morning light—in Daphne, it would still be pitch black. But here, there was a whisper of predawn light. In Colorado, the light came much earlier at this time of year. She reached over and turned on her bedside lamp.

Today was Sunday. Not the Sunday of her childhood, replete with a frilly dress that pleased her mother and half a day of church activities, which served as an antidote for the loneliness of being an only child. She felt close to her mother during those early years of church programs: the choir, bake sales, Sunday school, and the mutual conviction regarding matters of right and wrong. But these certainties, along with the mother-daughter intimacy, deserted her with the onset of adolescence.

Here she was today, with her own adolescent daughter, attempting to find closeness in the womb of a church. How ironic! Having fled her own church during a time of despair. Thinking a church, of all places, was the way to find community for Star.

The unexpectedness of it all. The church service, which did not use the word God. Trudi, with insightful green eyes, had grasped the essence of what Mariah sought—a lack of "churchiness."

Reverend Eddie would have condemned a church that allowed its members to pick and choose beliefs. Even the slightest expression of doubt triggered scorn, as if it were a serious breach of faith—in fact, a sin. Throughout high school, doubts flooded her, lodging a great lumbering guilt deep within her chest. In earnest she prayed as insurance to protect against a vengeful God who punished those who doubted.

In high school, Mariah had found herself drawn to Sherry, the "wild" girl, an outsider who briefly attended their church when she visited her mother in Daphne. Sherry's parents were divorced. (Mariah's mother never used the word *divorce* to describe her own situation. She preferred a different verb—Mariah's father had "left.") Mariah was both shocked and captivated by Sherry, who stood out among "the indoctrinated" with her fishnet stockings and Lycra mini skirt.

My God, she thought, *Sherry would have fit in at the Unitarian church.* Sherry asked questions no one else dared to ask. Why would a loving God allow innocent children to die, such as Sherry's brother, who drowned at age two? She used the f-word (but not in front of Reverend Eddie) and talked of wanting to try out sex: "What's wrong with having fun and pleasure? Why would *God*"—pronounced in a demeaning manner that made others gasp—"not want his creations to enjoy living?"

Was this the lure Mariah had experienced? Someone courageous enough to ask the very questions she and the others had avoided?

Star would never have survived in Mariah's childhood church.

In the kitchen, Mariah bunched the sheer white curtains that hung over the sink to either side. The natural light seeped in and saturated the dimly lit places. Even at six in the morning, in the smudged dark greens and browns outside, she could make out the activity of birds. She opened the window to the fluid notes of a robin's song. If Star were awake, she too would appreciate this. She liked to feed the crows on her way to school.

Was it the birds or the trees and the silence she valued most in living here? Twelve years ago, all that had mattered was a new start. A step forward from a fairy-tale past that had ended in torment.

At once, she heard her mother chanting a cheery little quip she had curled her lip to: *Today is the first day of the rest of your life.* Indeed, Mariah sensed a welcoming change taking place in her life.

She made a pot of coffee and placed two slices of bread into the toaster. Trudi had to have sensed her longing to take part in a fresh version of church school when she invited her to be a classroom volunteer with the youth.

"All you'd need to do," Trudi had explained, "is ask questions and listen. Stay neutral and allow the youth to have space to explore." This was not unfamiliar. In fact, no different from her individual counseling sessions. However, most of her clients truly needed direct advice.

She had often used questions with Star. To no avail.

When Star was seven years old, Mariah had asked, "What do you mean you no longer want to do swim lessons?"

"I think it's unlikely that I'll accidentally fall off a boat or a dock and drown—I know how to dog-paddle."

"But you enjoy the lessons. I mean, aren't they fun?"

"No. I feel like a guppy being bullied by a prima donna mermaid. I'd rather stay home and read."

When Star refused a burger at age ten, Mariah asked, "Why don't you want a burger? You always like Dick Tracy Burgers."

"I no longer want to eat anything that has eyes and can look at me."

"Wait a minute. My hamburger can't look at me with eyes. Just last week you slathered mustard and added cheese and said it was great."

"Mom. It's a cow. In India, they're sacred. I can no longer be a part of killing animals. What if dog meat were called hamburgers? Can you imagine Jeffrey between a bun? It's gross."

Today, Mariah invited wholeheartedly the opportunity to see Star with a group of peers. It had been years since Mariah was required to chaperone Star's class field trips.

Upon finishing her third cup of coffee, she checked her watch for the fourth time. Five after ten. She had made it clear, up by ten. She waited another five minutes before delivering three loud raps, followed by, "Star light, Star bright, time to rise and shine."

A good fifteen seconds later, the muffled voice of a sluggish Star announced, "I don't want to."

Staring into the face of Einstein plastered on Star's door, Mariah called out, "Sweetie, you're forgetting, we're going to church together."

"Mom." The dismissive tone clarified it was time to enter the room. How could Star sleep so late? It had to be the computer. Mariah yanked the quilted comforter off and gave Star a less-than-gentle shake.

"You promised you would give UUCB a chance. We need to leave in twenty minutes. I've made your favorite breakfast."

Star squirmed and sat up, rubbed her eyes, and groggily asked, "Do I have to?"

"Yes. A promise is a promise. Besides, I know you'll enjoy this—it's nothing like Aspen Creek."

They found a parking spot at the far end of the lot, which meant time to walk together. Mariah refrained from saying something about Star's cell phone. Thankfully, the phone went into Star's pocket as they crossed the lot and moved onto the walkway.

Mariah was about to say something supportive when Star made a decisive wide angle to the right, avoiding an older, disheveled person with a backpack, hair in dregs, who approached from the opposite direction. Mariah also veered, to stay close to Star. And then Star swerved back onto the walk.

"What was that about?"

"That person wants to hurt someone."

"You don't know that. Star, it's rude to so blatantly go out of your way to avoid someone for no reason."

"But I had a reason; I didn't want to feel his anger."

Mariah stared at her. Did she really feel something?

Inside, the classroom door was open. Four adolescents occupied a corner, teasing and chatting. Don adjusted chairs in a semicircle around a couple of rectangular tables.

Six more teens entered, and the room filled with the warmth of unruly chatter born of bonded history. Star shuffled to the back of the room. Mariah checked in with Don and then stepped aside to scan the students. An unusually tall girl—a good two inches beyond Star's five-foot-eight-inch frame—moved with awkwardness toward the back of the classroom. Her shoulder-length black hair was striking next to her pale and pasty skin. Black was clearly not her natural hair color.

The girl kept her eyes cast down and sat in the space at the far end of one of the two tables. And then Star, who had been pacing in the back, seated herself next to the girl. Mariah waited until the last student was settled before choosing a seat that kept her in the mix while keeping a watchful eye on Star.

In the middle of discussing standing up for what one believes, a boy with hair longer than Star's turned to Mariah and asked, "Do you think it's fair that some schools do random backpack searches without warning?" She tossed the question back, asking what he might do about this. She glanced in Star's direction, wondering if Star saw her engagement with the boy. But Star and the tall girl were chatting, oblivious to all else.

Don concluded the class with a light tap to a bronze bowl held in the uplifted palm of his hand. The tone emanated forth, blanketing the room in a calming silence. Don's expanding smile took center stage. He thanked the students and invited them to reflect on the gifts they offered to their community.

Everyone stood up, except Star and the tall girl, and the room filled with a pleasant cacophony as students began leaving the classroom. Star and the tall girl, who had said nothing during class, making it impossible for Mariah to learn her name, continued to talk. Mariah held back, afraid to interrupt an exchange unlike any she had ever observed between Star and a peer. And then Star stood up and said, "See you next week." Star radiated a rare brightness, and when she turned to Mariah, she made direct eye contact and smiled.

In Mariah's perfect world, they would have walked out hand-in-hand to the parking lot. This was only slightly less than perfection. They held each other in a cocoon of nonverbal unity, stepping in sync down the hall and out the back doors.

The brisk fall air felt invigorating rather than chilling, calling up several of her favorite comfort foods—bean chili, roasted potatoes; she too could easily shift to vegetarian, except for the occasional burger.

Three steps out from the church she asked, "Was I right? Not like Aspen?"

Star smiled and glanced away, causing Mariah to take in a calming breath and hold the many other questions inside. Finally, Star turned to her and said, "Well, it wasn't what I expected." Star beamed. "You were right—I like it. And I think I have a new friend."

"It sure looks that way. And what's her name?"

"Jen. And she's heard of David Bohm, which is rad because, really, he's not someone kids my age know about unless they're planning on becoming theoretical physicists, which she isn't, but she's interested in all sorts of cool stuff."

"That's exciting." They walked in step across the vast parking lot as churchgoers parted in waves. Drifting in reverie, Mariah lost track of her whereabouts. She slowed to scan her surroundings and caught sight of that familiar frame: the man with the baseball cap was striding in a determined manner a few steps ahead. The silhouette of a man permanently etched in her memory. Mariah's heart quickened and she halted.

"Mom. What's wrong?"

"Oh, it's nothing. Just. I forget where we're parked." Once she said this, she saw that the man was headed right for her car. In fact, the red Subaru Outback just to the left of her car appeared to be his. He pulled a set of keys from his pocket.

"It's right over there." Star pointed.

"Of course." But she stood fastened to the pavement. Her chest drummed. And then her body took over, walking her at a strong clip toward the car. She needed to see his face—the face that had haunted her ever since her first visit to the church weeks ago. She wanted confirmation that this was merely a look-alike.

When he reached for his car door, she stood at the back of hers, immobile.

"Mom," Star said in her what's-wrong-with-you voice, nice and loud. He turned toward Star. She knew she could slide right into her car in a heartbeat and be off. Instead, she took a closer look.

Their eyes met. Recognition flooded her. She squeezed her eyes shut momentarily and then gazed beyond his familiar frame. She had conjured scenes like this for years—randomly running into Devin (never at a church, though). Aware that her heart was hammering way too fast, she surmised that this could be some wild hallucination. The steady part of her recalled the advice she doled out to clients: *Take a deep breath.*

She did. And there he was. She took another deep breath. He took a step closer. She then did what seemed the natural thing to do: she called out his name. In that moment, he too called out. The words Devin and Mariah collided as they both exhaled.

Chapter 13

Devin smiled. A smile as familiar as the slight dimple in his left cheek and his ocean-blue eyes radiating a mysterious depth. How could a smile travel across two decades and remain the same?

"My God," he said, moving away from his car and toward her. "What has it been—twenty years?"

"Almost twenty-one." She bit her lower lip. Why had she been so precise?

Devin had grown even more handsome with time. With her additional twenty pounds and a face filled with anxiety lines, how was it he had even recognized her? Her face flushed. Oh God, why had she chosen to wear such a matronly dress?

"Mom." Star's certain-sounding voice brought her back to the church parking lot. Star stood at the passenger door, waiting for her to click it open, but the key fob had disappeared into the depths of her purse. She waved Star over to her side of the car. Perspiration dampened her underarms. She hardly recognized her squeaky, thin voice.

"My daughter, Star." Her hand shook as she clasped Star's hand, pulling her close. "We moved to Ash Grove . . ." Her brain went blank. Was it ten years ago?

"Twelve years ago," Star chimed in.

"Yes, twelve years," she said with a nervous trill. She gave a smile—the quick kind she'd flash at Gretchen on her way to retrieve a client.

"Do you live here?"

"Yeah. It's been about five years," he said. "I always knew after CU that I'd be back." He took a sweeping view of the horizon. "I love the high altitude and mountains."

Her heart swelled. On that first visit to Boulder more than twenty years ago, she had also fallen in love with this place. But what would bring him to this church? Or any church? The Devin she had known would never have attended a church, even a church that professed not to believe in a God. She took a step closer to her car and said, "I heard good things about this church, so we're checking it out." And then, "It's our first Sunday here." The fast-paced pounding of her heart brought on a light-headedness. She glanced at Star, who was donning her sunglasses even though the sun was very much absent.

Devin rocked back and forth. "It's a friendly community, all right." His voice was stiff. Was he embarrassed? He added, "I've been coming most Sundays for a little over a year."

Star had returned to her post, waiting to get inside the car. Mariah peered into her purse, snatched her keys, and clicked open the doors. "I'm volunteering with the youth program. Who knows, maybe we'll cross paths in the parking lot again." She yearned to say more, but what and how seemed an impossibility.

As she reached for the handle, he called out, "Mariah. It's nice to see you again."

She faced him. Her heart beat violently; she inhaled. His words, genuine, entered as liquid gifts. "Yes, it's a pleasant surprise," she said.

He pulled out a tan leather billfold and handed her a card.

"You're still a journalist."

"Yeah. I was lucky to have found my calling in ninth grade. With the internet, I can do my work most anywhere. Why not choose paradise?"

She flushed. It was paradise when they had come together. Later she had struggled to untangle the strands that had to do with him and those that had to do with the mountains. She stayed focused on the card as he continued.

"If you're ever in Boulder and want to meet for coffee, it would be fun to catch up. My number's on the card."

"So I see. Thanks." She met his eyes before turning away, and for a bright, hot instant, wonder and light gushed within her.

While Mariah navigated out of the parking lot, hands trembling, Star gave her the gift of silence. Once they hit Highway 36, Star asked, "Mom, who was that?"

"An old friend from high school."

"You mean your ex-boyfriend."

Mariah kept her eyes steady on the road. She squashed the impulse to fire back a curt response. "I didn't say that. Yes, we were friends, and it was quite shocking to see someone I knew over twenty years ago."

"Almost twenty-one years ago."

"Yup."

"So you knew him in college too."

"Sort of. He went to school here, and I went to San Diego State. Then we lost touch."

Star took out her cell phone, and relief swept through Mariah. She replayed the moment Devin had turned toward her, the moment when she knew, without a doubt, that it was him. Embers from the past flickered. She saw the part of Devin she had never let go of, the person she had cherished. His lips brushing against her cheek. Making out as a bonfire warmed a chilly evening.

All these years, she had assumed him to be happily married to Nicole in New York. Was he still with Nicole? She had glanced at his hand to see if he wore a ring, but she couldn't tell without staring. He had been very much alone in that parking lot.

Abruptly, a familiar fury at the God who had failed to save Charlie and Markus surged inside her. The same God playing a cruel trick in parading Devin through her new community. Devin, who had wanted nothing to do with churches. Devin, who had stepped out of her life when she would have given anything to be with him. Now he strode back in while she was in the thick of motherhood. There he stood, gorgeous as ever. And she, a middle-aged blimp.

"Mom. Why are you driving so slow?"

She startled to attention and sped up. Oh God, she had forgotten she was driving.

"That was amazing synchronicity," Star said.

"Amazing what?"

"Synchronicity."

"What's that?"

"I've told you. You've heard of Carl Jung."

"I have a degree in psychology . . ." And then she remembered—that was the odd word she had tried to recall the other day when the subject of church popped up twice in a single work shift. *Synchronicity.*

"He's the one who did research proving it. It's when events come together because of *meaning*, not just chance. Think about it. What are the odds of Devin showing up at the same time we did and parking next to our car?"

"Truly unexpected." Mariah couldn't suppress the smile that welled up.

"He must have been on your mind. That's how it works."

"Call it what you want, but don't be so sure about what's on my mind."

"It happens to me all the time."

"What happens?"

"Synchronicity."

"Well, sweetheart, I think you're very good at noticing coincidences."

"Especially meaningful ones," Star said, and returned to her phone.

In ninth grade, when Mariah had first gotten to know Devin and learned that, like her, he had no father or siblings, she had thought it extraordinary that they had this in common.

Then, in tenth-grade journalism, in an intense conversation about allowing the freshmen to have as much space in the opinion page as the juniors and seniors, he came alive, arguing on behalf of the underclassmen. Devin understood how fundamental it was to include differing perspectives. A concept that struck Mariah as vital. He had always been far more mature than the other insufferable teenage boys.

As juniors, Mariah and Devin were united in their outrage about the banning of gay couples from the senior prom. (Her own mother found their outrage to be ridiculous—but his did not.) Like the layers of an onion, layer upon layer revealed that they were more alike than not. Most mysteriously, his features changed and, in what seemed like overnight, he became handsome. And she could not see enough of him.

In college, at age twenty, she thought she understood the meaning of tragedy. She was alone in her room when Devin revealed on the phone that he had met someone at CU Boulder and ended their long-distance relationship. He was in love with Nicole. As she hung up, tears streaming down her naïve face, she wondered if this was God's punishment for losing her virginity with him. Later she would dismiss this "tragic" experience as merely a bump in the road.

As Mariah pulled into their driveway, Star asked, "Are you going to call him?"

The question sent a ripple of energy through her. She turned to Star and said, "No."

Chapter 14

My Journal of Hidden Truths
September 30, 2012

Everything changes, and anything can happen. Today is total proof of this, and you, Journal, are the first to know. I met someone at UUCB who I'm sure will be my forever best friend. Her name is Jen and, get this, she knows about David Bohm! How amazing and totally extraordinary is this? I declare it synchronicity.

I agreed to try this church out just to please Mom. Okay, truth is, I had to go. Once I realized this, some small part of me wondered, Wouldn't it be crazy wonderful if I met a cool person who thinks like I do? I giggled at myself for considering such outrageousness—in a church of all places. And then the impossible happened!

For starters, I must admit, Mom got it right. Not sure how she figured out that UUCB is unlike any other church. And it's nothing like Aspen Creek. Our teacher, Don, is cool. He turned every lame question thrown at him into a conversation more meaningful than any I ever hear in school. And, unlike the teachers at Aspen Creek, he wasn't making it his mission to control conversations. OMG, if only Mr. Haze could witness what a real teacher is like.

All the kids are mega cool. Especially Jen. She's one of few girls my age who are taller than me. And I could tell she wasn't into wearing stupid fashion clothes. As soon as we locked eyes, I knew she would get me. I sensed something different about her. Like when I met Mr. Seng or Jeffrey. An old soul. I could see both sorrow and brilliance within her.

Her choice to sit outside the discussion circle was my choice too. It didn't surprise me to see an empty chair perfectly placed next to her. She swiped her hand through her long dark hair, smiled, and said, "Are you into religion?"

"Nope. I'm a scientist. I study the works of David Bohm. My mom made me come." My head tilted toward Mom, who obviously stood out as a newcomer. The only parent. I wondered if I looked like her daughter. Our hair color is different, but we both have waves. Except she irons hers out. Scanning the room, I smiled. For once in my life, I blended in. As if I had always belonged.

Jen and I half paid attention to the discussion about projects aimed at making life better for everyone, including squirrels. In between bits of group chat, we leaned in and shared with one another small pieces of ourselves, as if they were undiscovered jewels waiting for the right recipient.

Jen said, "I'm totally not religious. But my parents made me come when I was . . ."

I saw her hiccup, and I scooted in closer. I peered at her and knew she wanted to tell me a hidden truth. Just as I share with you. She glanced around the room. I stayed focused on her. She then drew in her lower lip and pressed both together. When she turned to me, I knew she'd made up her mind.

"Way back when I was a boy."

These words fell on me in a bundle of dense energy. My body yearned to hug her for that raw honesty. Something I rarely encounter. Instead of hugging her, my jaw went slack. This must have been why she looked away.

"How long ago?"

"Last year. My name used to be Jacob."

"No, I mean, how long ago did your parents bring you to UUCB?"

"Since I was six." Jen quickly smiled at me and then looked away.

"Wish my mom had brought me here when I was six." She gave me an odd look, and it made me want to say more. "I hate junior high school." She nodded, and I returned the nod.

"Me too. I'm doing it online now cuz I can't stand all the posers."

Wow. Okay, Journal, we are going to need to figure out a way to get Mom to let me do online school. OMG, I'd get through school so fast and easy if I didn't need to sit through all the drama and stupid classes.

When Jen told me this, my leg swiveled and tapped hers. She met my eyes, and I couldn't help but grin at her. My heart swelled. I wanted to say, *You are so amazing! All the sorrow in your life has made you so real.*

Jen is wise. She gets that this is her life, and if something is wrong about it, it's up to her to fix it. Even if the grown-ups can't. She understands that if she doesn't try to make it right, she could die without experiencing living a real life. This is a hidden truth Jen and I both have.

Not only did I experience synchronicity in meeting Jen, but Mom too had the experience. And Mom being Mom totally missed it.

I'm sure, given Mom's horrid experience of growing up in a church that threatened hell, she would question if trying UUCB was the right thing. Well, she got her answer smack in front of her in the church parking lot. Of course she was clueless.

This guy from twenty years ago, who obviously was involved with her, happens to park right next to her car. OMG, what are the chances? For sure it's a sign! Mom acts all surprised, as if it is the oddest coincidence around.

Mom views life as a series of random events with no relation to anything. Just like the little boy who crashed our lunch yesterday. Obviously he meant something to her, or she wouldn't have practically barfed up her lunch. To her, life presents a set of meaningless coincidences. I declare that her meeting a former boyfriend was a coincidence meant to happen.

In Mom's world, me being who I am and being her daughter came about by sheer happenstance. Some arbitrary sperm penetrating an available egg. I refuse to think this way. If I believe myself to be nothing more than the outcome of some chance alignment of DNA, then nothing in life has meaning. All of life must be equally accidental and, therefore, meaningless. So why take any part of life seriously if one truly believes that what you see is a bunch of arbitrary events?

My new friend Jen understands this. She understood the hidden truth of who she really was, even while everyone else could only see a boy named Jacob.

Journal, and whoever You are reading this, I'm excited to have met Jen, and I know this wasn't some random, meaningless coincidence—I was meant to meet her. This too is a hidden truth.

I liked that guy Devin. I could tell he was into Mom, in a way different from anyone else who might like her. I had a hard time looking at him because his energy was so strong. I needed to wear my sunglasses even though there was no sun. I kept flashing on this scene of moonlight and warm weather and teens making out. For sure it must have been them, but this was way too weird to allow myself to see and feel. Anyway, that might just be my imagination.

Did You catch that, whoever You are? Deep down, I'm not sure what is real and what is my imagination. People like Jen give me hope. She figured out what is real for herself, even with everyone saying and seeing differently. Since I can't tell for sure what is real—David says reality is hard to grasp—I will try to believe my innermost self.

Chapter 15

Mariah jerked herself up in bed, her chest heaving in a silent, unrelenting cry. She rubbed her eyes and shook her head, trying to release the nightmare that had plagued her for the past twelve years.

January 8, 2000, had begun with a promising blue sky, though she and Charlie were tasked with the usual Saturday chores. Laundry spilled out of the hamper, the kitchen floor was a sticky mess, handprints marked the pale-blue family room walls.

Charlie was ready to pitch in to help restore some basic level of cleanliness. But there was three-year-old Markus to entertain, and Milly, who, at four months of age, needed constant attention, so Charlie suggested he take the two children. Drop Milly off at Olivia's, and then he and Markus would go to Dove Tail Park, five miles up the road. When she wrapped her arms around him in thanks, Mariah realized how desperately she needed this time alone to regroup. A tantalizing three hours to herself.

She held the generous bundle of Milly on her right hip while Markus raced ahead, showing off his skill in opening the car door. Milly's arm stretched out in front of Mariah's face, close enough to kiss her tiny finger pointing at the early-blooming pink camellias. The erupting flowers were intoxicating as Mariah leaned forward, allowing Milly to draw in the scent.

Mariah waved goodbye to her family. The aging Ford Taurus made its way out of their cul-de-sac at 11:30 a.m. She squinted at a twisted quilt of cloud crawling over the sky and briefly considered a little gardening before stepping back into the chaos of her house.

Once inside, she loaded up the CD player with favorites: Fleetwood Mac, Abba, the Spice Girls. The rhythmic music pulsing through her body turned laundry sorting into a dance. She mopped the floors, elated with the change from speckled goo to glistening, all the while unaware that the quick, ready-to-wave-goodbye kisses she had delivered to Charlie and Markus would be the last. That her rushed, inadequate expression of love would replay over and over. This deceptively beautiful January day in the little town of Daphne held no warning signs of an impending tsunami.

Her sense of being on a vacation amid putting her house in order abruptly ended at one o'clock with Olivia gasping into the phone and the sound of Milly shrieking.

"What's wrong, what's happened to Milly?" Mariah's legs gave out, and she fell into the couch, prepared to hear of a head split open or a broken bone.

"Out of the blue," Olivia said, gasping, "she started screaming. I checked her entire body—no rash or bee sting. I've been rocking her for twenty minutes. She's inconsolable. I'm about ready to swaddle her in a blanket."

"Mom, Charlie will be there soon. Try taking her outside—put the phone to her ear." She began singing "This Little Light of Mine" to no avail. She switched to a bedtime chant: "Momma loves you more than the distance of stars, the sun, the moon." Her voice spoke into a vacuum. Without intending, she yelled, "Milly!" But the only response had been a shrill scream.

Mariah switched on her light, reached for the TV remote, and began flipping through channels. She landed on a nature show. With glazed eyes she watched scene after scene of predator and prey while the narrator spoke in a soothing, paternal voice, and she finally drifted off.

Eventually, the TV screen turned to a gray snowy buzz. Mariah rubbed her eyes and glanced at the clock—3:00 a.m. She turned off the TV and nestled under her blankets.

Two hours later she awoke with a familiar throbbing in her head; a splash of color danced mockingly around her room. Even before squinting to read the numbers on her clock radio, she knew there would be no escaping her nemesis.

She forced herself up, planting feet on the carpet, holding at bay the thick taste of nausea that wrapped itself around her throat. Once in the bathroom, she fumbled, found, and consumed four small white pills that served as her only defense.

She all but crawled into bed before reaching for her phone. Her voice slurred, but her message was clear: she would not be in today. She buried her throbbing head under her pillow, anticipating the pills kicking in.

"Mom."

It was Star's voice, but the face of Markus. She reached up for him, and he faded into a thick fog.

"Mom."

She glimpsed the soft curls of his blond hair, his rosy cheeks. The painful pounding in her head had softened. The migraine had traveled downward; it was her heart that now ached.

"Mom."

She turned toward the distant yet familiar voice. She willed herself to answer but couldn't move. Light hands wrapped around her shoulder, rocking her back and forth. She was on a beach, asleep as the tide rose to her limp body, tossing her to and fro. Mariah lifted her right arm to part the surrounding fog. She reached out for the auburn curls framing Star's fear-drenched face.

"Your alarm was ringing. Are you okay?"

All that came out of Mariah's mouth was a moan.

"Do you need a doctor?"

She shook her head, breaking through the medication stupor. "Sweetie, I'm fine. It's one of those horrible headaches. I took some medicine. I'll be okay." She moaned and turned away, but the hand that had grasped her shoulder returned. With eyes shut, speaking into her pillow, she said, "You need to get ready for school, and I need to rest."

"I'm not going."

Moments passed before Star's words sank in. She felt the weight of Star sitting immobile on the side of the bed. "You have to," Mariah said.

"You couldn't hear your own alarm. I won't leave you alone. School's boring, and I have a horrible stomachache. If I eat anything, I'll throw up."

Mariah lifted her limp body to a modified sitting position. "What's going on? You know I get these headaches."

"You dreamed about him!"

"What are you talking about?"

"The little boy. We saw him Saturday, and you dreamed about him."

"No . . . I have a migraine. I need to rest, and you need to go to school." She didn't wait to hear Star leave the bedroom before burrowing under the covers again.

Later, Mariah opened her eyes to the sun filtering through her curtains. Squirming around, bedsheets twisted, she saw that it was two o'clock. No wonder her stomach was growling.

Star always got stomachaches when Mariah suffered a migraine. Why had she responded so harshly? With a light touch, she knocked on Star's door while staring into the eyes of Einstein. She rolled her eyes at the poster's proclamation: "Imagination is more important than knowledge." Star obviously had both. Holding her breath, Mariah cracked the door and, seeing Star's absence, exhaled. Star's stomachache couldn't have been all that bad, or she would have insisted on staying home.

She lingered in the doorway. Stuffed animals strewn across a twisted sea of sheets and blankets. A dangling replica of the solar system, poised to glow in the dimness, graced her ceiling. Her computer desk oddly neat. And then, temptation. Star's journals.

She went to Star's nightstand, where those journals lived. A pang of guilt swept through her when she saw that the cork-covered journal was there. Her hand twitched while an insidious voice whispered, *Hypocrite.* Her head pounded. She took a step back. She needed to return to her bed.

Turning away, Mariah caught her image in the full-length mirror—a contorted, unrecognizable version of herself. She slunk back to her room, crawled under the covers, and shook. Who had she become?

Forcing herself up again, she stumbled into the narrow hall. She needed to view the self the world sees. That Devin had seen. She turned on the light and stepped toward the hallway mirror.

Her creased face framed by Markus's blond hair, now yellowed with age and dried out in attempts to tame it straight. And her hips—they were just like her mother's, wide and expansive. Tears streamed down her cheeks. She had become a twisted image of her mother.

The storybook excitement upon encountering Devin vanished into waves of anguish. How could she have dared to stretch her imagination, fantasizing a fit, younger self? A self that might have been able to rekindle the magic that had never left her. Standing before this mirror, without blinders, she saw the raw, painful truth.

Chapter 16

Star's silence during dinner that night was immoveable. She refused to discuss anything about school. Annoyance grew so much within Mariah that she felt relief when Star excused herself and retreated to her bedroom.

Mariah paced around and ended up drinking a half bottle of merlot while giving her mind over to *America's Got Talent*, followed by *Glee*. When she finally turned off the TV, a marinated sadness settled on her. Guilt over enjoying Star's absence circled her like a snake, ready to strangle. She knocked on Star's door and when she heard no answer, she cracked open the door and found Star lying on her back, staring at her dimly lit universe.

"Just checking in to say good night."

"Good night," Star replied with eyes pinned to her ceiling.

"Is everything okay?"

Star remained motionless. A drunken sentimentality swept over Mariah, and she slipped in and sat on the side of Star's bed, yearning for some form of pardon.

"You're awfully quiet . . ." She reached over, grazing Star's silken cheek and causing her to twitch as if a fly had alighted. "Are you sure everything's okay?"

Star's complete disregard soured her mood. She stood up, vexed and at a loss. When she moved toward the door, Star finally answered.

"You tell me what's wrong, Mom. You're the one who stayed home with a migraine."

Stunned at first, and then incensed, she flashed on her own mother—intrusive, insisting she attend one church function after another. Overbearing and marching into her room without even a knock. Still, Mariah never would have spoken to her mother with such sarcasm. Now here she was entering her own daughter's room with caution, tiptoeing around.

There are no perfect parents.

Mariah shouted back, "Don't you ever talk to me this way. You have no idea what I've been through. I hope you never have to suffer a migraine." She stormed out, slamming the door.

Unable to sleep, she lay in bed with the TV droning on until the morning alarm rang way too early. With hot water spraying from the shower over her body, shame consumed her. Had she outright slammed Star's door as she left? She could recall only the quick flare of anger and her uninhibited release, courtesy of too much wine.

When she arrived at work, the heaviness kept her marooned to the seat of the sedan. She flipped the visor down and peeked into the mirror with trepidation. God, she looked a wreck. The soft area below her eyes remained puffy. Her makeup appeared completely made up—made up, propped up, to fill this role. She would get through the day and on to another.

Stepping into the gleaming, fluorescently lit building, she encountered Gretchen. Mariah wanted to scurry away like a mouse bumping into a cat. She surely looked as if she had been in a bar all night. Mariah fixed her face with resolve.

"Mariah."

Her stomach knotted.

"Missed you yesterday."

"Another migraine," Mariah said.

"Sorry. I understand they can be hideous. Have you had them your entire life?"

Hadn't they already discussed this? Mariah sweated uncomfortably. "For the past twelve years. Thank God they don't happen often."

"I've heard rubbing peppermint oil on your forehead can help."

Mariah took a step forward and squelched the impulse to say something nasty. "Ha. I'll have to check that out."

Gretchen trailed after. "I know. Sounds bizarre. But maybe? So . . ."

Mariah stopped, turned toward her supervisor again, and braced herself for a testimonial about peppermint oil.

"How's Star doing these days?"

She faced Gretchen's intense amber eyes. This was not an innocent question. "She's hanging in. Junior high is a big transition." Mariah blocked images of the humiliating meeting with the counselors. Gretchen's eyes remained fixed on her, and something inside Mariah quivered. "Why?"

"Tilly said Star is being teased."

"Oh?" Mariah crossed her arms.

"Evidently, she made quite a commotion in science class."

"They have science together?"

"No. It's just, well, you know how gossipy teens are." Gretchen rolled her eyes.

"Oh God, yes," she said, though she herself had not experienced that. At least not to the extent that would involve her mother. "Star told me what happened in lab. Quite frankly, it was an understandable mishap." Mariah dreaded what Gretchen might say next.

"I'm sure it was," Gretchen said. "Tilly also said that Star sometimes acts strange and doesn't seem to have any friends."

"You know Star. Highly imaginative. And an introvert."

"Right. Well, the girls hadn't seen each other in a while and Tilly tried to connect with her. But, as you know, they seem to be cut out of different cloth, so to speak."

"Oh yes, I do know." Oops. She had not intended this to sound sarcastic. Gretchen narrowed her eyes. Mariah hurriedly said, "I mean, let's admit it, Star marches to a different drummer. Recently she's made a new friend . . . more friends would be nice . . . but her major complaint is being bored with school. Mine is whether she's being challenged enough." Raising her brows in sync with a nod, she turned away and resumed her stride down the hall to her office.

How *dare* Gretchen describe Star as *strange*? Why not *unique*?

At noon, Mariah considered snagging her leftover mac and cheese from the fridge in the staff lounge and eating it cold in her office. Yet congealed cheese held no appeal.

Richard stood in front of the microwave, staring at a revolving bowl of soup while the timer flashed numbers in reverse. He turned to her. "Hey there, how's it going?" Before she could answer, he said, "Looks like no salad today. I'm also breaking with tradition—trying soup. It's soup weather after all."

"Sure is. It's leftover mac and cheese weather too."

"Are you feeling okay?" he asked.

Ugh. He must have taken a good look at her face. "I was out yesterday with a brutal migraine. Still feeling a little under."

"Sorry." He removed his bowl of soup. "You'll join me, right?"

She nodded as she placed her lunch in the microwave, and he sauntered off to a small table in the corner, away from where most of the staff gathered.

When she joined him, Richard stretched out one arm and then another. "I can't believe how sore my arms are. I finally joined a gym. Guess I overdid it."

"Really? What prompted this?"

"Well," he said, placing the palms of his hands on his substantial girth. "I like to eat. Building muscles burns more calories."

"Okay . . ."

"Yeah, so, given a few more muscles, I'll burn fat cells even while relaxed in my therapist's chair."

"For real? Just a few more muscles?"

"Theory has it that every pound of muscle burns fifty additional calories."

"Hum . . . and I wonder what it takes to create a pound more of muscle."

He gave a shoulder shrug and then took a spoonful of soup. "And I wouldn't mind bringing back a little more, uh, definition—or tone."

Bring back? Was it ever there in the first place? He just seemed so naturally soft and tending toward roundedness, she assumed he'd always been this way.

She said, "I can't fathom how anyone working full-time could find the energy to work out. I'm totally spent, just happy to be home. Pure torture it'd be to drag myself to the gym."

He gave a quick smile and assembled some crackers and cheese to go with his soup. "A brutal migraine, huh?"

She nodded and made her eye contact brief.

"I have no idea what your experience of a migraine is, I can only guess based on my limited, painfully clear memory of having something like a migraine happen."

She looked up. "When?"

"Just after Joey died."

"I forget, how old were you?"

"Sixteen. He was fourteen. For the next six months, I had the most god-awful headaches. Missing school three or four times a week. Had to make up classes over the summer."

Richard had lost his brother to a lethal combination of pills and alcohol. He had told Mariah, years earlier, when they were dating, that the experience led to his decision to become a counselor. But he had revealed nothing about migraine headaches.

"My doctor diagnosed it as a migraine. I had all the classic symptoms—bright flashes of light, depression prior to onset, nausea, and vomiting . . . but now I question the diagnosis."

"So you suffered migraines?"

"That's the thing. I didn't."

She hadn't either until shortly after moving to Ash Grove. Before, it was depression that had consumed her.

"It's mysterious," Richard continued, "but not really. Nothing worked in terms of medication. And then someone my mother knew suggested a therapist who specialized in trauma and mind-body connections. Within a month the headaches stopped."

"So what changed?"

"For starters, I was given a safe, contained place to grieve and address the guilt I had as Joey's older brother. As I began to work on this, the headaches lessened." Richard peered down at his soup. "You know, there's lots of literature with interesting evidence that the body will act out unexpressed emotions."

She nodded and took another forkful of food. Of course she was aware of these so-called theories—but migraines?

"I think it's unlikely that I had a sudden-onset migraine whose disappearance just so happened to coincide with me releasing the pain and guilt I had been carrying." Richard raised his eyebrows as he looked at Mariah.

Was this in deference to her—thinking she might consider it dubious? She did, and she struggled to remain impassive.

He gave a tight smile. "Toward the end of my time with the therapist, my parents had several sessions with him, and . . ." He slowed down. Had he told her this before and she missed it? She held his gaze as he spoke in measured words. "If it weren't for my headaches, well, I'm not sure my family would have come together or healed. My so-called migraines brought the three of us back together as a family."

"And therefore, you chose to be a therapist."

"Absolutely. Therapy changed my life and my family. I only wish . . ." Pain filled his eyes. "I guess there's no telling. It's easy in retrospect to analyze what wasn't working. Who knows? There may have been nothing that could have kept him from following along with his peers. My parents were doing their best—given everything."

Mariah's whole heart welled up and she was afraid to say anything. She had yelled at Star for no good reason last night.

"In the end, I'd say it was forgiveness that saved our family. My parents needed to forgive themselves." His voice lowered to a whisper. "As did I." Richard took a few more sips of his soup and munched on another cracker. Mariah stared at her mac and cheese.

Richard said, "I think I recall you saying you've had migraines for about twelve years?"

"They don't happen all that often. I manage them." Mariah scooped a forkful of food but couldn't bring it to her mouth. Was it his tragic story or his question that triggered the mammoth lump in her throat? She pulled in a deep swallow of air and held it for a moment or two. She blinked her moist eyes.

"Mariah," he said, his voice tender, "you've experienced a loss unimaginable to most of us. Something unspeakable. I . . ."

She met his gaze and pleaded wordlessly with him to stop.

"You know I care about you and . . ."

Mariah's napkin was now twisted so tight it could serve as a stir stick.

"I just wanted to know that it's possible. These headaches. Your body may be reacting to emotional trauma. It's never too late to heal."

Chapter 17

My Journal of Hidden Truths
October 2, 2012

Why is it I get these horrible stomachaches whenever Mom has her migraines? It's not fair! Mom of course thinks I'm faking, because nothing could be as violent and painful as her migraines. I should've known with my stomach somersaulting from the moment I woke up that Mom was out of it.

Her alarm clock woke me. I dashed to her room, and there she was all doped up in bed, alarm ringing—she didn't even hear it or me. For a moment I thought, *This is it! She's gone!* Which majorly freaked me out until I remembered the sleeping pills or whatever it is she takes for her monster headaches. Even so, she's all I have.

Once I figured out what was going on—the headache, a bad dream—I decided it wasn't worth staying home since I'd be sharing the house with her all day long.

I'm getting better at staying in my bubble at school. My goal—to not be noticed. Avoid drama. I keep watch, and when I see or feel someone coming who might upset me, I move. The hardest part is advisory because Tilly's in it.

At first, I needed to act all surprised to see her and be friendly since our moms work together and I sort of know her but have never been friends with her. Except now, even though I no longer need to be polite and make eye contact, she keeps pushing herself into my space. She's hard to ignore.

"Hi, Star, you're in with skipping advisory on Fridays so we can have an extra-long pep rally, right? Who doesn't want that?" I looked away, and she declared her answer: "My choice, if they'd give us a choice, is to shorten all the content classes on Friday so we can have advisory *and* the pep rally. Advisory's good—gives me a chance to catch up."

Catch up on gossip, that is. I gave her the answer she expected. "Whatever."

In Mrs. Severson's class today, I turned to the door just as Jasper was walking in. I try not to notice him because his sadness spills all over me. Today was different. I felt his smile coming, and I wanted to take it in. When I turned, our eyes caught one another's. Neither of us could hold back the smile. I then imagined him saying hi to me as he passed my desk. No one other than Tilly says hi. Then I heard his voice.

I wanted to jump up and tell him, "I agree with you. Science doesn't have all the answers. You're brave to have shared about your mother." Except I lost my nerve. Besides, science is way more complicated than having answers or not. Science is process. Sadly, school is all about right and wrong answers—as in, one way of viewing reality; a way that misses everything important.

Lately, I've been thinking how cool it is that some entities go on for thousands and thousands of years—actually, millions—and stay the same. Like stars. Here's what's amazing: the same sun that tans me in the summer did the same to David Bohm and Buddha. I like trees for the same reason—they can live hundreds of years. And imagine this—some of the most intelligent creatures don't even have brains, like starfish. They're so rad—if they lose an arm, they know how to create another one. Wish we humans could do that.

Most of what Mr. Haze teaches in science is old-school party line about what's real and what isn't. Because he's a teacher, he feels obligated to pretend to know more than he does, so much so that he forgets how little he does know. If he was a real scientist, he'd be interested in finding out more about how Jasper's mother healed herself from cancer.

Anyway, I try to get in touch with this staggering reality of the universe—stars, planets, and infinite space—by staring up at the version pinned to my ceiling. If I lie flat on my bed and keep my thoughts from wandering—focusing on the phosphorescent stars and planets—I can let go of all the crazy stuff that seems so irrelevant.

That's what I was trying to do last night when Mom interrupted. Okay, I was majorly pissed off at her. We had dinner, and she acted like everything was normal. But it wasn't. I know she saw the little boy in her dreams. She couldn't even get out of bed. I could tell she was relieved when I went off to my bedroom.

Staring up at my planets and stars, I imagined the thousands upon thousands of other galaxies. Then I tried to imagine the implicate order as David Bohm describes the underlying connection. Like what I had with Jeffrey—a being of an entirely different species, and still, we could communicate and understand one another. How can this be?

Regardless of differences, we're all made from the same stuff. Just as Carl Sagan said, every living thing is composed from stars—carbon, nitrogen, oxygen, and hydrogen. And David Bohm then takes it a step beyond the physical into the realm of consciousness. I don't understand all of David's ideas. But I know he's right that thoughts are more than neurons firing in the brain. Thoughts are powerful transmitters of information. Jeffrey, even a dog no longer living as we know it, understands my thoughts. Something of him remains alive. I have sensed his presence and spoken to him. This is my hidden truth.

Staring up at my bedroom universe, I was understanding all kinds of profound ideas when Mom interrupted. As soon as she knocked on my door, I suffered the sucking, needing whirlpool of her energy. Even though I didn't invite her in, she stepped into my room anyway. If I had been at school and sensed this vibe, for sure I would have moved away and not made eye contact.

She's drinking too much. It pulls her down. She became mad way too quick. It hurt when she yelled back at me. She holds the answer to my questions. I'm angry at her, but I can't stay that way. She's all I have. I miss Jeffrey more than ever.

Chapter 18

Mariah waited outside Adeline's Café along with a half dozen couples milling at the entrance. She and Richard had once been one of those couples leaning in close to each other, remarking on the warm breeze and the expected forecast of high temperatures. Now she stood solitary among this group of confident, connected people awaiting Sunday brunch.

She glanced at her phone—four minutes early. She could stroll around the block, and that way Devin would be waiting for her. How ridiculous. What in the name of God was she doing here? She took in the carefree faces surrounding her. Women wearing clothes that screamed *free spirit*: colorful draping tops, leggings or jeans that clung to the contours of thighs and calves, sandal-clad feet with polished nails. That her closet was empty of anything fashionable was no surprise.

Last week, stepping out of the UUCB classroom, she had run smack into Devin. It was no different from meeting him in the parking lot the previous week. She was flustered and entirely unprepared to meet him amid ushering a gangly group of adolescents out the door.

"Mariah," he gasped.

"Oh, hi." Despite her resolve to not call, to drop this whole notion of reconnecting, she felt an explosion of delight. But when he asked if she wanted to join him for brunch, her answer came quick—and later (she played it over multiple times), she knew it had a sharp, defensive edge to it. "No. Star. We have plans. I'm sorry, not today."

He persisted. No sign of disappointment. "How about next week? Star can come too."

She glanced back into the classroom, where Star sat in conversation with Jen. She took a breath. "Next week is perfect. Star plans to hang with her friend." Arrangements fell into place. They would meet at Adeline's.

After church this morning, Mariah had given Star a crisp twenty and watched with wonder as she and her new friend—tall, skinny, awkward Jen—sauntered out of class with conspiratorial grins. She imagined them ending up at Poppy's and then at Soothsayers, where Star might make a purchase. Star would wait for Mariah to call, and then they'd meet two blocks west of Adeline's at the corner of Ninth and Pearl. This was perhaps the most normal experience Star had had and the easiest playdate Mariah had ever set up. Indeed, there hadn't been many.

Now, her watch showed almost five after. She turned toward the wait list with a sense of purpose. And then caught sight of him striding toward the café. His gait had not changed in twenty years—both urgent and calm, long legs gliding forward in a synchronized fashion. He moved with a familiar resolve, as if on a mission. She turned away to not seem overeager.

A calculated moment later, she turned back, and, like magnets, their eyes found one another. An undefined smile played across his face as he made his way toward her.

"I guess everyone had the same idea." He scanned the crowd. "I didn't expect this, though I suppose I should have. The food is excellent." His shoulder grazed hers as he turned to face her again; she caught a musky scent of aftershave. It was the same scent Charlie had used. "Should we get our name on the list?"

"Sure," she said, and he weaved his way through the small crowd and slipped through the doors. The smell of coffee and bacon wafted out.

Devin had no trouble fitting in here in his casual long-sleeved gray button-down shirt. He had always easily fit in, and he had always had a plan. How common is it to know in high school what you want to do with your life? Mariah, on the other hand, had fallen into psychology and only later realized the practical implications of it. She wondered about this older version of Devin as she watched him make his way back to her.

"I left our name off—wanted to first check with you. It's a good forty-five minutes before a table opens." Again, he scanned the crowd. "In all honesty, I was hoping for a quieter place."

"I agree. Forty-five minutes is a bit much."

"How would you feel about a step back in time—Shiva Lotta Latte? They continue to do a fine job with coffee and pastries." He gave a shy smile and said, "Do you remember?"

She nodded and whispered, "I remember."

He looked away, a smile still playing on his face. She felt light-headed at the prospect of drinking coffee twenty years later at the same place where they used to openly kiss.

The coffee shop was almost empty. On the blackboard behind the barista was a sparse menu of yogurt, granola, and pastries. The full-bodied scent of freshly ground coffee beans perfumed the air.

As they walked up to the counter, Devin said, "I come here at least once a week."

Mariah debated telling him that she'd also visited the café, but she was saved from the decision by the barista who asked for their orders. She ordered a cappuccino with cinnamon-walnut bread, and he ordered an Americano and yogurt with granola. They slid into opposite sides of an oak booth, its firmness forcing her into a straight-backed position. They adjusted coffee cups, bowls, and plates, and for endless moments seemed helpless in piercing the silence.

At last, in a soft whisper, he spoke. "Twenty years is a long time." He reached over for the honey jar and dribbled a translucent golden line into his granola.

All she could do was nod. Two decades. How could they have anything in common? She speared a corner of the sweet bread with a fork—were she alone, it would be her fingers twisting off the corner and popping it in her mouth.

He offered a strained smile. "I don't know where to begin." He gave a little laugh. "You were the last person I expected to see at UUCB."

"Tell me about it. You, who poked fun at my churchiness, show up in a church parking lot?"

"And you, who were so, uh, well—"

"Straight-laced? Conservative Christian?"

"Yeah, and in Boulder, at the Unitarian church—hardly the center of Christianity."

"I admit, it surprises me too." She almost added, *I planned to never step foot in a church again.* She took a sip of her cappuccino. "Clearly, we've both changed in two decades." Devin was the first and only genuine atheist she had ever met.

"It's hard to remember who I was. Other than my mother and journalism, I've let go of most everything from my past." He looked in her direction, but not at her, as if seeking guidance from Shiva herself. "And now, here I am, back in this café"—he turned his gaze to her—"with a significant piece of my past."

What was he trying to express? Regardless, it felt courageous. Intimate. He smiled at her, and twenty years fell away; she saw the two of them sporting sunglasses while walking hand-in-hand down Pearl Street.

"So . . . ," he began, "are you . . . does Star have . . ."

"A father. Yes. But, like yours and mine, he's no longer in the picture." She hoped he didn't notice how quickly she spewed out the last sentence. Her eyes dropped.

"Sorry . . ."

"Me too."

"Are you still Mariah Palmer, or did you take a new name?"

"Same name. But . . ." She stirred the froth on her cappuccino. "I'm not the same person." Glancing up at Devin, in a moment of dizzying collision, she was in both the past and present, but the pieces no longer fit. She took a deep breath. "So, is, uh . . ."

"Nicole."

"Are you still together?"

"No. She passed." He said it matter-of-factly and then took a sip of coffee. Did he mean he was over Nicole and she was in the past—but no, that made little sense.

"I'm so sorry," she said, studying his face. But there was no change in his expression. Clearly it hadn't been a sudden loss, like hers. She knew what a sudden loss looked like, even disguised in one's face.

"Ten years ago. Ovarian cancer. We weren't together. As a couple. In fact, three years before, I was on the verge of leaving her. And then. Well. It's complicated." He sighed and glanced around.

Was he uneasy talking about it with her? The distant clanging of pans and whirring of espresso machine created a veiled privacy. She wanted to know more but was afraid to say anything. She thought back to her own life ten years ago; it had been one of the loneliest periods of her life. Jeffrey and Star, her primary relationships.

"The thing is, after a couple of years in New York, I longed to get back to the mountains, the sunsets, nature—Central Park just didn't cut it." He picked up his coffee cup and took a few sips. "But I was caught in her web and couldn't leave. I was relieved she didn't push for marriage, which was disturbing. After all, that had been the plan."

She nodded. Years ago, that plan had devastated her. "So, you *didn't* marry her?" Devin slowly shook his head. A rush of heat swept up her neck. She clasped her napkin and patted her lips in case the cinnamon-walnut bread crumbs had bunched in the corners of her mouth.

"Prior to the diagnosis, I was ready to call it quits. I convinced myself she was having an affair. There was this gentleman, at least twenty years older. An art collector who frequented the museum where she worked. He had the balls to flirt with her right in front of me." His jaw tensed, and her heart went out to him. "The truth is, it didn't bother me as much as I let on. My annoyance was like . . . a facade of anger. It wasn't real. I was no longer in love with her." He picked up his cup and glanced off, drew in a long sip of coffee. When he turned back to Mariah, he had the same earnest look she remembered from high school. "I'm sorry to go on like this. You're probably not dying to hear all these details about me and Nicole."

"Please. Continue." She chided herself for using her clinical voice. Yes, she wanted to hear all the details.

"Well, this supposed affair was really just my out. Making it easier to do what I had wanted to do for years—leave Nicole and come back to Boulder."

"But you didn't leave?" Mariah said. Devin's disclosure stunned her. She had always imagined him happily married. A reality she had invented. What other nonexistent realities had she created?

"No, because out of the blue, it became clear something was really wrong. With her. When the cancer diagnosis arrived, she fell apart. Almost overnight she lost everything. Her hair, her job, even Mr. Hoity-Toity stopped calling. It was heart-wrenching, like witnessing a beautiful marble statue turn to sand." He bowed his head. "I was all she had—other than her dysfunctional family."

Without thinking, Mariah reached across the table. She clasped his hand, gave a light squeeze, and he responded in kind. It felt so natural.

"I don't regret staying with Nicole," he said as she withdrew her hand. "I experienced a part of her that I'd rarely seen. She let go of all the sharp judgments that kept me defensive. And that fictional love affair?" He gave a quick smile. "It disappeared like smoke. All in my imagination. She changed in profound ways." He inhaled slowly and added, "So did I."

He picked up his spoon as if to take another bite of yogurt, but he returned it to the bowl. "Is this too much?" His blue eyes again captured hers.

"No," she whispered.

"The last year, when it became clear nothing was working, she began praying, meditating. It was all so foreign to me." He shook his head. "My mom came to be with us during what turned out to be Nicole's last week. That was a shocker. She had been furious when I followed Nicole to New York. In the end, it was a gift, having her there."

Mariah nodded slightly, jolted by hearing him say *mom*, when he had always called her Candice.

"Nicole was in hospice care, hooked up to drip bottles, pale as a sheet, and barely breathing. But she'd have these lucid moments. She'd say that she was meditating and would talk about all kinds of weird stuff that made no sense. Like . . ." He turned his eyes upward. "How everything was perfect, that there was no need to be upset." He glanced at Mariah with a modest smile. "I guess you could say she was at peace."

Mariah opened her mouth—nothing came out. She and Devin had both lost loved ones, but in such dramatically different ways. A toxic mingling of anger and jealousy welled up. The universe had bestowed a kindness to Nicole and Devin, whereas she and Charlie had had no warning. No silver lining to Charlie and Markus's violent departure. They had loved the life they had; there was only more growth ahead of them. Hot flames of anger singed her heart. With practiced discipline, she numbed the pain.

"My mother understood everything Nicole was trying to express. She has changed over the years," he said. "I'm actually enjoying her." He smiled at Mariah's look of skepticism. Devin swallowed the last of his coffee and asked if she would like another. She nodded, and he slipped out.

Mariah couldn't imagine the woman she knew as Devin's mother in this caring role. Once, in high school, he had called to tell her he was sick and wouldn't be at school the next day. His mother was away at an important conference at the time. Mariah fretted over who would take care of him. After she hung up the phone, she turned to her mother and said aloud for the first time, "My boyfriend," and asked for her mother's help. That evening, they had delivered a dose of her mother's homemade chicken soup.

Now, as he returned with two full cups, she tried to recall the adolescent Devin, the boy who showed up at his front door in a robe, looking pale and sick but grateful to receive chicken soup.

Handing the cappuccino to Mariah, he said, "Growing up, I felt ripped off in not having a real mother." His cheeks reddened. "I mean, I liked how on top of things your mother was."

"Not if you lived with her. Overbearing is what you'd get with my mother. Or a more apt description—majorly intrusive."

He gave a short laugh.

She added, "Oh yeah, I remember you pouting about how she never brought birthday cupcakes to school or even made you a cake."

He rolled his eyes, yanking her back to the younger, unrecognizable version of who she was. She giggled.

"But I liked your mother," Mariah said. "Maybe for the same reasons you had issues with her. To me, she was, well, honest . . . and exotic."

"Exotic?"

"Yeah—so different from my mother," she said. "I'm glad you're feeling closer to her." Mariah thought of Star and the multiple ways Star was so different from herself.

"Me too. And she lives here in Boulder now," he said. "She left her position at UCLA and moved here for some sort of grant research project with Naropa." He gave a wry smile.

"Naropa?"

"It's a university here in Boulder, named after an eleventh-century Tibetan Buddhist sage. It's fully accredited, legit, and is Buddhist inspired."

Her head spun. She pinned her vision to the Shiva relic. "Dr. Quinn?" She hadn't intended to say this aloud, it just spilled out.

"Yup. She's no longer the staunch atheist I grew up with. She describes herself as spiritual. She's the one who suggested I check out the Unitarian church—I had no idea a church could be so non-churchish."

Mariah slowly nodded.

"Yeah. She meditates, she's a vegetarian. This research project at Naropa . . ." Devin sighed. "It's unconventional. Something to do with psychics."

"Okay," she said, working to make her voice steady while her mind whirled.

He gave her a tentative look, and then took a breath as though reconsidering whatever he was about to say. Her heart raced; she was certain he would ask about her past. She twisted her napkin on her lap and braced herself.

"I wonder . . . do you still consider yourself a person of faith?" he asked.

She laughed with relief for what he hadn't asked, and her cheeks reddened. "Truth is, I came to UUCB searching for a community for Star. She's brilliant, but she struggles to make friends. I'm thrilled she's already made a friend. That's who she's with now." Saying this made her smile. At this very moment Star was with a real friend. "I only considered UUCB *because* of its non-churchishness."

His smile came quick and polite. "When Nicole was dying, I thought of you. How assured you were that there was a heaven. I desperately wanted to believe it."

Her eyes fell to the table; she had no reassurance to give him. "Heaven is no longer real to me," she said. A cold sweat sprang up under her blouse. She willed herself to stay seated through an unbearable series of seconds. She glanced at her purse—if only Star would call.

"It's none of my business . . . ," Devin said, and Mariah felt every part of her body go still. He spoke softly, guiding his words delicately. "I'm wondering . . . I mean, how did you end up here, so far from where you grew up? What brought you here?"

Of course he wanted to know her story. As if it could be told like a fairy tale. No. This story was so horrific, she had failed to find a way to tell it to her own daughter. She took in this older version of Devin, the one who'd been elevated from his spiritual experience of losing a love he had already decided to leave. He had shared this "tragedy" with Mariah, but what did he know of true tragedy? Nicole's death had been peaceful and planned and complete with his mother swooping in to bring about a reunion. The anger she'd been able to tamp down earlier now surged within her.

"Life is not fair," she sputtered.

He flinched.

She thought of Nicole, Charlie, Markus. "Nicole didn't deserve this." Her heart pounded so fast she was breathless.

He drew back with a stunned look. "Nicole was at peace."

"No. You can't know that." Her voice louder than intended. The blond woman two booths away turned her head. "Okay, maybe she was, but not everyone is as fortunate. Death can be brutal." Her mind screamed, *It's not fair.* "No. I no longer believe in a God that creates heaven. Nor fairy-tale endings." The energy that coursed through her body made sitting impossible. She stood up so fast she pitched forward and slammed her palms on the table, narrowly missing the coffee cup. She shimmied out of the booth, turned to him, and said, "I am left alone with a daughter to raise. I had to leave the community that brainwashed me." She shuddered.

She dove her hand into her purse, yanked out her phone, and announced, "I need to go."

Chapter 19

My Journal of Hidden Truths
October 14, 2012

Okay, Journal, I'm a complete wreck. I had no idea today would turn out as it did. This must be what it's like to fall in love.

Mom gave me twenty bucks, expecting Jen and I to get pizza and hang out at Soothsayers while she had brunch with Devin. But we weren't hungry.

So we started toward Soothsayers. Walking side by side down the street, I could tell she was as excited as I was to have an entire two hours to ourselves. I had to calm the urge to skip. Roaming around Boulder without Mom, a totally cool friend by my side, made me insanely happy.

Jen was dressed in black leggings, a short skirt, and boots. She had this rad nylon undershirt with sleeves that made her arms look tattooed. From a few feet off, it would have fooled me. She said it was the closest her mother would allow to the real thing.

Jen is the first genuinely cool person I've walked around with. Part of me imagined the fun of running into Tilly and a few others, just to show them that I'm not as nerdy as they think. Jen said she likes my retro way of dressing. Mom of course thinks I dress weird. Truth is, I just put on what feels right and comfortable in the moment.

Just as we passed Clutter Consignment and Bodywork Bistro, a beautiful gray-and-white mutt caught my attention. He was sitting with a bright-red leash wrapped around a bike rack, obviously waiting for his person. His eager eyes reminded me of Jeffrey, who would wait for me every day after school. He had Jeffrey's wavy hair and a stub tail. I had to stop and pet him. Jen understood. "You're missing Jeffrey." I nodded and turned away to hide my damp eyes. "Hey," she said, "let's skip Soothsayers. I have a better idea for where we should go."

She was right. Soothsayers and tarot cards no longer seemed important. Jen took me to the Boulder Humane Society, where she had met her best friend, Rachel.

My stomach was a twisted wad as soon as we stood outside the building. I wondered if this was what it was like to have a blind date. My heart ached for Jeffrey, knowing there would never be a replacement. I held back, and Jen said, "Star, I know you miss him. Please, let's just take a quick look. If I hadn't come here, I never would have discovered Rachel."

No way did I expect this place to feel like visiting a jail (even though I've never been in a jail). Bars, pleading yelps, the smell of dog pee mixed with ammonia. There were curled-up furry bodies tucked tight in corners, dogs running crazy in small confines as if on steroids, and a dank atmosphere of abandonment. After seeing three distressed mutts in a row huddled in the corner of their cells, I turned to Jen and begged, "Please, let's leave."

She held my hand, met my eyes, and spoke slowly. "Your. Job. Is. To. See. Beyond. Appearances." My lips trembled. Merging feelings coursed through me. "Star. You're good at seeing deeper." Then she said, "You can see me." And then I understood. I wanted to hug her, but instead I pressed my shoulder against hers. "Keep your heart open and you may find the one who can fill the empty space Jeffrey left." This made me flinch. She noticed. "I know. It's the best way I can say it. Trust me."

We made our way down row upon row of yelping, desiring, wanting dogs, and my trust in her conviction began to evaporate. Sadness filled my heart as I looked over sweet dogs showing up grungy, smelly, and resigned to the back corners of their cages. I forced myself to pause and take quick glances. Deep down, I knew I was trying to find a dog that looked and felt like Jeffrey. Soft curls, a body that wiggled with tail movement, no yelping, just a mooing and moaning, a deeper way to communicate.

The barking and howling overwhelmed me. I would have left if it wasn't for Jen, who kept a hand on my upper arm, guiding me forward. When we came to the last kennel, relief washed over me to finally be done.

I took a deep breath and made my eyes travel slowly into the confines of the miniature jail cell. At first, nothing registered special—another mixed-breed smallish mutt quivering in the back of its cage.

I took a closer look, thinking I was only doing this because Jen was so sure I would find a Jeffrey replacement and this was the last caged mutt. All at once, my heart began beating overtime. Creating the same sensation when I first caught sight of Jen at UUCB, and when Mr. Seng suggested the recycling project.

When I refocused on her, she felt my gaze and lifted her head. We held each other's eyes—hers, deep brown, watery, and full of desire. I wanted nothing more than to comb my hand through her beautiful brindle hair. My heart surged.

She looked nothing like Jeffrey.

Jen tugged at my sleeve and pointed to the name tag. The Humane Society makes up names for their abandoned guests. I had disregarded these made-up names. "Star, look!" The name typed out on the card read "Stella."

I smiled at this sweet-sounding name. When I turned to Jen, I could see she was waiting for some other reaction. At last she blurted out—"Don't you get it? *Stella* is Latin for 'star.' She has your name!"

Jen glanced around—we were the only ones peering in at Stella. Jen unlatched the cage door, and Stella leapt forward to greet us. The rules were that we needed to let someone know which dog we were interested in before meeting them. Jen is good at breaking rules for the right reason.

Stella's curved half-moon tail, with the tip almost touching her back, wagged so hard it almost straightened out. I squatted down to be at eye level. She boldly charged right into my lap and tried to lick my face. She was so sure I was the one for her that I knew she was the one too.

Jeffrey, part cocker spaniel and part poodle, had unmistakable heritage. Stella is hard to pin down. Longish body, legs that seem too short, eyes that are huge, ears that flop. Her body is a third the size of Jeffrey's, with bristly straight brindle hair. She must have come from a diverse family. Beagle, Chihuahua, terrier-something. Totally unique.

All I know is that her joy wrapped around me. For a moment, she lit up that empty place in my heart where Jeffrey had lived. And she's so different from Jeffrey or any dog I've ever met. Jen is right, appearances don't matter at all—it's the inside that counts. I fell instantly in love with Stella.

And then, my cell phone rang. It was Mom. I couldn't wait to tell her.

"Mom!"

"Meet me at Ninth and Pearl in about ten minutes." Her voice sounded as stressed and strained as the dogs locked in cages waiting to be chosen. I shook.

"But. Can't I have a few more minutes, like, another five or so?"

"Okay, five. But that's all. See you in fifteen minutes." Her tone fetched a gloomy shadow of dark colors that swirled around me. One I never argue with.

Jen had seen the chemistry between me and Stella. As soon as I turned towards her, she hugged me. "See?"

"You were right. I just needed to wait until the end to find her."

"So why didn't you tell your mother?"

I rolled my eyes. And knew Jen would understand.

"Mom evidently had a difficult lunch date."

Chapter 20

Early Monday morning as she got ready for work, Mariah found a note from Star in the kitchen. "Mom, your coffee's ready to go—I set it up! Hope you have a good Monday. I'll make dinner tonight. Love, Star." She had drawn a heart next to her name.

She must have written it after Mariah had settled into her room last night. Star never go up earlier than necessary. What could she be up to?

Mariah now realized that Star had been empty-handed the day before. In her state of turmoil the previous day, she hadn't even noticed. Had Star set her eyes on the priciest tarot deck Soothsayers had to offer? Was she planning to ask for an advance on her allowance?

Not a word had passed between them the entire ride home. Star had been busy with her phone, and Mariah had the sense that Star knew exactly what her mother needed: to use her full attention to halt the trembling in her body; to drive safely. It was early afternoon, and she yearned to be home, to have a glass of wine and call it a day.

Later, she and Star settled into a simple dinner of mac and cheese. Mariah had experienced a detachment—oddly forgetting to ask Star how it was strolling through Boulder with her new friend. Star had not brought it up. The only thing Star commented on was Jeffrey. She hadn't said a thing about Jeffrey for about a month now, so Mariah had assumed that, with adjusting to school and meeting Jen, she was over the loss.

"Mom, would it be hard for you to accept a dog that is different from Jeffrey? I don't think we can ever find another one like him."

"You're right, sweetie, we can't. He's one of a kind. We shouldn't even try."

"I agree," she said, and added, "that is, we shouldn't try to replace him."

"Of course not."

"But it would be nice to get to know another dog, even if we end up with a dog that's nothing like Jeffrey."

"Yes, it would. We need to be open to new relationships. Let's give it some thought."

At 11:40, Mariah retrieved her lunch from the cafeteria refrigerator and settled into a corner table. Moments later the cafeteria doors flew open. An unmistakable melodic humming told her it was Richard. She flashed him a smile, and he slid into the yellow vinyl chair across from her. He looked as though it were the Friday before a Monday holiday.

"So?"

"So what?" he said with a grin.

"So what wonderful event is springing up in your life?"

He grinned wider and glanced around the cafeteria. "You noticed."

"It's hard to miss." She reflexively stirred her salad with no appetite.

"I'm that obvious?"

"Let's just say the humming in sync with the tippy-toed movements, as if you were about to break out in dance, is, well, a slight giveaway." And then it hit her. "Are you in love?" She almost blushed at her own question.

"Mariah. I can't believe—"

"I'm teasing."

"No. That is, I don't think I am."

"Well?"

"Finally I had a decent date."

No wonder he enrolled in a gym.

"That's fabulous, Richard. You deserve this." She glanced at her salad but reached for the small bag of crackers she had brought. "So, who's the dame?"

"Someone I met on Matchup. We happen to have a lot in common. She's also divorced, no children. She's into birding, something I've often considered."

"Really?"

"Actually no. But. Sounds like a great way to explore a little countryside."

Mariah focused on giving Richard her attention, her face fixed, even though she felt numb inside.

"Anyway, it's nice to meet someone with similar interests. Unfortunately, she lives in Denver." He unwrapped his sandwich and asked her, "So, how was your weekend?"

She allowed the question to settle while staring vacantly at her salad. "A rather odd thing occurred a few weeks ago."

"Oh?"

"Yeah. I ran into this guy from high school. Here in Boulder," she said. "My daughter calls it synchronicity."

"Oh, Carl Jung, right?"

"Yep. I'm the psychology major who needed my thirteen-year-old daughter to remind me of this word's meaning. Star tends to find meaning in every event—regardless of how random it is." Mariah couldn't help her dismissive tone.

"I say, there's no telling." Richard leaned forward with a glow in his face.

Why the hell did she bring this up? She tossed her eyes around the cafeteria hoping he'd get the clue: there was nothing more to say.

"So . . . is this guy someone you dated, a former boyfriend, perchance?"

"Yes. Twenty years ago. Believe me, I'm nothing like I was two decades ago."

"I imagine the same can be said for him?"

"Oh yeah. He too has changed." She recalled her amazement in instantly recognizing him.

"Are you going to meet up with him?"

"We did. Yesterday. Brunch in Boulder."

"And?"

She immediately saw Devin's stricken face. "It was a disaster." She winced and shifted her weight on the rigid chair. The ache in her back needled in deeper. "I mean, really, Richard, can you imagine meeting someone you dated in high school at our age?"

"Hell no. But then, I was a total nerd. Here's the embarrassing truth, I never dated in high school. That's why I fell so hard for Debbie. Unlike you, I had little experience."

"The point is, we grow up. We change."

"Thank God for that." Richard took a mouthful of his sandwich.

Mariah's stomach rumbled in the ensuing silence. But she couldn't eat. Even the crackers tasted like cardboard. She attempted to shift her focus to her afternoon schedule. Except she couldn't recall her schedule.

"Perhaps, if you give him a chance, it might be you both have changed in compatible ways."

She stopped herself from shaking her head no. She forced a partial smile, and asked, "So, what's her name?"

"Lynelle. She's a fitness coach."

Oh no. Richard was not an image of fitness. But maybe this would be the inspiration he had been waiting for. She met his smile. "I'm happy you found her."

He beamed, and she checked her watch and readied herself to leave. As she stood up, Richard said, "Hey, you too deserve to have a nice relationship. Don't let yourself spoil it."

At home that evening, Mariah had barely slid her coat off her shoulders when Star showed up and took it from her. She couldn't remember the last time she had been greeted by anything other than an empty room. Star, with an irrepressible grin, announced she had dinner planned. The house smelled heavenly, like something baking.

Star almost danced into the kitchen, where she opened the oven door to reveal drop biscuits. "I made them from scratch—we had all the ingredients. I looked it up on Allrecipes dot com." She then poured Mariah a glass of wine, grabbed a plate with crackers and cheese, and ushered her into the living room while she prepared the rest of dinner. Scrambled eggs and veggie sausages.

"This is a beautiful meal, Star. Let me guess, you want an advance on your allowance."

"That would be nice . . ." But Star shook her head.

"You're wanting a new cell phone?"

"No!"

"You found the perfect tarot deck?"

"Mom. This is much more serious than tarot cards."

Star's eyes thickened—for a moment Mariah panicked. What in God's name did this child need?

"I, I met this most amazing, wonderful dog. Her name is Stella! That's Latin for 'star.' I need to have her."

Chapter 21

Mariah left work early that Friday to pick up Star and go to the Humane Society. Her excuse: a dentist appointment. She never got a free pass for outright lying. Her conditional upbringing always injected a hefty dose of guilt.

Although she had expected they'd eventually get another dog, she had imagined the two of them spending evenings surfing the internet with conversations of which breed would be the best match. It hadn't occurred to her that Star might decide on her own to go to the Humane Society. Yet it made perfect sense. Star's new friend, Jen, understood Star's immediate need to have another dog.

Waiting for Star in the Aspen Creek parking lot, without a looming date with the school counselors, Mariah felt giddy. When the obnoxious school bell rang, Star was one of the first to race out. She slid into the seat next to Mariah with a conspiratorial grin. Mariah experienced a rare burst of delight in joining her daughter.

When they reached the Humane Society, Mariah said, "Are you sure they're open?" The parking lot was empty.

"Yes. I called earlier today. Stella knows we're coming for her." Star's face stiffened. Her eyes fraught with potential tears.

Before Mariah could unbuckle her seat belt, Star strode ahead to the entrance. She held the door for Mariah with eyes fixed inside the building. Mariah entered to the muted sounds of persistent barking and the smell of ammonia and was transported to her practicum in a psychiatric ward. Like homeless dogs, so many of those patients had longed to experience an intimate home life.

The young woman behind the check-in counter grinned at Star. "You're here for Stella!"

Star beamed and nodded.

"I'll get her," the woman said. "I know she'll be excited to see you again."

Star turned to Mariah. "Mom, you'll love her. She's different from Jeffrey, but that's okay. I can tell she's the right one for us."

Yips and barking ensued, and Star moved toward the door to the kennels.

"She hears me!"

Once Stella was placed on the ground, Star fell to her knees, and the yips subsided. Small gripping whimpers followed. Stella shoved her nose into the creases of Star's clothing, ignoring Mariah's sweet talk and gestures.

Star was right. Stella was nothing like Jeffrey. And the stark contrast clarified that something new was on the horizon.

On Sunday morning, Star's bedroom door creaked open as Mariah finished her third cup of coffee. The brindled bristle-haired mutt who had claimed Star as hers wiggled in circles around Mariah's slippered feet. This homely, odd-looking mongrel couldn't have been more opposite in appearance to Jeffrey. The tapered, curled-up tail moved so vigorously that Stella's attempt at moving forward resembled a drunken swerve.

Star emerged in tie-dyed flannel pj's, ushering Stella out the kitchen door. Star up from bed before nine was an impressive feat. Life, or at least routine, had changed since Friday afternoon.

Three blocks from the Unitarian church, Mariah's hands slipped on the steering wheel, her palms sweaty as she scanned the intersection and forced herself to slow down her breathing. She inched through the four-way stop. It had been two weeks since she'd experienced these maddening symptoms of anxiety.

"Mom, what's going on?"

"Nothing. Too much coffee—had a hard time sleeping last night—it's making me jittery."

Star made a guttural sound while twisting her head to the right, as if suddenly she found the landscape of parked cars fascinating.

Mariah asked, "So UUCB is a good choice for you?"

"I already told you. And I can tell you're nervous."

"I'm just checking in, that's all. I won't be in class today. I'm attending the lecture upstairs," Mariah said. Star pulled away from the window and gave Mariah a suspicious look. "Besides, Don does a great job of managing everyone. I'm hardly needed."

"Except when Bruster and Forest start acting all weird, dominating the discussion."

"Star, even you agreed Don is quite talented at keeping the conversation on topic." And Mariah wondered, did Star enjoy her presence in class? Had her attendance reminded Star of the old days when Mariah had no choice but to sit in on Star's classes?

"What's it about?" Star said.

"What's what about?"

"The lecture."

"Oh." Mariah searched her memory. It wasn't the topic that had caught her attention at all. It was the presenter. The word *reconcile* was what she remembered from the title. "It's, um. I think it's a scientist talking about how to reconcile one's faith in the unseen with the facts of science."

"You're interested in *that*?"

"Maybe. I thought a change would be good."

"If whoever this scientist is has studied David Bohm, the answer would be obvious."

"Who?"

"David Bohm. A famous physicist. Don't you remember? Mr. Seng told me about him and gave me one of his books."

"Oh, that's right. Well, perhaps."

Once parked, Mariah flipped the visor mirror down and decided one more application of lipstick wouldn't hurt.

"Mom, I wish I could bring Stella to class to meet everyone. I wonder if they allow dogs."

Mariah smiled. "I guess you'll have to ask."

They hustled in silence toward the classroom. When Star's face lit up at the sight of Jen coming down the hall, Mariah felt a pulse of calm through her body. She touched Star's arm and pecked her cheek.

Turning the corner toward the stairs, she ran into Trudi balancing an armful of construction paper. "Let me help." Mariah reached out her hand.

"No problem." Trudi unloaded the paper on the supply counter several steps away. "Looks like you're skipping out on class today." Trudi grinned.

"All's well in room seven. Thought I would slip into the lecture and see if I might learn a thing or two."

Trudi had filled her in on the lecture option when Mariah had swung by the church earlier in the week to help put together introduction packets for potential new teachers and volunteers. Mariah typically entered through the basement door that led to the classrooms, so she hadn't seen the sign in front announcing Reverend Scott's sermon topic or the guest lecture. But on that Thursday evening, the parking lot had been full, and she ended up circling around, parking on the opposite side of the basement entrance. Even parading past the front of the church, she still would have missed the reader board were it not for the name that brought her to a stop.

She asked Trudi about the lecture.

"Each week we have a guest lecturer, and people can choose whether to attend that or the sermon. Dr. Quinn was here last year, and she packed Nathan Hall discussing quantum physics. I'd go if I could. She used to teach physics at UCLA. I hear she's got some sort of hush-hush research project going on with Naropa." She gave Mariah a quizzical look. "Do you know her?"

"Sort of . . . it's a long story." Mariah had shifted her gaze away.

Now, three days later, Trudi was congratulating her for attending a lecture instead of volunteering in Star's class.

"It should be a tad more interesting than discussing how stereotypes get started with teenagers," Trudi said.

"Perhaps," Mariah responded, though in fact, she had been looking forward to the topic. The students, including Star, all had such unique takes on life. She had never been exposed to these subjects at any level of school.

"By the way, that daughter of yours seems to have settled into UUCB quite nicely."

"She sure has. I'm so pleased." She considered sharing Star's desire to bring her newly adopted dog for show-and-tell and decided to leave that up to Star.

"I didn't mention this the other night," Trudi said, "but I'm especially glad to see her connecting with Jen. He's had such a hard time."

"He?"

"Oops. I've known her since she was five. Until last year, she was a he."

"My God. I didn't realize kids this young—"

"She's so much happier."

"Oh. It's just . . ." What could she say? She cast her eyes past Trudi to the window and noted, even on the grayest day, light saturated that part of the hallway. Trudi stood motionless, brows raised, seeming to want to hear more. "I guess what I'm saying is—I had no idea." *But does Star know?*

"Jen would be glad to know that. Her transition was the right thing. As soon as I met her in kindergarten, I realized this was a little girl inside a boy's body."

But did Star have any idea? She must. They'd become best friends.

Trudi continued, "Her parents are so brave. The kids here have been accepting, but it's especially nice to see a true friendship develop. Star is quite special."

Trudi collected her materials and headed into the classroom, and Mariah traveled up the stairs with the parents who had dropped their children off at Sunday school. Most proceeded down the hall to attend the church service. She veered left, entering an austere space with the same beige metal folding chairs that had graced the basement of her childhood church. For a moment she reconsidered—should she join Star and the other youth? She glanced back toward the stairs. A sense of safety, encouragement, had fused together in the confines of the classroom. Yet something unfinished niggled in the pit of her gut, urging her toward the folding chairs.

How could someone as solid as Candice Quinn have changed? Her own mother, for sure, had softened, which seemed more like a melting than a changing.

Fifty or so chairs were arranged in a semicircle facing an unadorned podium. Two-thirds were full. Why did she feel this need to see the new version of the woman who had totally intimidated her?

She chose a chair in the back row, off center. No need to make herself visible to Candice. Surely, Candice would not recognize the anxious, insecure eighteen-year-old who had dated her son.

Polite chatter filled the air as Unitarians spanning several generations settled in. Mariah sat straight-backed, forcing an open expression of friendliness. She had no business being here. It wasn't the topic that drew her: "Reconciling faith with the facts of science." Her interest was self-serving. What did a changed version of Candice look like twenty years later? And how *does* an atheist pull off a talk about faith? Faith in what?

Within minutes even the back row filled up. At 11:00 a.m., a church official wearing a stole with an image of a light above a chalice stepped up to the podium to introduce Candice. Mariah's heart pounded as she scanned the front, waiting for Dr. Quinn to enter. At age eighteen, she had viewed anyone close to her mother's age as old; Candice, though, had had a timeless appearance.

Candice approached the podium with an unrecognizable gait—weightless, gliding forward in a state of serenity. This was quite the change from the no-nonsense straightforward stride she used to display, as if she were on a mission, and always with confidence. And her hair now was long and freely flowing, a shimmering brilliant gray that could be mistaken as blond. So very different from the tight wrap—or bun—that used to bob behind her. She had let it go—or let it loose. And it flowed with every step.

Her chiseled features remained. Unlike Mariah's mother, who had become increasingly round with time, Candice had become more defined. She looked a bit like the famed photographer Annie Leibovitz. She even had the same piercing, stern eyes.

From the doorway, Devin's familiar frame entered and he wove his way through the front row. One spot, center-front, remained open. Mariah watched him maneuver into his seat and felt a pang to the left of her breastbone. They hadn't spoken since Mariah had stormed out of the coffee shop a week ago.

Candice placed her palms together and did a partial bow. She then scanned her audience, as if on a mission to make direct eye contact with each individual. Mariah shifted in her chair, dodging Candice's eyes by lowering her own. She then anchored her hips into the metal frame and focused on what Dr. Quinn had to say.

"In 1902, famed psychologist William James concluded that the brain does not create consciousness but is merely its filter. Eastern philosophies have taught for thousands of years that we live in a sea of unified consciousness. Our personal consciousness exists both in and outside our bodies. And now physics has demonstrated at the level of the most basic building block that there is an interconnectedness that is real and verifiable."

These words, *interconnectedness*, *consciousness*, twirled and spooled in Mariah's mind. She couldn't reach or hold the concepts, but something inside her applauded the barely grasped notions. Candice's face glinted with lightness, a sparkle in her eye, as she espoused the recent discoveries of science, confirming something grand, beyond what Mariah could ever comprehend.

Even so, Mariah noticed a lifting within herself—including her lips into a partial smile. She reminded herself that this was the same woman Devin had spoken of being present at Nicole's bedside.

Mariah stared in bewilderment as the audience collectively nodded, including Devin. They all were taking in some profound and foreign language. Her head throbbed, and she turned toward the exit. But if she were to leave, everyone, including Candice and Devin, would notice. She gripped her chair and took the advice she gave her clients: slow, deep breathing.

"We now have a theory to support the presence of something that used to be considered ludicrous." Candice paused, and the stillness pulled Mariah's attention back to the podium. "The next time your phone rings and you know who is on the line, take a moment to consider an alternative to coincidence."

Candice eyed her audience, and Mariah again avoided her gaze. She thought of Star's pronouncements of synchronicity. Stella, the chosen one, who happened to share her name. But for Star, even small, insignificant coincidences were meaningful.

"Some of you have felt, seen, and heard phenomena that have no physical explanation, that is, within the framework of Newtonian physics. What if our connection with one another is as fluid and present as the very molecules we exchange moment by moment in the air that we breathe?"

My God. Has Candice totally gone off the deep end? The air that we breathe? Mariah furtively glanced around. Everyone appeared riveted by Candice, and many were nodding. Were all these people appeasing her? Or did they experience a reality vastly different from Mariah's?

Candice closed by saying, "Thank you for listening with open minds and hearts."

For a lingering moment, all Mariah could hear was an in-and-out of breathing. Then collective clapping. She surprised herself by moving her own hands in sync, as if joining something larger than herself. And then everyone, including Mariah herself, stood up while continuing the applause. As the clapping dropped off, a cacophony of conversation filled in.

Mariah scanned the group to find Devin's tall, angular figure. Her heart pulsed. His defined jawline, so much like his mother's. He and his mother had grown closer with time, while Mariah had drawn back from her mother. She twisted sideways, excusing herself as she edged past the couple to her right. Devin gave a slight bow to Candice and then moved toward the exit, leaving his mother surrounded by adoring Unitarians.

Mariah shimmied her way through the crowd to reach him. Why had she raged at him? As she was about to call out, a tall slender brunette stepped toward him. Mariah froze in a swirl of confusion.

Devin's face expanded into a generous smile. The same smile that had greeted her outside Adeline's Café. A moment later, they were animated in conversation, clearly on the same wavelength, grasping all that Candice had delivered.

Chapter 22

My Journal of Hidden Truths
October 22, 2012

So, yesterday, Mom skipped class and listened to a scientist give a lecture about something to do with faith and science. I could tell she didn't like it and probably was clueless about what they said. She refused to talk about it on the way home.

Mom doesn't like to consider realities beyond what she can see and touch. It's not like her to even go to such a lecture. Maybe she's bored with what goes on in our class—no. That's not it. I can tell she's really into our discussions. Hum. I wonder if it has something to do with meeting Devin?

To her credit, she totally got it that Stella knew I was coming for her and that I had made it clear to Stella that I am hers. Like Jeffrey, Stella connects to my thoughts. Mom's been trying to bond with her—she gets down on her knees, makes these kissy sounds, and coos to her while rubbing behind her ears. I can't help but smile.

Here's my hidden truth: Everyone sees and feels things way before their minds can figure it out. Such as me meeting Stella. And knowing Jen would be my friend. Even Mom. Like whatever happens in her mind before those migraine attacks. I know they come after certain dreams. But it's just like Mom to not want to talk about what she can't see but feels.

Mom for sure would have a hard time with how my day went, which is why I only trust you, Journal. I'm still wrapping my mind around today's bizarreness.

What happened in advisory was synchronicity-plus. Like always, I was minding my business, trying to stay in my own bubble. I took out my notebook, which I use as a sketch pad, and prepared to pretend to listen.

Advisory is a lame waste of a class period. Mr. Humphrey stands in front and reports extracurricular activities, gives a stupid lecture about what it takes to be a successful student, and opens it up for comments, which turns out to be a bunch of complaining with no solutions. This, thank God, is the only class I have with Tilly.

Tilly sits three seats behind me, so she always walks by my desk because she's racing in as the bell is ringing and thankfully ignores me. Today she was slightly late—the bell had rung, and she was scrambling by while digging in her suitcase of a purse. A tightly folded piece of paper fell next to my desk. I should have left it alone. But I picked it up.

Once it was in my hands, I knew not to open and read it. I didn't need to. Without looking, I saw Curtis Orloff, the eighth-grade class president and Mr. Hotshot. I almost threw it at Tilly, but Mr. Humphrey was already standing in front of the class, sizing us up. So I stuffed it in my backpack.

I returned to my sketch of the solar system as perceived by a giant whose shoulders reach the sun. But my pen drew Curtis laughing at Tilly, plus three other warped dudes who hang around him. And then, without wanting to, I understood. It was a bet. Curtis knew Tilly had a crush on him. He was lying to her. He only wanted to make out with her to win a bet with his insipid friends, one who knew her from church and witnessed her take the abstinence oath, which I can imagine Tilly doing. Tilly doesn't look like most seventh graders; she looks more like the eighth graders she hangs out with at lunch.

For a moment I couldn't think straight—totally not knowing if I made this up or if it was like other times when I just knew stuff and it was somehow related to synchronicity, which I sort of understand. Either way, touching the note made me queasy, and I couldn't wait to get it out of my pack. I grabbed my Sharpie and drew a firm black *X* through the drawing of Curtis and each of his sick friends.

Mr. Humphrey was rambling on about stupid preparations for the pep rally and choosing a new student council member. I shot a quick look behind me and saw Tilly rifling through her purse, looking for the lost note that I'm sure she had already read. Inside my head, I yelled at her to put her purse down. Sure enough, Mr. Humphrey also saw her. My face turned red when he announced: "Ms. Higgins, you appear quite engrossed with locating something rather important in the depths of that suitcase of yours. Put it under the desk or chair until class is over." I dropped my head and covered my ears—I didn't want to hear the other kids giggling.

I followed her out of class because it's the only time I see her except after lunch, when we pretend to not see each other going to different parts of the forest. She knew I was close behind her, so she turned and said: "What do you want?"

"You dropped this." I held out the note. She yanked it from me. I then stupidly said, "I didn't read it."

She glared at me and said, "Yeah, sure. Just mind your own business."

I almost left. That's what I should have done. But just like that crazy impulse of picking up the fallen note instead of leaving it, I blurted out to her, "Curtis is only using you. Don't go."

Her eyes widened. I felt her hand slap my face, and my cheek stung—except her hand didn't leave her side, it only twitched. I turned and dashed off to social studies, holding my breath so I wouldn't cry.

Chapter 23

At Star's insistence, they left early for Sunday school the following weekend. The church parking lot had plenty of spaces and Mariah scanned the lot for Devin's red Subaru, but there was no sign of it. She felt both relief and melancholy.

Star strode ahead through the lot with a plastic bag of props tucked under her arm for a surprise performance. She waited for Mariah, holding open the back door to the classrooms.

Outside room 7, Jen stood among a handful of UUCB youth. Star merged into the mix, her voice blending into the animated chatter filling the hall. Mariah stood at a distance, wishing it were possible to be a fly on the wall and simply observe.

"Hey." Mariah turned and met Trudi's eager face. "Looks like another exciting class in store for room seven."

"I barely downed my second cup of coffee before Star was up and ready to go."

"Don's a master at stirring up positive energy," Trudi said, smiling.

"I must admit, stepping into UUCB was one of the best decisions I ever made." Mariah met Trudi's emerald eyes and her heart swelled. Trudi had no idea how close to the cliff she had found herself with Star.

"So . . ." Trudi cocked her head. "How'd it go with Dr. Quinn's lecture? I heard she was her usual awe-inspiring self."

Mariah sighed as the image of Devin talking it up with Ms. Beautiful

Brunette seized her mind. Pushing the image away, she flashed on a snippet of a dream. She, in the middle of the lecture hall, noticing her shirt was on backward. She gave a little laugh, and Trudi responded in kind.

"Truth is," Mariah said, "everything she talked about was foreign to me. Yet . . ." She glanced up at the ceiling. "I don't know. I sort of understood . . ."

"She's definitely eccentric," Trudi said.

"For most who attended, she was awe inspiring." Mariah kept her voice light, hoping Trudi wouldn't pick up on the mishmash of emotion coursing through her.

Inside room 7, everything had been rearranged. The tables were set against the back wall, providing an open space in the center. Because she'd missed the previous Sunday, Don caught her up. The youth, in groups of three or four, had prepared skits to show their own experiences of stereotyping.

Star's threesome, with Jen and Caleb, titled their presentation "Judged by appearances—we're not who you think we are." First up was Jen. Had it not been for Trudi's disclosure, Mariah would not have recognized the teenage "boy" who sauntered across the room in torn whitewashed jeans, an oversized hoodie with the hood up, hiding the loose strands of dark hair. This presentation enthralled Mariah. She knew it was Jen in disguise, but what played over in her mind was, *This* too *is Jen.* How incredibly brave of Jen to walk out in the guise of her former self.

Mariah, like her mother, had always been wholly governed by appearances. She had attempted, at age thirteen, to assert herself, announcing that she would no longer wear a dress to church—after all, she never wore them to school. Why should it matter to God? It had been a tentative foray into feminism, without a single mentor to support her. But this assertion had turned into a painful confrontation with her mother.

"Don't you dare walk into God's sanctuary wearing pants like a man."

"Why should I dress special when God supposedly sees me all day long? It's unfair to have to wear a dress to please God." Mariah drew her line—a weak one—and refused to attend unless she could wear what she wished: culottes. Her mother was mortified.

In the end, it was the response from the other kids that caused Mariah to back down. That was when she realized it wasn't part of her character to go astray. She had lacked the will to stay strong, the conviction to rise and be true to herself.

Now, she wanted to stand up and cheer for Jen's bravery. She held back, afraid of embarrassing both Jen and Star.

Star was up next, dressed as she did for school—"lazy clothes," as Mariah would say, glorified pj's. Since Star left for school after Mariah went to work, there was nothing she could do about it—not that she should. Star's role in the skit was startling and effective. She added an overcoat, grabbed a laundry bag, hunched herself over, and shifted into the likes of a homeless person.

Star's presentation moved Mariah as much as Jen's had, and with an ache of humility, she further realized she was the target audience, the one with the tendency to judge by appearances—be it Star, Jen, or the disheveled stranger on the street. Ah, even Stella would have fallen victim to her critical judgment.

Later, as they left the classroom, Mariah slipped her arm around Star's waist and gave a tender squeeze. Star's soft smile soothed the knotted place in Mariah's chest.

Several steps down the hall, she caught sight of Devin intertwined among the parents. *What is he doing here?* She felt unsteady; she barely breathed. His cobalt eyes fixed on hers, and he gave a shy smile.

As he eased his way toward them, a relentless desire to draw close swelled within her. She glanced away and recalled the eagerness in his face at the end of Candice's lecture, a fervor that burst into zeal as he engaged in conversation with Ms. Beautiful Brunette. She imagined him coyly yet full of charm telling the woman, "My mother's giving a lecture in Nathan Hall; something you might find fascinating."

"Mom. Devin's here!" Star's smile was bright and wholesome.

Devin grinned too and said to Star, "You must have had an awesome class."

"Way awesome."

"Such as?"

"Well, we got to be the teachers. This never happens at Aspen Creek."

"Cool . . . so what was the lesson?"

"Stereotypes. The basics. Just because someone looks different doesn't mean they're different on the inside. We did skits showing how stereotypes mess up ways of seeing what is real."

"Wow, that's the kind of Sunday school experience I wish I'd had at your age."

Mariah tilted her head in his direction, raising her brows. He gave an apologetic half smile and a hasty shrug—he had no Sunday school experience. And was well aware of the stifling nature of hers.

"So, hey," Devin said, "it's a beautiful fall day . . . I'm planning on going to the Museum of Natural History. Would you two care to join me?" He turned toward Mariah. "Have you been?"

Star's enthusiasm was palpable.

"It's been on my to-do list," Mariah said.

"I heard they have an exhibit on crows," Devin said.

"I study crows," Star blurted out. "I even have some crow friends." She glanced at Mariah as if divulging a secret. "I feed them on my way to school to study their behaviors."

"I'm also a fan of crows," Devin said. "They're fascinating." He gazed at Mariah, silently asking permission.

She was surprised by the invitation, given that she had stormed out on him, for reasons that remained confusing. They had laughed, talked about how Candice had changed. Why hadn't he invited her to hear his mother speak?

Mariah took in Star's bright eyes focused on Devin and made her decision. "Since crows have been my nemesis, perhaps I'll benefit from learning more about them. Yes, we'll join you."

Walking along the Boulder Creek path toward the museum, Star pointed out unusual birds. Birds Mariah had no time or attention to notice. Devin leaned into Star, nodding. They chatted back and forth as though best of friends. Mariah wondered how Charlie would have responded to his unusual daughter. His passion had been music, something she had easily slid into. She had kept Charlie's favorite CDs but couldn't bring herself to play them.

Star suddenly stopped on the path and scooped something up from the ground, some creepy crawling bug she then delivered to an orange-red bush. Devin turned and caught Mariah's eye. She smiled without thinking. The effortlessness of it startled her.

In the museum, Mariah walked through in reverie; she had little interest in the exhibit. It was the wonderment in her daughter's eyes that mesmerized her as Star jetted from exhibit to exhibit. And the man who had once been the love of her teenage life, moving in step, whispering, nodding, and pointing to the next display.

Again she flashed on Ms. Beautiful Brunette, who had surely grasped the fullness of what Candice had to say, while her frumpy self stood on the sidelines barely clutching the concepts.

Why had she not thought of taking her daughter to the museum? Or at least summon the enthusiasm to share the experience with her?

Afterward, as they strolled across the creek toward an inviting expanse of green, Devin said, "Don't know about you, but I'm hungry."

"Me too," chimed Star.

"Well, it just so happens my favorite digs for lunch is down the road—Mustard's Last Stand." He grinned. Mariah cringed inside and then Devin turned to her and, as if answering her thoughts, said, "Don't judge the lunch menu by the restaurant's name." He gave Star a quick wink.

Mustard's Last Stand turned out to be the consummate hot-dog capital of the world. Mariah had always liked hot dogs—she had fond memories of roasting hot dogs on a stick over an open flame—but Star did not. Before Mariah could suggest something different, Star pointed to the picture of a soy veggie dog, which Devin ordered for her. He and Mariah indulged in polish sausages with onions and sauerkraut. They smiled at one another, and Mariah was transported back to high school; it was as if a cord extended across time, somehow lassoing them to the present.

But then a breeze kicked up as they finished their lunch at a picnic table in the park, hinting at the winter to come. It sent a stinging chill through Mariah. She turned toward the glacial peaks of the Rocky Mountains.

At once, like a gut punch, she understood. He hadn't mentioned his mother's lecture because he knew it was beyond her comprehension. And this was why he had left her for Nicole and New York. He had only known the youthful Mariah, the girl incapable of seeing beyond the world of Reverend Eddie's.

But Mariah had chosen to attend the lecture, had listened intently to cascading incoherent sentences that everyone else seemed to grasp. She even permitted a wild notion or two to flicker uncomfortably before settling into the space of plausibility.

She too had changed.

Chapter 24

A week later, Star asked for the second time, "When are we going to dinner?"

Devin had made the suggestion over ice cream at Glaciers at the end of last weekend's outing. The three of them had laughed like teenagers when the top of Star's three-scoop cone of Funky Donkey plummeted down, splattering on the Formica tabletop. While Star grabbed a pile of napkins to clean up the mess, he leaned toward Mariah and said, "My mother would adore meeting Star. Can you both come for dinner next Sunday at her house?"

Mariah had been wholly unprepared for such an invitation and surprised herself by accepting. Now, as she finished folding a pile of clothes, her thoughts skittered between what to wear and whether Candice could have possibly recognized her at the lecture. There had been way too many people for Candice to have taken in everyone—and besides, Mariah was twenty-plus years older and light-years beyond the awkward eighteen-year-old Candice had known.

Mariah picked up a stack of clothes and said to Star, "Devin suggested we come around five thirty."

"Mom."

"Yes?"

"Is it Devin's mother who you listened to instead of coming to class?"

Mariah's pulse quickened—how did Star pick up on so much? She had not said a thing about the talk to Star. Was this what Candice meant when she suggested there might be more going on when the phone rings and you know who is calling?

"Actually, yes."

"She's a scientist! Does she know about David Bohm?"

"Honey, how in the world would I know?"

"Because you went to her lecture on science and faith, right? That's a topic David Bohm would talk about."

"Well, she didn't mention his name."

"Maybe you forgot. What I remember was your silence the whole way home, as if you didn't like what you heard."

Mariah's memory was one of relief at gathering Star and managing the preliminary bouts of a migraine. Her focus was getting herself home and in bed.

"Truth is, I enjoyed the lecture. It was all so new to me. Dr. Quinn is brilliant, and I know little about physics. So we're going to meet her for dinner, and I'll expect you to be polite and not bring up the lecture."

"Why not?"

"Because Devin wants us to get to know his mother, and she wants to get to know us. There's no need to talk about me attending her lecture. Am I clear?"

As Mariah pulled up to 500 Berry Knoll Drive, her panic spiked, and her thoughts returned to the lecture. The rawness of Candice's gaze—like a spotlight moving across the gathered faces while Mariah had squirmed to make herself small and unnoticed. Devin sliding into place center-front.

She turned off the ignition. *What the hell am I doing here?* The wasted time pondering over what to wear. Who was she fooling? Devin's interest was to introduce Star to his mother. Mariah was merely the means.

Star quickly jumped out and announced, "I like this place." She was gazing up at two large silver maples a short distance from the house. "Look at the beautiful trees!" Each had a few tenacious leaves clinging to umbrella-like frames; below were soft mounds of yellow-gold foliage.

Mariah looked past Star to the cerise-colored Craftsman with stone pillars, cantilevered porch, leaded and stained-glass windows. Her knees weakened and heart quickened as she moved forward. The last time she'd spoken to Dr. Quinn, decades ago, she'd been an insecure, monosyllabic, small-town girl hyperaware that her mother was a dental hygienist who had barely made it out of high school. And now, Candice Quinn's dinner guest? What would she say to keep the conversation going?

Five steps led to a generous front porch bathed in ambient light from the surrounding windows. Mariah stood on the fifth step and looked back to see Star captivated by a crow scrounging through a tuft of leaves. On cue, as if watching all along, Devin stepped out. The brightness of his face startled Mariah. She stepped forward. His expansive smile brought her eyes downward. He reached for her hand but they ended up in a full-body embrace.

"Star," he called out. "Have you been observing the flying patterns of crows?"

"Not particularly. I've been noticing how they imitate the sounds of other creatures, the variety of their voices."

"Interesting. You'll make a great scientist."

"I can't wait to be done with school so I can go to a university and study to become a scientist."

"Well, in the meantime, maybe we can go back to the museum. Did you know they have a different exhibit every month? And since it's November now, we can check it out later this month."

"Yay!" Star shouted.

The front door opened, and Candice strode onto the porch, her long gray-blond hair draped over a crimson batik tunic. Mariah caught her breath. This version of Devin's mother was so different from the one Mariah had previously known, the woman who had worn only stiff fitted clothing. Still, Candice's presence stopped the flow of conversation.

"Who have we here?" Candice's smile was probably intended for everyone, but her eyes zeroed in on Star, who was midway up the porch stairs.

"Mother," Devin said, "you remember Mariah."

Mariah gave a labored smile; her entire body tensed in the familiar grip of both fearing and respecting this woman.

"Yes, I remember," Candice said as she turned to Mariah. "Not only from high school, but from my lecture two weeks ago."

A ferocious blush swept across Mariah's face. She turned away from Devin.

"And this must be your lovely daughter. She has your beautiful hazel eyes."

Star stood fixed to the steps, staring at Candice. "Star," Mariah whispered. Had she been alone she would have said, *It's impolite to stare.* Star proceeded up to the porch and reached out to shake hands. Candice held Star's between her own for a second or two.

"Mom says you're a famous scientist. Do you know of David Bohm? I plan to study physics and specialize in the nature of reality."

"I don't know about the famous part—but yes, I'm a fan of David Bohm. So glad to meet you, future scientist."

Star beamed into the twinkling eyes of Candice, who then turned toward Devin and Mariah and gestured for them to head inside. They walked through a foyer, down a hallway, and past a polished wood staircase to a large living room.

"If you don't mind," Candice said, pointing to a woven container filled with slippers and shoes. Mariah saw that Candice herself was wearing a pair of ballerina-like slippers. "I'm rather fond of the rug—I try to limit as much outside debris as possible."

Mariah slid her feet into a pair of generous red slippers. An engraved plaque on the wall read "When all your desires are distilled, you will cast just two votes: To love more and be happy." Hafiz. Her heart pulsed and she wavered between wanting to weep or joyously dance. Of course she did neither.

"Make yourself at home. I'll be back shortly." Candice scurried off.

The Persian rug was gorgeous, with a dense pattern of indigo, brick red, and sunset gold. In the center was a floral design that resembled a lotus. The room itself was sparse, which Mariah found pleasing. The one quasi couch—a futon—sat low to the floor and was adorned with multicolored pillows. Mariah drove past the futon store on her way to work and always questioned why anyone would choose this furniture. She loved her overstuffed recliner sofa. Yet this modest wisp of a couch positioned around two Amish knotty-pine coffee tables and a colorful wingback chair worked in this setting.

Next to the sitting area, against the wall, was a four-foot Buddha dipped in gold. Buddha's undisturbed state wrapped Mariah in a blanket of tranquility, just like Shiva had at the café.

Devin walked up next to her with an amused look. "Who would have guessed my mother would have a gold-plated Buddha sitting in her living room?"

"Certainly not the Candice I knew a few decades ago." She couldn't suppress her smile.

"Nor the mother I grew up with," he said. "She was quite taken with her journeys to Thailand, where there are many Buddhas in gold." Was it pride or dismay she heard in his voice?

"There's something about the contentment in that face . . . ," Mariah said. "It's infectious." Maybe a small Buddha in the corner of her living room would help her relax.

Candice reentered with a tray of crackers and cheese and a pot of tea. Devin gave a nervous chuckle. "Mom doesn't want any dirt on her carpet, but cracker crumbs and splashes of tea are permissible."

"Well, for Christ's sake, it's not hanging up, which is a ridiculous location to keep a rug." She laid out a spread of crackers and cheese. "This is a fabulous herbal tea I discovered when I was in Thailand. But if you'd prefer, I have a bottle of seltzer in the fridge."

Mariah hesitated, hoping she heard incorrectly. No wine? How would she survive this without a glass of wine?

"Tea sounds perfect," Mariah said. She glanced at the statue, willing a calmness. Again she thought, *What the hell am I doing here?*

Star was meandering around the room. No surprise. She was slow to adjust to new spaces. The first day of class at UUCB, she had wandered from corner to corner before settling in at the back near Jen.

Mariah was unsettled by Star's behavior, but Devin and Candice paid no attention to Star's roaming as they discussed the origin of the tea, where the rug had come from, and the wonders of Boulder, a topic Mariah chimed in on. She wished she could ask them how two devout atheists found a community in a church.

"Star," she called out. Her voice sharp, urgent, drew the attention of both Candice and Devin. Mariah adjusted to a softer tone. "Sweetie." Star looked at Mariah. "You'll try some tea, won't you?" Star turned away and moved in front of Candice, who fixed her focus on Star.

"When my dog Jeffrey died, he missed me as much as I missed him. I needed to let him know it was okay to move on. What was your dog's name?"

Mariah started to stand up, to reach out and take Star's hand, to pull her down next to her. She stopped herself. An uncomfortable silence blanketed the room. Devin darted his eyes between Candice and Star.

Candice set her teacup down and stated, "Hafiz. It's been a little over a month since he passed."

"I like that name. Who's he named after?"

"A Persian poet who lived a very long time ago. One of my favorite quotes . . . let's see . . . there are so many." Candice hesitated with eyes half-closed.

Mariah felt light-headed, as if she had taken in too much wine. *Is this really happening?*

Candice looked at Star and said, "'I wish I could show you, when you are lonely or in darkness, the astonishing light of your own being.'"

"That's awesome! When I feel the light, it's wonderful." Star twirled around as if to release the exuberance coursing through her body. "Your Hafiz must have been very special to be named after someone so wise."

"He was definitely a light being."

Star then went to the large floral-printed pillow next to the statue and plopped down.

"He liked to lie right there." Candice nodded in agreement.

Was she placating Star? Mariah turned to Devin; his expression remained neutral. She gazed at Star—her tall, lanky body relaxed; the corners of her lips gently turned up; eyelids half-masked. The silence coiled like a spring.

"Star," Mariah said. "Do you want some tea?" Mariah poured a half cup and set it aside. Star shook her head. Mariah then turned to Candice, who was still focused on Star. "Star has quite an imagination. I never know what she'll come up with. But she has for the longest time talked about wanting to be a scientist, right, Star? And she gets very good grades." Mariah took a sip of hot tea. It singed her throat. A bead of perspiration developed on her forehead.

"Actually," Star said, "I want to be a physicist who studies either how the universe came into being or, like David Bohm, the fundamental nature of reality and consciousness." She crawled off her pillow seat and crouched next to the coffee table, sipping the tea Mariah had poured. She then looked up at Candice and asked, "Did you ever get to meet David Bohm?"

"I'm afraid not. By the time I became familiar with his work, he had been run out of the country, thanks to the ludicrous spectacle of the

McCarthy hearings. This, my dear, took place nearly fifty years before you were even born. Tragically, we lost one of the most significant theoretical physicists of the twentieth century."

Mariah's chest tightened, seeing Star spellbound by Candice.

Candice then added, "I'm especially fond of this particular quote: 'The ability to perceive or think differently is more important than the knowledge gained.' He was a veritable genius—completely misunderstood. So how is it that someone your age is familiar with Bohm?"

Star beamed. "From Mr. Seng."

Mariah's heart dropped. The janitor. Why didn't she ever meet him? And why hadn't she ever pursued a serious conversation about physics with Star? She clasped the small teacup, preparing to hear a string of supportive words from Candice.

Star said, "He came here from California, but actually he's from Cambodia, where he was a physicist. I first got to know him in fifth grade, when he helped me get recycling going in my school. When I moved on to junior high, he gave me a copy of *Wholeness and the Implicate Order.*"

"That's a challenging read for anyone."

"Yeah. There's lots I don't understand. That's when I miss Mr. Seng the most because he's good at explaining." She took another sip of tea.

"Star, would you like to look with me in my library? I may have some recommendations for you," Candice said, and Star shot straight up. Candice turned to Mariah. "Please excuse us. We won't be gone long."

Mariah forced a smile while her jaw clenched. This woman had no idea what it was like to raise a brilliant child who was so ridiculously sensitive to everything. She lowered her eyes to the intricate patterns of the carpet, tracing the perimeter of a lotus with her red-slippered foot.

"I knew my mom would adore Star," Devin said. "Your daughter's amazing."

"I agree. And, at times, maddeningly so."

"She knew Hafiz had recently passed, and she was right on about his favorite place to lie."

Mariah's mind raced. But wasn't this because of losing Jeffrey? Star had correctly assumed that Candice had lost a dog too. And, duh, just like Jeffrey or any dog, Hafiz would have liked the cushion.

She said, "Star picks up on things. I don't know how much to read into it. I mean, sometimes it's total imagination." She considered sharing Star's experience of conversing with Jeffrey in school, insisting the incarnate dog was present, but this was way too crazy to reveal.

Devin stood up, stretched, and said, "Mom's been doing a research project through Naropa University having to do with psychics. She's become an expert in these kinds of things . . ."

Mariah smiled dismissively. "So I gathered from her lecture." She wanted to add, *Do you actually believe in this woo-woo stuff?* "I mean, I know your mother is brilliant, and it's clear she has a new perspective on it all." Mariah pushed her back against the flat futon, swung one leg over the other. "I'm surprised you didn't mention she was going to be a guest lecturer."

Devin was quiet for a moment, his face tense. Then, in a soft tone, he said, "I didn't have a chance." He looked directly at her. "We left Shiva, or rather, you left Shiva . . . in a rush."

Her face reddened. Why had she said anything or even attended the damn lecture? And she *knew* why he hadn't invited her; he had invited who he wanted—Ms. Beautiful Brunette.

"I planned on letting you know," he said, "but I wanted a chance to prepare you. I mean, even I'm trying to get my head around who she is these days. She's become quite unconventional."

In a flash she tasted her rigid late-teen self, trying to confront the ridiculous notion of the devil while inside she quaked with fear of reprisal. She winced and assured herself she *had* changed. She wasn't the insecure, gullible pansy Devin had suffered in the past.

"I'm not the same person you knew twenty years ago. You were concerned I couldn't handle the gravity of her ideas?"

"That's not what I said."

"It's what you implied."

"No, it isn't. What I'm saying is, you never gave me the opportunity. You left before I had the chance to tell you."

She crossed her arms. A numbness washed over her.

"You must have seen me at the lecture. Why didn't you say anything?"

"Yeah, I saw you." Her heart hammered wildly. "You were busy with someone else. I didn't want to interrupt."

Devin gazed at her with a blank look on his face. And then, the beginnings of a smile emerged. "Oh. Right. I was nabbed."

"Nabbed?" She lifted her brows, recalling him in animated conversation with the woman, who could have been a model.

"Yeah. That was Ginger. She's quite the fan of my mother's."

And a fan of yours, she thought. "Clearly you both were taken up by your mother's lofty ideas."

Devin cocked his head and gave a belittling smile. "It may have looked that way from a distance, but you have no idea." A long pause followed. Devin shifted uncomfortably. "Since you're irritated about this, why didn't you bring it up last week?"

"I guess it became clear that you had no intention of mentioning Candice's lecture to me."

"Like I said, you didn't give me the opportunity."

"Truth is, I've been preoccupied the past thirteen years." She uncrossed her legs and leaned forward. "You have no idea what it's like raising a child as a single parent—a child who is unusually sensitive."

She stood up, wishing she could leave. She no more belonged here than she had in his childhood home two decades ago. The hell with Candice. Devin appeared pale, frozen in time. A small aching part of her trembled, and she was on the verge of tears. She frantically searched for a way to mend the ghastly rupture.

"I'm happy for your mother," she said.

He gave a quizzical look.

"That she has time to study the nature of reality. And clearly, you and your friend also appreciate her work." She almost stopped right there. "I'm not so sure I can fit such vast pondering into my busy, small world." She turned away just as Candice and Star entered the room.

Chapter 25

Glowing with delight, Star held up a book. Devin smiled, amplifying her joy.

"Mom has quite the collection of books," he said.

Star turned to Candice. "Someday I want a library in my home as large and wonderful as yours. I love books!"

"Did you get another book by David Bohm?" Mariah asked, straining to be cheerful.

"Hey," Devin said. "I'll be back shortly."

Star's smile faded, and Candice's lips tightened as they watched Devin leave the room. Star stared at Mariah.

"Well?" Mariah asked.

"It's not written by him, but it is about his ideas. Him and another famous scientist, Karl Pribram. It's called *The Holographic Universe* by Michael Talbot."

"Oh my!" Mariah exclaimed, though she wondered what the hell the book was really about.

Candice said, "The book is an exceptional extended essay bringing together two giants in the field of science. It's too bad the author has passed. He was quite talented and lived a fascinating life." She smiled as she watched Star, who had plopped down on a pillow, absorbed in the book. Turning to Mariah, she said, "You have a remarkable daughter. She'll enjoy this book." Candice then stepped toward the hall and called back, "Shall we move on to dinner?"

Mariah nodded as Candice left the room, and she said to Star, "Did you hear Dr. Quinn? It's time for dinner. You'll need to put the book away."

In the brightly lit kitchen, the smell of fresh-baked bread failed to seduce Mariah. Her stomach lurched and she swallowed the thickness. Under the thin soles of her borrowed slippers, the floor tiles pressed against her feet, hard and cold. She wanted her shoes back on.

Candice led them into an alcove where a rustic rectangular table with four place settings lay waiting. She gestured to the seats with the upturned palm of her hand and disappeared into the kitchen.

Mariah would either be facing Devin for dinner or sitting side by side. She chose to sit facing the kitchen.

Candice reentered the dining area with a large colorful salad and a side plate of nuts and cheese.

"Dr. Quinn, have you ever seen a hologram?" Star said.

"Star, please call me Candice. Yes, I've seen holographic photographs. I'm sure you have too."

"Only little ones, like on cards or key chains. I'd love to see large ones." Star circled the table twice before seating herself directly opposite Mariah.

"Well, you're quite right," Candice called back from the kitchen. "They differ greatly from the trinket variety."

Mariah's stomach rumbled as if she were hungry, yet food had no appeal. She took a sip of the lemon ice water and welcomed the cool, numbing sensation.

Candice placed a loaf of thickly crusted golden-brown bread in the center of the table and said to Star, "Given what you know, any idea what aspects of the hologram inspired Bohm and Pribram to use it as a metaphor for the universe?"

Devin stepped into the alcove then, and Star turned to meet him.

He laid a hand on her shoulder as he passed and slipped into the chair to Mariah's left. She felt, or imagined feeling, the heat of his body just inches away. She took another sip of ice water.

"Maybe. . . ," Star mused with a grin, "they used holograms as a metaphor because they create an illusion of being three dimensional. We're made almost completely of space, but we all believe we're solid." Star then playfully pinched her right arm. "Ouch! It's a really good illusion."

Mariah caught the humorous glint in Candice's eyes as she chuckled. She couldn't tell if Devin had also joined in the levity. The prospect of turning toward him tied a small knot at the base of her spine.

"Star, you're exactly right," Candice proclaimed. "You'll learn in reading Talbot's book that there is another remarkable aspect to holograms." Candice turned to Mariah. "Please, help yourself to salad and bread."

Mariah eyed the fresh, crisp salad laced with strawberries and avocado and the sliced bread, still warm from the oven; the pat of butter Star spread on her slice melted at once. The cheese and nuts alone would have, under any other circumstance, irresistibly drawn her in. Yet her stomach churned.

Candice continued, "Every fragment of holographic film contains all the information recorded in the whole. Just like our DNA. I'm sure you've heard of acupuncture, which has been around for about three thousand years. It's based on the same premise that the whole body can be represented in the microstructure of each organ and bone."

From within Mariah, a surge of resentment roiled—she was back at a lecture, but one she had never agreed to attend. Is this what Devin had had to put up with his entire life? And then she stiffened as she felt his focus on her. She didn't know how, but the sensation was as real as the pounding in her chest.

If only he was seated across from her, it would have been easier to inconspicuously glance his way now and then. But as it was, she had to turn to her left. She heard him munching on salad, and in her peripheral vision, she caught a flicker of motion; she quickly turned toward him, thinking it safe to steal a glance.

But her timing was off. His ocean-blue eyes found hers, and they clung. She pulled away with a stab of remorse. Her heart ached so distressingly she feared she would faint.

"Mom, are you okay?" Star asked.

Candice looked at Mariah and then glanced toward Devin. Of course, Candice would know Devin was upset.

Mariah wished she could blink her eyes and be home in her recliner with a full glass of chardonnay. She took a slow deep breath. "I'm fine. The salad is lovely. But I'm afraid I'm having a small allergic reaction to the avocado." And she did feel sick, her mouth coated, as though she had ingested some sort of poison.

"Can I get you anything?" Candice asked.

"Oh no. I'm going to pass on the salad. The bread is wonderful." She took a nibble and caught Star's suspicious look. To Mariah's relief, Star turned back to Candice.

"Who is Karl Pribram?" she asked.

"Oh, my dear child, Karl Pribram is a giant in neuroscience. He's responsible for developing the theory of quantum consciousness in collaboration with David Bohm."

Star fired off additional questions, bringing about another lecture from Dr. Quinn. "Nonlocality of information . . . this, my dear, is what makes it possible to have that sense of someone looking or thinking about you before your rational mind has had an opportunity to dismiss it . . ."

Mariah took a piece of cheddar and ate it with bread. Her insides remained a twisted mess. Even with her dismissal of Devin's gaze, the heat of it continued to pierce her.

Dr. Quinn's authoritative voice continued, "The web of subatomic particles composing . . ." At least there was no expectation for Mariah to say a thing.

Eventually, Candice reached for the plate of cheese and nuts, and Star reached for a second slice of bread. The "lecture" had come to completion.

"Devin," Candice said, "I suspect Star would take an interest in your telescope. Why don't you take her to the roost?"

"You have a real telescope?"

Mariah glanced to her left, catching Devin's attentive response to Star. He nodded.

"I've always wanted to look through a real telescope." Star stood up, leaving her plate unfinished. Devin saluted her in mock solemnity. A moment later they were gone.

Alone with Candice, Mariah sprang to her feet and began collecting the empty dishes.

"No need to worry yourself with that," Candice said.

"Oh, no problem at all." Mariah stacked the four plates, piled the silverware on top. "This has been a wonderful dinner, and you have been so kind to Star." Candice remained seated in an ominous stillness.

"Mariah," Candice called out as Mariah entered the kitchen. She placed the dishes on the counter next to the sink and slowly returned to the table. Mariah sat down, resigning herself to the attention Candice wanted. "Your daughter has many gifts—"

"With all due respect, Dr. Quinn, you've only just met her."

"You're right. And I haven't a clue what it's like living with a child who is brilliant and has native psychic ability." Candice smiled.

"I understand she was right about your dog having passed," Mariah said. "But this isn't typical. I've been called many times to meet with teachers and counselors concerned about her mental health. I sometimes wonder—"

"Wonder what?"

"Well . . . she's quite different from other children. Sensitive. Excessively. Not in a normal way." Why in God's name was she sharing this? Candice had no idea; she had barely raised Devin.

"I dare say, *normal* is a highly subjective, overrated concept." Candice looked directly at Mariah. "But then, it all depends on how you interpret *normal*." She tilted her head and lifted her brows.

Mariah looked away as a wave of heat rose up her neck and reddened her face. She gritted her teeth. Of course. Candice viewed *her* as the abnormal one.

"I . . . can only imagine the challenge of having a daughter so advanced and misunderstood."

Tears of frustration caught like a solid lump in Mariah's throat. She refused to give Candice eye contact. She tried to swallow the surge of emotion.

Candice continued, "Star *is* extremely sensitive. Picks up on dimensions of reality that pass most of us by." She then stood up and moved toward the kitchen. "Can I get you some tea?"

"No thanks." Mariah followed her into the kitchen with the leftover salad and bread. Even with her hand shaking, she plunged in. "I'm confused. You're a scientist. ESP, psychic—they've been around forever in folklore . . . no one who has a college degree takes this stuff seriously. I mean, you're the expert, but I was always taught it doesn't fit with any known theory of science." She had, after all, obtained a master's at San Diego State. She had done an internship on a hospital psychiatric ward. A good number of these folks claimed to have extrasensory powers.

A softness spread across Candice's face. She dunked a tea bag into a steamy cup of water before answering. "I used to agree with you. In fact, I've written papers about the implausibility of the so-called sixth sense. But I've come to my own senses." She smiled and rolled her eyes upward, as if this were some private joke. "Innately accessing information—such as the fact that I had a dog who recently died and had a special place where he would lie down—does not fit with our current, albeit obsolete, theory of reality and consciousness." She paused and met Mariah's eyes with a hint of warmth. "But, mind you, this hasn't stopped the CIA, FBI, Homeland Security, to name a few, from hiring a bevy of psychics."

Mariah nodded out of respect. But if this were true, why wasn't it common knowledge? Why hadn't she heard about it?

"I've heard from multiple colleagues who, quite frankly, think I've gone off the deep end."

Mariah followed her out of the kitchen and back into the alcove, heart beating overtime. She herself had wondered the very same thing about Candice Quinn.

Candice turned and held her eyes. "Quite to the contrary, Mariah. I didn't go off the deep end. I delved deeper into the implications of our most current understanding of science—quantum physics. I began connecting the dots that I've denied my entire life. They've come blaring back at me in research that can't and shouldn't be ignored. Believe me. Your daughter is not imbalanced. She's connected. She's a sensitive soul who . . . who needs . . ."

Mariah turned to the window and cast her gaze somewhere far over a darkened horizon. What Candice was about to say would not surprise her. Star needed her undivided support. She braced herself to hear the shameful truth Candice was about to share—her failure to give Star what she needed.

But Candice didn't finish her sentence. Her words . . . *who needs* . . . floated into suspended silence. Mariah turned back to see Candice's eyes thickened with tears. Her cheeks were soft apricot in the muted light. A mixture of grief and guilt surged through Mariah, and she caught her breath, blinking her own moist eyes as tears began to form. With the sleeve of her shirt she attempted to dry them.

"I'm so sorry," Candice murmured.

Mariah's mind swirled in confusion. Why was she apologizing?

"I sense it's been a difficult decade—in fact, devastating."

"Star is all I have," Mariah said, looking directly at Candice. Before she could stop herself, she said, "Everything—beautiful, precious—can be destroyed without a moment's notice."

Candice's arm rose as if to reach out. And then retreated. A heavy stillness settled in the space between them.

Finally, Candice spoke. "Life can seem capricious. Even the most adept psychic can't predict final outcomes. Nevertheless"—Candice pursed her lips and cast her gaze beyond Mariah—"living in terror is hardly living at all. I think Einstein had it right when he suggested that the most important decision one can make is whether the universe is a friendly place."

Chapter 26

My Journal of Hidden Truths
November 3, 2012

Remember, Journal, when I proclaimed this would be a year of consequential events? Well, I predict meeting Dr. Quinn is as important as when I met Mr. Seng. I'm glad to be recording this date. And whoever You are, I am sure You'll agree with me. Meeting Dr. Quinn is destined to be life changing! She totally gets me. And she picked out the perfect book for me to read—*The Holographic Universe*! It's so much easier to read than *Wholeness and the Implicate Order*. Now, more than ever, I want to understand all of David Bohm's writings.

Dr. Quinn wasn't at all bothered about me noticing Hafiz. I practically saw him in the room—I sort of did—but I knew it was like when I saw Jeffrey in Mrs. Severson's class. He wasn't really there, but enough so that I could feel his energy. I would have spoken to him like I did with Jeffrey, but I could tell Mom was all uptight and this would have totally freaked her out, so I just settled in and sipped my tea. But Dr. Quinn understood.

When we were alone in her amazing library, she talked to me in a way no one else ever has.

"Star, do you sometimes get overwhelmed from feeling the energy that surrounds you?"

I nodded. This was such a great question. "Yes. I feel calmness in your house. It's so much different from all the crazy energy I feel at school."

"Being familiar with Bohm, you understand that everything is made up of vibrations. Energy is real and perceivable."

At that moment her vibrations shot through me, and before I could stop myself, I stood on my tiptoes and proclaimed, "I want to be a scientist like you." My face then heated up, as if I felt her embarrassment. Or something.

Dr. Quinn spoke with tenderness. "Star, you're quite skilled in picking up emotional energy."

All I could do was nod. No one has ever talked to me this way. It was as if she knew the part of me I keep hidden from everyone.

Then she said, "People who respond to energy more intensely are biologically and psychologically wired to sense what others miss. It's a gift that you have."

I nodded at her but didn't understand the gift part. All I know is that the hardest part of school is being around the sadness other kids feel.

"Is this true for you too?" I asked. At first, she didn't answer. I thought it was because I was asking something too private. But then I figured she was busy thinking about it. She started to walk towards the door, and I followed.

Before we returned to the living room, she caught my eyes and said, "Yes. It's true for me. But I dismissed it." I gave her a confused look, and she said, "For a very long time. And now I'm back to honoring my true self."

I didn't understand that either. But her honesty wrapped around me, and in that moment, I knew anything was possible. I hope to have another chance to be alone with her.

Back in the living room, everything had changed between Mom and Devin. I had wanted to spend more time with Dr. Quinn, but I could tell Mom wanted me with her. I had to work hard at not letting it wreck my evening.

Later, Devin showed me his telescope, which was way cool and would have been even better if the sky had had fewer clouds and his sadness had not settled onto me. I said to him, "Your mother's so cool. It must have been special growing up with her. She's so smart!"

He sort of nodded. I hoped he'd tell me what it was like having her as a mother and that he would be happy just talking about it, but instead he said, "I met your mother before she had any idea that you would come into her life. I can tell she loves you more than you can imagine."

Chapter 27

Cold sweeping rain blew through the parking lot, pelting Mariah's windshield like peppercorns. The rain turned everything into a dismal dreariness, matching her mood. Before heading inside, Mariah blasted the heat in her car to try to stave off the chill running through her. Plus, she'd arrived at work a bit early. If she entered now, she'd surely run into Gretchen with an update on Star.

The drive to work, with dimmer light than the week before, had made it clear that winter was closing in. How was it possible to feel anything other than despair during this season? In her first year at BHP, she'd noted that her clients fell apart within the second week of November—a trend that repeated itself year after year. The expectation to be grateful in November followed by cheery in December was too much for anyone suffering the distress of life gone wrong. But Mariah had no choice but to keep herself together. More than together, she had to assume a veneer of cheerfulness, or at least neutrality, while putting up with excited chatter from coworkers about holiday plans and the staff party.

The holiday season, as inescapable as weather, seeped into every environment, including the air in one's own home. A miscalculated turn of the radio dial filled her kitchen with a Christmas carol, stirring memories of Charlie singing "Rudolph the Red-Nosed Reindeer" to Markus while bouncing him on his shoulders. The unavoidable garish lights strung on trees and homes never failed to summon Milly's downy head and alert eyes and Markus's nose pressed to the window as they wound their way through the posh neighborhoods of Pasadena. All the while, she and Charlie belted out Christmas songs, certain of a future where Milly and Markus would sing the same songs to their children.

For the past twelve years, Mariah had avoided traditions of Thanksgiving and Christmas. A dozen Thanksgivings collapsed in memory as a single blur, overshadowed by the vivid final Thanksgiving with Milly, Markus, Charlie, and her mother. They had a twenty-pound turkey that year. She and her mother stuffed it with her mother's favorite recipe. It had been their last family gathering. At the time, Mariah had marked it as a first. The first time she and Charlie had not been guests at her mother's house, the start of a new tradition. The lovely part was that her mother, while resistant at first, proclaimed it to be the nicest Thanksgiving she had ever experienced.

Since then, Mariah and her mother hadn't shared a single Thanksgiving. When they'd last talked, on Saturday, Mariah had ended the call without a commitment to having Olivia come for Thanksgiving or Christmas, although Thanksgiving seemed the obvious choice—much less bother. Upon saying goodbye, Mariah found that she missed the closeness she had experienced with her mother when Markus was born. A mutual initiation into the mystery and terror of giving birth. Charlie had been wonderful and supportive—but her mother kept her afloat.

Markus was a dream child in so many ways. A stuffy nose now and then, and a disposition so bright he could hurl a spell of joy on her and Charlie amid the gloomiest of moods. She had thought only caffeine could perk her up—Markus proved her wrong. His dimpled smile, his irresistible cherub face framed with curly blond hair, his outstretched arms powered her like a double espresso.

Parenting him required nothing more than the basics, which Mariah discovered were underrated. Meals three times a day, snacks in between, day-care arrangements, cleaning up every twenty minutes. Legos, Cheerios, dirty socks, leaves, and debris of all sorts scattered mercilessly across the floor. And unending piles of laundry. Bedtime routines, which she looked forward to, left her in a final state of depletion and barely able to crawl into her own bed.

"All consuming," she had confided to her mother, who agreed. Charlie did his best to help on weekends, passing on music gigs when the travel time was over forty minutes, offering to get groceries or do a load of laundry. Imagining her mother raising an only child without the support of someone like Charlie deepened their closeness.

Milly, three years later, made Mariah's previous life with just one child seem like a piece of cake. Unlike Markus, Milly was planned. Growing up an only child, Mariah had longed for a brother or sister. She was intent on giving Markus what she had yearned for—a sibling.

She had insisted they not find out the gender before birth. When Dr. Trimble proclaimed "You have a lovely baby girl," her whole heart swelled with joy. She lifted her eyes upward and gave thanks to a God who listened to her deep desires—even when she was filled with sin. As she held the crying infant, she whispered to Charlie the name they had agreed upon—his late sister's, Mildred.

Within the first week of Milly's birth, Mariah sensed something wasn't right. Milly never slept through the night as Markus had. She'd wake screaming for no apparent reason well past her second month. It took a good hour to get her settled. And then, as dawn arrived, if the slant of light entering her room was too bright, or if the morning brought the pattering of rain or gusts of winds, the same hysterics would again pull Mariah from her bed. She knew there was an undiagnosed medical condition causing her daughter to cry and fuss nonstop. Mariah consulted her pediatrician, who diagnosed Milly as having colic.

"But what causes this? You mean there are no medical explanations?"

Dr. Trimble attempted to reassure her with a smile. It wasn't at all soothing. "No one knows the exact cause of colic. But we know that children who have colic as babies do not differ from others."

"But how long will it last?"

His response was less helpful. "Three or four months."

Those first jaw-clenching, scream-filled months had brought Mariah to her knees, weeping with exhaustion, frustration, and—most debilitating—guilt. Clearly, she was being taught a lesson she needed to learn. More patience, understanding, flexibility. With each comparison of how perfect Markus was and why Milly was so challenging, guilt's razor-sharp edge buttressed the fact of her inadequacies.

Mariah turned her car off and checked the time. Gretchen was likely settled into her office. She glanced at herself in the mirror, applied another layer of lipstick, and strode toward BHP.

The morning client sessions passed with ease. She listened and offered advice. On her way to lunch, she previewed her afternoon—the hoarder group (the "pack-rat syndrome," Gretchen had quipped). Advice-giving never worked. The group members demanded a nuanced approach, facilitation. She faced the afternoon with dread.

As she walked into the lunchroom, Richard, munching on a sandwich, looked up and smiled. His eyes sparkled.

"An enjoyable weekend?" she asked.

"Bingo." He flushed. "Lynelle and I spent the weekend together."

She popped the lid off her salad container and drenched it with dressing.

"And you?" Richard took another bite of his sandwich.

"It was interesting . . ."

"Such as?" He set his sandwich down and swiped a napkin across his face.

"Devin invited Star and me to his mother's house for dinner."

"Hmm. That does fit the definition of *interesting.* Was it . . . like a date?"

"Absolutely not." She crammed a forkful of salad into her mouth. Her thoughts returned to the ambient light of Candice's porch, the way she had held her hand out, and he had pulled her in. Devin's musky scent, his arms wrapped around her torso, pressing her against his chest. Why had she attacked him about the lecture? "Since we knew each other in high school, I sorta knew his mother, who has also moved to Boulder. So . . . think odd reunion, with mother of former boyfriend and my daughter."

"Got it. Complicated."

"Yes. With a capital *C*."

"So?" Richard asked as he took another nibble of his sandwich.

"Star likes Devin, which is saying a lot. She was thrilled to be invited. And his mother, well, she's . . . gee, what can I say? Otherworldly?"

"How so?"

"That's not quite the word. She's a scientist. Actually, a brilliant physicist who taught at UCLA."

"Okay . . ."

"Except . . . she parted with tradition and has a rather unique view of reality."

Richard put his sandwich down and looked at her intently.

"Star was all over her—and she likewise. It was . . . uncanny." She replayed the moment Candice entered the porch, locking on to Star while barely noticing her. "It was . . . as if two people destined to meet finally found each other." She gazed upward, trying to collect the right words. "Like, this eerie energy between them."

"Wow," Richard said.

Mariah took a nibble of her salad and then put her fork down. "Star did this odd thing. Somehow she knew Candice's dog had died. I thought it was her imagination. Or a lucky guess. And it turned out she was right. Not only that her dog had died but also where he liked to sleep."

She took a deep breath and glanced around the cafeteria, unable to escape a deep discomfort. "I was the only one who didn't know she had it right. The fool mother, thinking it was my daughter's imagination." A wave of heat washed across her face. Devin had been impressed. She had dismissed it.

"How could you have known otherwise?"

"Right. I mean, this daughter of mine will talk about the wildest of things. I let her have conversations with Jeffrey, after life, because that's what she needed. Later I'm called to school because she's talking with Jeffrey in her social studies class, freaking out her teacher who hears her. Jesus. I don't have a place to park this weird stuff. If I was her teacher, I'd also think it was a psychotic breakdown. Or drugs."

Her hands had turned the paper napkin in her lap into a twisted wad. She needed to calm herself. She looked at her soggy salad drenched in ranch, then at Richard, who remained quiet. "You see, I grew up believing so-called psychics were people who listened to the devil." She shook her head. "I know it's backwards." When Mariah was in middle school, she came to realize why she struggled to fit in. Her new classmates didn't attend church all day long every Sunday. No one believed in the devil. That first year, outside the boundary of her small enclave, she had learned that everyone in her middle school class would laugh if she said what Reverend Eddie made clear: it was a sin to kiss a boy.

"But, honestly," she said to Richard as she speared a few leaves of lettuce. "When you got your master's at Colorado State, did your science professors discuss additional dimensions—the sixth sense? And what about your counseling and psychology instructors, did any of them ever report on the crazy client who wasn't crazy but psychic?"

Richard shook his head, a consoling response.

A tear traveled down her cheek. Had she truly missed an entire dimension alive and well in her daughter and others? With her napkin a twisted mess, she used the back of her hand and mumbled, "I'm sorry."

"No need. Star's always been a challenge. She would be for any parent. Don't be so hard on yourself."

Richard wasn't a parent; how could he know?

He continued, "You may be right . . . Star's off the grid. Who knows, maybe there are dimensions of reality you and I don't pick up on but others do. Think of it this way: I grew up with a cat and you a dog, and we both knew our pets understood how we were feeling and responded in kind. Years later, scientific studies verify what we've known all along—they pick up on our feelings."

She stopped herself from saying "too simplistic" and instead considered a coincidence she had often dismissed. "Jeffrey always knew when Star was coming home."

"So, was he psychic?"

A laugh gurgled up from her belly. She let it come and it grew bigger, spilling out in waves of tears that moistened her cheeks. He handed her his unused napkin. Maybe she could wrap her mind around this foreign concept. Considering Star psychic would be so much easier than thinking psychotic.

"You're right," Richard said. "The word *psychic* was never uttered inside the walls of Colorado State. They relegated it to folklore. Wouldn't surprise me, though, if there aren't a few clandestine studies supporting what they taught to be crazy beliefs—psychic, ESP, or whatever. Seems like the concept has been around forever. There's got to be a few renegade scientists studying this stuff."

"Yes." Mariah nodded. Candice. Her arm extending to touch Mariah and then withdrawing. With brimming eyes, Candice had murmured, *I'm so sorry*. How could Candice have changed so radically?

"Star may be one of those lucky ones who has a special radar for picking up on dimensions of reality the rest of us don't key in to."

Richard gave a quick smile. "Even so—and I know you know this—she's still a kid who needs your love and understanding, which you have given her."

He had no idea about her level of irritation with Star. Star's odd sensitivities, insistence on feeding crows, and wearing sunglasses to avoid acknowledging others. What were the words Candice had used to describe Star? *Sensitive* and *connected.*

"I get it you're worried for her," Richard said.

Mariah sighed inwardly. *No, Richard, you don't,* she thought. No one knew what she was going through.

"So, I'm wondering," Richard said, "how much harder would it be to view Star as, well, psychic?"

Her head moving toward *no* preceded her verbal response that stuck in her throat.

"She's the same challenging kid—but now, perhaps you have a little more understanding of where this so-called highly imaginative behavior is coming from."

Again, she shook her head, opposing the open-minded reply she sought to give. Richard had no clue how convoluted her life had become. How complicated life was with a child. She stood up and dumped her pitiful salad. She forced herself back down and waited while he finished his sandwich.

"So?" Richard asked.

"It scares the shit out of me," she whispered.

"Because . . . ?"

"You're not a parent, you wouldn't understand. You're suggesting I'm to assume she can read my mind whenever she wants."

He gave a partial smile. *Is he humoring me?* And then he tossed out, like a shoulder shrug, "And would that be so bad? If you accepted the fact that she can sense what's going on or has gone on around her?"

The word *fact,* hard and unforgiving, made her flinch. Had it now become a fact, solid and unmovable? She met his patient face, awaiting her answer. "I need to figure out how to . . . to take this additional aspect of Star into consideration." Mariah glanced at her watch. This was eating into her prep time for the hoarder/clutter group. "If you had a child, you'd understand how crazy-making this is!" She bit her lower lip. "I'm sorry. You're right. Acceptance. It's just . . . this psychic stuff has added a whole other layer to the . . ." Her mind flashed to Star's multiple screaming fits over what appeared to be nothing. They were rare now, but not the moodiness. "The complications I've had with her."

Richard kept his gaze on her. He knew she kept secrets. Silence surrounded them even as the cafeteria filled. If only she could go home and crawl into bed.

"You're right," he said. "I have no idea what it's like to be a parent." He hesitated and then met her eyes. "But I do know what it's like to be an adolescent in a family that keeps secrets."

Chapter 28

My Journal of Hidden Truths
November 5, 2012

Journal, I knew this would be a year brimming with horrors hurtled from the bowels of Aspen Creek. Today confirmed this. Whoever You are reading this, it's because I can't take the dreadfulness of school.

Today, Tilly's anger came at me cerulean blue, the color of the ice pack Mom keeps in the freezer. It smacked cold and hard as she swept by my desk in stupid advisory class. She had met with Curtis and discovered I was right.

Knowing her business was not my choice.

I pulled out my drawing pad and sketched Jeffrey meeting Hafiz. For a splintering moment a gladness swelled inside. I wish I could have met Hafiz.

When Tilly passed my desk, I "heard" her yell nice and loud, "Stop!" And then felt her melt into a swampy pool of tears. I shut my eyes, shook my head, and then figured out what happened: her church rules are strong. For sure, she wouldn't have let Curtis do it. It was Curtis she yelled at.

When she pulled her chair out, the back of it slammed loudly into Simon's desk. The anger that flashed between them made my muscles spasm. Mr. Humphrey's face grew grim. He called on her and embarrassed her when she refused to answer.

I knew she planned to lay into me. I waited as long as I could before leaving class. Five steps into the hall, she showed up in my face. I took a step back. She wanted to yell but didn't dare.

"How'd you know?"

I shrugged my shoulders.

"Who told you?"

"No one."

"Someone must have."

I looked away, trying to escape the blaring blue anger. I stared at the place where the linoleum floor met the metal locker. Looking up, I noticed it was a dented locker with an ugly scratch down the center. Puffs of dust and tight curls of dirt collected between the linoleum and the locker, and I thought of Mr. Seng and his tedious job of cleaning. Sadness weighted me down. I took a quick look at her and then murmured, "I'm sorry."

"How did you know?"

"I just did."

"What do you mean?"

"I don't know. I just could tell."

"Did you hear voices inside you?" Tilly's question drilled into me and would not stop boring in until I answered. The words *voices inside* confused me. People think voices happen outside their ears, but everything happens inside our heads, where the brain translates the nerve impulses into something that makes sense to us, like words and images. I couldn't explain this to Tilly, so I nodded.

"It must have been the devil."

"What?"

"You heard the devil speaking to you." Tilly took a step backward. She looked at me oddly, like I was an alien. "It's not normal to know stuff with no one telling you."

I had nothing to say about this. It's sort of like synchronicity but it's not. Tilly would never understand synchronicity anyway.

Tilly turned to leave, took several steps, and then spun around to face me. "That's the devil speaking. You had better be careful, he's trying to take your soul."

The bell rang, we were both late. Tilly moved quickly to get somewhere fast, away from me.

Dr. Quinn is the only person I know who can make sense of this. She understands *The Holographic Universe* and David Bohm's ideas of an implicate order. Okay, whoever You are reading this, I pretend I understand, but I know I'm struggling with this. Therefore, I want the opportunity to study physics like Dr. Quinn and David Bohm.

I used to not question myself so much. But now, I wonder if something's wrong with me. More than ever, I want to see Dr. Quinn again. She might understand. I know where she lives . . . but I can't imagine a way to get there without freaking out Mom. For sure, Mom doesn't get her.

Chapter 29

Mariah scurried into the hoarder/clutter support group a few minutes late. The irritation with Richard evaporated when she saw her clients seated and pleasantly chatting with one another. Georgie, in particular, appeared settled.

During Georgie's first six weeks in the hoarder/clutter support group, she had provided supportive comments to others and revealed what her choice collections were—dolls and stuffed animals—but shared little about her life. When she began announcing "Messies, be gone" at the end of each session, Mariah held no expectation of meaningful change.

Three weeks ago, Mariah had been shocked to learn that, in her pursuit of collecting, Georgie had acquired a debt that could cover the price of a new Prius. Georgie's announcement today was even more shocking: "I made my last doll purchase." Mariah waited before responding, looking expectantly at the women to contribute something supportive.

Kelly was the first to speak up. "Georgie, that's a big step to take. To tell us this. Even if it isn't the last one, at least you spoke it." Others nodded.

And then Angela said, "That's what I said six months ago about all the craft items I store. As you all know, I never have time to do craft projects . . ."

Again, Mariah held back before commenting, and then Georgie

said, "Now I understand why I keep collecting what I do." This disclosure was even more unexpected.

Darlene spoke next. "I don't trust my understanding anymore. It's all in my head. True knowing has more to do with my spirit." Darlene was a committed hoarder who came only to satisfy her daughter. Several of the women rolled their eyes. "I know I'm supposed to keep all these magazines cuz they got something in them that someone needs to read, and that someone is me."

"Darlene. You ain't Georgie," said Thelma. "She says she has an understanding. We need to be respectful, right, Mariah?"

Mariah nodded and invited Georgie to continue.

"My little girl, Jasmine, loved dolls and stuffed animals."

Mariah went numb and clinical. She straightened her back and pushed against the rigid chair.

Georgie continued, "When I bought a doll this week, I felt filled with sadness. This has never happened to me when I go to purchase something. When I pulled this sweet baby doll off the shelf, sadness choked me. My hand shook. I knew I needed to keep this doll but for reasons different than the hundreds of others." Georgie teared up, and the entire room shifted.

Mariah waited, biting her lower lip, wondering if she should facilitate before Darlene or Angela jumped in to dismiss this.

Georgie went on, "It was during the drive home that I understood. I've been saving these baby dolls and stuffed animals for Jasmine. It's my way of not letting go. I don't want to lose her." She began weeping.

Mariah was the only one dry-eyed. Her back ached from her stiff posture, as did her thighs, pressing her knees together.

Between sobs, Georgie plowed on. "But I have. She died two years ago last week. She was the most precious part of my life."

Kelly and Thelma circled around Georgie, gently embracing her.

"I was clueless about the hoarding. It made me feel good, for the moment. I know that's what we're supposed to learn here, that the feel-good never lasts, but now I get why. Hanging on to things she loved in this life won't bring her back. Jasmine is teaching me. I need to let go to live."

When Mariah was on her way home at the end of the day, Georgie's last sentence played over in her mind as she slowed to the stop sign, made a hard right, and accelerated, noticing tree after tree transformed into brittle sticks, with a handful of tenacious leaves clinging to wispy branches. *I need to let go to live.*

Would Georgie have had this realization if she had not hung on so long? Was there a balance between hanging on and letting go?

Mariah knew nothing of her clients—of anyone, really. Her own daughter wasn't the only mystery.

At home, the smell of Top Ramen infiltrated the house. Mariah knocked on Star's door, heard her chatting away. Star cracked her door, holding her cell phone away from her head, and whispered, "It's Jen. Have dinner without me, I'm not hungry." Stella nudged the door wider with her nose, demanding contact. Mariah squatted down and rubbed behind her floppy ears. Having been satisfied, Stella slipped back through the door, which Star promptly closed.

This had to be the teenage behavior other parents bemoaned. Behavior foreign to her own childhood experience of setting the table for two, sitting down, wanting only to eat in silence and instead being peppered with questions. At Star's age, she had done more than set the table; she often made the meal. How unexpected that she now welcomed this behavior from Star—a refreshing resemblance of normalcy.

Mariah turned toward the kitchen, satisfied Star had a friend. Everyone appreciated Jen's contribution to class discussions. Last week she had presented a compelling argument for how a mass conversion to paganism could save the environment and reduce the amount of warring.

How had her parents let go of having a son and welcomed a daughter? How devastating if they hadn't let go. Mariah and Star had the benefit of welcoming Jen as herself: a bright, sensitive young woman. Jen deserved relationships in which she was accepted for who she truly was, not who she had been. Didn't we all deserve this? The choice to leave behind who we were before? Did the baggage of the past necessarily have to be factored into our present selves?

Late that evening, Mariah stood facing Einstein's eyes. She smiled. Then gently tapped three times on the door.

"Yeah."

"It's your mother."

"Duh."

Mariah sighed while inwardly laughing at the whole notion of knocking and waiting to be invited in. It was both odd and funny in a sort of perfect way. She entered to find Star sitting on the floor, back against her bed, in flannel pj's and the fluffy slippers Mariah had gotten her for her birthday. Stella lay draped over her lap. Star looked up, cradling her journal. Mariah joined her on the floor.

"Just thought I'd check in before heading to bed. Haven't seen you all evening."

Star closed the journal with a velvet marker.

"So . . . how was school?"

"You know I can hardly stand it. It's boring, and I hate all the drama."

"The drama?"

"Kids making a big deal out of nothing. I just try to mind my own business. It's like being in a whirlpool—I feel the suction from vibrations.

The teachers are mean. I hate how teachers try to find out who's not paying attention and then pounce on them."

Star mentioning vibrations was not new. But now Mariah wondered whether she should inquire. She made a mental note to come back to this. "Were you pounced on today?"

"No. But I don't like watching it."

"I'm sorry. So, no new friends?"

"Jen's my friend, and she does school online, which means she can work at her own pace without drama or teachers bugging her."

Mariah pressed her hip to Star's. Doing so, she rubbed against Stella, who groaned. Her fingers combed through Star's lush auburn hair. Star did not pull away, creating a pulse of comfort.

"I'm sorry it's so hard, sweetie."

"Mom," Star said. Mariah pulled her hand back and braced for the onslaught about the benefits of online schooling. "Did you ever believe there was a devil?"

"That's an interesting question."

"Some kids actually think the devil exists and takes over people's minds."

"Hmm. Well, I guess I'm not surprised. Lots of religions believe in the devil."

"Do you?"

"Not anymore."

"So you did."

"A long time ago. I belonged to a church that taught you either listened to and believed in God or you listened to the devil and got into . . . trouble." The word *hell* ripped through her mind. "There were lots of rules about good and bad."

"That's totally creepy. I mean, all voices are in a person's head, and who knows how they get there, where they come from."

"I suspect the devil was made up to scare children into behaving in certain ways."

"What about *The Exorcist*?"

Mariah startled, recalling her own mother forbidding her from ever seeing it. "When did you see that?"

"I don't know, sometime last year on Netflix. It was too gross to watch all of it."

"So you know it was completely made up. There's no such thing as a devil."

"Yeah. It looked all fakey, mostly because it's such an old movie with sad special effects." Star placed her hand on Stella's belly and gently caressed the silky skin. She then looked intently at Mariah. "Even so, it's based on a true story."

"Oh, I'm not so sure about that."

Star gave her a challenging look.

"Well, that may be," Mariah conceded. "But it doesn't necessarily mean the child was possessed by the devil."

"If you google *exorcism*, you'll see lots of people believe in the devil."

"Star, you and I both know there's lots of crazy stuff on the internet that isn't true. I sometimes think if someone works hard at believing in most anything, like the devil or bigfoot or the bogeyman"—Star cracked a smile at this—"people can talk themselves into believing anything's real. But we have no need for the devil, do we?"

"No. I just don't get why people would choose to believe it."

"Humans like to have explanations for things they don't understand. Sometimes that means they make things up."

"That's why I like science. Scientists must prove through experiments what they say is real and true."

Mariah stroked Star's hair, gathered it up in her hands, and then leaned over and kissed her cheek. This was why she had made the decision to leave the reaches of Reverend Eddie and the specter of hell.

Chapter 30

In her own bedroom, Mariah flicked on the bedside lamp and reached for the TV remote. She aimed it at the screen and then tossed it aside. What had prompted Star to ask about the devil?

Mariah had been well into adulthood when she had stopped believing in God. But the devil? Certainly, she didn't believe in a being with a red-pointed tail, ready to pitch you into the fires of hell. Evil, however, was another matter.

When she began questioning the whole God business, she realized that prayer had been her insurance against evil. An insurance that had failed to protect her family. Did Georgie also blame God for her loss?

She left her room for the kitchen, where her cell phone lay charging. Perhaps there was a missed call. But the cue came up blank. Did Devin think she was still mad at him? She wasn't. Not at all. Her fury was with herself. She poured another glass of wine and returned to her bedroom.

With the wineglass nearly empty, she was drawn to the far reaches of her closet. The right upper shelf, where a long-abandoned box waited patiently for her return.

The image of Georgie recognizing grief's ruins hovered as Mariah stood on tiptoe and reached for the sturdy box, weighed down with a stack of sweaters she had long ago lost interest in wearing. A transcendent dizziness overtook her as she stretched up, tossed the sweaters aside, and shimmied the box out of its corner and into her hands. She nearly collapsed from the weight of the box.

The room spun as she placed the box on the floor. She dropped onto her bed, and the bleakness inside her expanded. An unbearable heaviness.

She returned the unopened box back into its vault within her closet and then turned to her glass of Riesling on the nightstand. She didn't sip; she swallowed a large mouthful of the sweet tang.

She didn't have to open the box to be transported back to that day, a sunny winter afternoon twelve years ago—her mother on the phone, with Milly shrieking in a frenzy in the background. Olivia had tried everything. The child was inconsolable.

Mariah told her mother Charlie would be there soon. She hung up the phone and a violent tremor seized her. The noiseless house bellowed an ominous, undecipherable warning, and all she could do was pace about in the hushed confines of her home, dumbfounded by the sudden and complete shift of atmosphere.

Fifteen minutes later, just prior to *the* phone call, she experienced the beginnings of a heart attack. She collapsed onto the couch and placed her right hand over her heart. It was beating out of control. Realizing her own panic would only make it worse, she tried to slow her breathing.

And then the phone rang.

Later she learned that Charlie and Markus had been at the four-way stop a half mile from the park. She imagined Markus jabbering away in his booster seat right next to Charlie. She never let Markus ride in front with her; Charlie, however, had insisted—"It feels like I'm a damn taxi driver. For Christ's sake, we're only going to the park." But in this case, Markus wouldn't have survived either way—the truck had come from behind at eighty miles an hour.

Thank God the driver had also been killed. Court proceedings would have been another kind of hell. The truck driver had Ecstasy in his blood. Lots of it. And his alcohol level was five times the limit.

Because her heart had stopped prior to hearing the phone, she fainted when she picked up the receiver. And in that stupor, she could see what they tried to convey in words.

A medic arrived. Seeing his clean-cut, youthful face, she knew it was not a dream. Again, she lost consciousness. It was Markus she heard, yelling at the top of his lungs—"Mommy!" He reached out for her but was swept away, as if he had been standing on a sandy beach and was pummeled from behind by a rogue wave. She was racing in that dreamlike state, where everything that urgently matters is rendered in slow motion. And for the briefest moment, Charlie's embrace enfolded her, swaddled her in his arms as she had done countless times to calm Milly. She had felt the weight of his body press against her and the softness of his breath.

Chapter 31

My Journal of Hidden Truths
November 6, 2012

I got to advisory class early this morning and so did Jasper. He smiled and I said "Hey" and he said "Hey" back. I wanted to say something meaningful because I noticed him not being sad and I liked the feel of his smile. "I think it's cool that you said science doesn't have all the answers."

He replied, "I like that you're different from all the others." His face reddened, and he looked away. "I mean, you do your own thing and stay out of the drama."

"You sort of do too. Like telling about your mother. That was rad."

He did a half smile and said, "Maybe. I mean, it's the truth."

"Mr. Haze doesn't know as much as he thinks he does. I know a real scientist. She's famous. And she'd understand what you said about your mother."

"Really?"

"Yeah. Her name is Dr. Quinn and she knows about David Bohm." I could tell he had never heard of him, but he pretended by nodding his head. "She loaned me this really cool book called *The Holographic Universe*. I'm not very far into it, but there is a whole chapter called 'A Pocketful of Miracles.'"

"Cool. Want to meet up for lunch?"

"Sure."

It was nice to not be alone during lunch. But we didn't talk about much. I tossed out a few ideas from *The Holographic Universe*, like how the brain creates internal holograms, which explains how the visual cortex allows us to see dimensional images, and how memories can't be traced to any one particular part of the brain. But I could tell listening to me talk about this made him uncomfortable.

We ate most of our lunch in silence, and all of a sudden, I missed Stella. Then I knew how to start the conversation again.

"Guess what? I have a new sister."

"Oh?"

"Yeah. She has four legs, whiskers on her face, and whenever she sees someone, even a stranger, she wags her tail. Her name is Stella."

This made Jasper giggle, and then he shifted back into his usual serious face and said he once had a dog that he considered to be his brother. I told him someday he could maybe come visit Stella and me.

After eating lunch, I wanted to go off to the forest like I usually do to visit the crows and other creatures, but because that's against school rules, I pretended that's not what I usually do. Jen would have no problem with this, but Jasper is different. Even though we didn't talk about much and we walked around the official boring school space, I liked walking with someone for a change. It's not something I want to do every day, though.

I'm glad Jasper's in advisory. Since Tilly got all weird with the devil in me, I overly dread advisory. So at least I now have a friend. It's totally bizarre to imagine Mom being my age and actually believing in the devil. Yet I sort of understand.

Sometimes I feel like a radio transmitter. Signals quiver in my mind, and before I give my mouth permission, I am doing the transmitter thing. That's what happened at Dr. Quinn's house with Hafiz. If my mind was completely in charge, I would have kept my mouth shut because it really was weird. And even though I could tell Dr. Quinn thought it was cool, Mom was shaken up. It made her mad. Same with Tilly. I should have kept my mouth shut about her stupid note. I get why some people might think it's the devil taking over when this sort of thing happens—because it does sort of feel like something that's not quite right is taking over.

Even more weird is to touch something of someone else's and know, without really knowing, what's going on. And I don't even care or want to know, so it's not like synchronicity, because it comes at me without me wanting to connect or have meaning or whatever. It's always been like this. But now others notice, and they think I'm crazy. Or that the devil has taken over. Which must be another word for crazy. Maybe I am. Kids now whisper and tell me this to my face. I used to not care. But now I sort of do, even though I mostly keep my thoughts focused on growing up as fast as I can.

I wish I wasn't Mom's only kid. She worries about me nonstop. If I had a human brother or sister, her worry would be thinned out and spread around. Actually, I know I have a brother. Except, like Jeffrey, he is no longer on planet Earth. But that doesn't mean he's gone. Something really sad happened to him. I can tell he wants to connect with Mom.

If Mom were more like Dr. Quinn, life would be easier. I hope she and Devin stay friends so I can see Dr. Quinn again. I only saw her once, and I already miss her. Meeting her was like synchronicity. Everything about her and me connecting seemed perfect. I hardly had to explain myself and she understood.

Chapter 32

Mariah passed through BHP's entry and saw Gretchen striding down the hall toward her. She considered rushing forward as if consumed in her work. But instead she turned to Gretchen and brandished a smile. "Good morning. How'd the new consultation group go?"

"Oh." Gretchen stepped closer, dimples forming in her lower cheeks as her smile expanded. "Quite nice. The new therapists all had brilliant questions. Thanks for asking."

Mariah relaxed into the detour she had created. She remembered being one of the new therapists—timidly posing questions, fearful of her ignorance. She had been older (but not wiser) than the others. Caring for Star had delayed her career.

Gretchen shuffled sideways into the alcove next to the main entrance desk.

"You know . . ." Gretchen eyed her before continuing, "We could use several of these groups. How would you feel about cofacilitating with me in the spring and, if all goes well, running your own consultation group summer or fall?"

Her own consultation group? Mariah was floored. "If you think I'm ready . . ." Her voice sounded mousy; she forced herself to stand taller.

"Ready? Goodness gracious. Who's ever ready. You're good at listening, and you're not afraid to speak your mind. So how about we give this a try starting in April?"

Mariah nodded, swimming in this stroke of support from Gretchen.

"I don't mean to be nosy, but, as one mom of a teenage girl to another, I'm wondering how Star's doing?" Gretchen said.

Of course, this had to be why Gretchen had buttered her up.

"Tilly is crying one minute, hysterically laughing the next—she's so volatile. I guess Tamara went through this as well, only I don't recall. It's possible I'm repressing the memory." Her eyes drilled intently into Mariah. "So is Star roller-coastering as well?"

"She's my only one. I'm assuming typical teenager. I never know if she's going to be in the mood to eat dinner with me or not."

Gretchen stayed fixed, seeming to want to hear something different.

"Honestly, I have no idea what's typical for Star."

Gretchen leaned back against the edge of the countertop, her vigilant eyes focused on Mariah, who restrained herself from spilling it all. The gulf between these two daughters had been enormous from the get-go—one trying out for cheerleader and the other being called out for talking aloud to her deceased pet. What was the worst that could happen if she said, *Star is psychic, connected, sensitive, and that sums it up*?

"Gretchen, you know my daughter."

"It's been a while . . ."

"True. Let's just say she continues to march to the beat of her own drum. Wears what she wants, not interested in joining school groups, and it's easy for others to view her as . . . odd."

"Oh, that's not at all what I was aiming at. I got it the second year she came to Thanksgiving that she was her own person."

"Well, no surprise—she continues to be." She sounded too curt. She softened her voice. "She doesn't like school. 'Too much drama' is what she says. Even though she's not personally involved in any of the drama. Hates witnessing it. She's lobbying me to let her do online schooling."

Gretchen's face turned pallid. She opened her mouth to speak, but Mariah had already begun her reply.

"I agree. No way."

When Gretchen's concerned expression did not budge, Mariah's annoyance turned to dread. Gretchen sighed and lowered her voice. "To put it lightly, Tilly's been histrionic."

Mariah fixed her face therapist-like, portraying compassionate understanding.

"Lately . . . ," Gretchen said, and the pause sent a wave of heat through Mariah. "A lot of Tilly's upsets have been about Star."

"What do you mean? Do they even have a class together? Star has said nothing of Tilly."

"Evidently they have advisory together."

"Advisory?"

"In theory, it's a time to check in and get to know a core group of kids that will have advisory together for the next two years." Gretchen's face made clear there was more. Mariah squelched the impulse to check her watch and announce a need to get going. "Like I said, Tilly's so different from her older sister. I'm in unfamiliar territory with her. I don't know quite what to take seriously. But you and I have known each other long enough we can both say that Star is extremely unique."

Mariah forced a nod, but the "you and I" part of the statement stirred resentment.

"Tilly said that Star reports hearing voices. Voices that compel her to say whatever she hears to others." Gretchen's face broke out in red splotches. "I know we have different faith traditions," she said, and she seemed to gulp the next breath of air before continuing. "Nevertheless, Tilly's convinced Star is channeling the devil."

Mariah almost busted out laughing, but Gretchen's pained face stopped her. She took a deep breath. "I don't know what to say." In truth, she didn't know *how* to say what she wanted to say—there is no devil! "I'll have a talk with Star and tell her she's upsetting Tilly. That she needs to keep her thoughts private unless someone is asking."

"Mariah, I . . . well . . ." Gretchen's face seemed on the verge of collapsing.

Mariah ached to get on with the predictable schedule of her work, but linger, she must.

"I know Tilly is totally hormonal." Gretchen shook her head at this. "But, just in case, I wanted to make sure you knew Star is reporting that she hears voices. And it freaks her peers out. Given Tilly's emotional bouts, I may be wrong. But I care about you and Star and, given her challenges, and now that she's a teenager—and as we know, adolescence is a vulnerable developmental phase—I . . . I'm thinking you might want to consider having her evaluated."

Mariah's body stiffened at the word *evaluated.* Evaluated for what? And then the *what* presented itself. Evaluated and diagnosed. The indictment of these joined words made her feel dizzy and countered all notions of Star being sensitive, intuitive, psychic. "Evaluated," she mumbled.

Gretchen's face shifted from a worried-mom expression into that of a professional clinician. "As in a mental health check. Star has teetered upon normal from the start. I know you've worked hard with her. That second Thanksgiving we spent together, while Star was having panic attacks right and left, you were doing everything to keep her calm."

"Wait a minute," Mariah said. How dare she? "You have her wrong. Those weren't panic attacks. She doesn't have an anxiety disorder. She was reacting to the bickering between Tilly and Tamara and worrying about getting the turkey fully cooked and her not liking the taste. She's over-the-top sensitive, and we—yes, I'm including myself—simply don't appreciate how tuned in she is."

Gretchen stepped back and eyed her as if she were a stranger. "Well, maybe I got her wrong." Gretchen paused, and Mariah braced herself for the rebuttal. When Gretchen spoke again, her tone shifted to one of self-assuredness. "It was a long time ago. But flash-forward, and she's announcing to kids, who she doesn't hang out with, the intricacies of their social life. When asked how she could know such happenings, she reports hearing voices. Mariah . . ." Gretchen cocked her head. "Maybe Star marches to a different drummer. But I care. If she were my daughter, I'd want to make sure there's nothing more going on."

Mariah winced, recalling her internship at the psychiatric ward in Pasadena. Normal-looking people reporting bizarre experiences. And hearing voices. The psychotic ones all heard voices.

Chapter 33

Not until she got into her car at the end of her workday was Mariah able to savor the privacy she had craved from the moment Gretchen uttered the word *evaluated*. A cold and callous word. So different from the words Candice had used.

Candice—who seemed to discern the depths of her daughter from only one encounter—used words like *sensitive*, *connected*. And, most startling, *other dimensions*. Disturbing concepts. But much less so than the term *evaluated*.

Star had been spot-on about Candice's dog. Whatever she had said to Tilly had to have been unnerving. And correct.

Do psychics *hear* voices? She could google this.

And then Mariah heard a voice; it was that of her mother, insisting she tell Star the truth about her family. She grabbed her phone and clicked on Star's name. Before she could cancel, Star answered.

"Hi, Mom."

"Hi, sweetie. I . . . I . . . had something I wanted to ask and forgot. Are you okay?"

"Yeah, I'm at home with Stella, talking to Jen—she's on hold."

"Oh, sorry, I'm on my way home."

Talking with Jen, a normal teenage thing. If Gretchen were to hear the full story about Jen, she'd likely also recommend Jen for a psychiatric evaluation.

At home, Mariah found a trail of everything Star had consumed for breakfast and snack. *Why is the kitchen a mess every time I come home?* She briskly cleaned the counter space before approaching Star's room. Pausing, hearing no conversation, she cracked open the door. Stella jitterbugged at her feet.

"So, how's Jen doing?"

"Okay. Can I hang with her after church this Sunday?"

"I'm sure we can work something out."

Star sat on her bed with knees up, resting her back against the headboard. She held up the book Candice had given her. "This is awesome."

"Glad you're enjoying it. And homework?"

"It's simple and lame. Since I'm getting good grades in all my classes, there's no need to keep asking me."

"Sorry. Guess it's habit." Mariah walked to the other side of the double bed. "Mind if I join you?"

Star's face lifted into a partial smile as she scooted a few inches over. Mariah settled in next to her and leaned back against the headboard, her shoulder pressing softly to Star's.

"So, things went well at school today?"

"Not as dramatic as usual."

"Hum . . ."

"I had lunch with someone I sort of like."

"Nice. Does this someone have a name?"

"Jasper." Star glanced back at her book, but she had a smile on her face.

"So what is it about Jasper that you like?"

"Well, he's . . ." She lowered her book and scanned the ceiling. "He doesn't pretend to be cool or anything. He's honest and not into drama."

"Sounds refreshing. Is he in some of your classes?"

"Science, social studies, and advisory." She returned her gaze to the book.

"Is Tilly in any of your classes?"

Star's face dropped. "Only advisory."

"I take it you're not friends."

"She's way too much of a drama queen for me. I try to ignore her."

"That's interesting."

"How so?" Star's eyes blazed. The book dropped to her lap, and she eyed Mariah with suspicion.

"You know I work with Tilly's mom."

Star nodded.

"She told me that you said some things that upset Tilly."

"Mom. Like I said, I try to ignore her. She gets in my space on purpose and says all kinds of crazy things." Star turned away.

"Well . . . it upset her when you said that you hear voices."

"*Everyone* hears voices inside their head. Tilly thinks it's the devil if you hear voices. She hates me because I don't try to be popular. Neither do Jasper and Jen. That's why I get along with them. They're honest about who they are."

Star sidled away, parting shoulders. Mariah stopped herself from further questions.

Star picked up her book again. "Just like Candice said, David Bohm had to leave the US. His ideas didn't fit what most scientists believed." Star briefly met Mariah's eyes. "I googled it."

Mariah nodded.

"Like my friends, he didn't give a flip what others thought. He refused to testify against scientists he admired, who McCarthy called communists. That's why he lived in London instead of the United States." She tilted her head back and mumbled, "That was insane." And then, looking at Mariah, "I wonder if Mr. Seng knows about this."

Mariah patted Star's thigh. This brilliant child. And so unusual.

Star was right. Mariah heard voices too. Voices of guilt and the voice of failure. Her eyes moistened; she turned her focus back to Star. "Have you studied McCarthyism in history?"

"Are you kidding! My history class is a pathetic version of the pilgrims coming to America. That's why I looked it up. So I could understand what David went through."

"Back then, things were different. But . . . our world has changed." Mariah's thoughts went to Jen. And the skit she witnessed . . . a presentation unimaginable in her own youth.

"Not enough." Star stiffened and turned to face Mariah. "People still diss anyone who acts differently. Of course they can't just go and send them to another country." Star glanced at the book lying facedown across her thighs. "Jen is always worried she'll someday meet someone she really likes, and they'll freak out when they know the truth about her. I wish people weren't that way."

Mariah let that sink in. She then wrapped her arm around Star and tried to pull her closer. "It must have been reassuring for Jen to know you're so accepting."

"Yeah. I think she chose to tell me right away, because if I had a problem with it, she would have held back from being my friend."

"Or maybe she trusted you from the beginning and wanted you to know all of who she is."

"Hmm. That's a nice way to put it." Star's shoulders relaxed. Moments lapsed. "I'll never forget walking into the classroom and right away noticing her. Everyone was new to me, but I could tell she was different in the right way. I knew immediately we would be friends."

"Sweetie, that's so special."

"Yeah. It was as if I already knew we would understand each other because we're both different from most kids."

"It's normal to feel different. Most of us feel different from one another—"

"But Jen really *is* different. How many girls do you know who used to be boys?"

"You're right. Being transgender is unusual. But she has more in common with everyone than not."

"That's *not* what I'm talking about. I mean, duh, we're all human. But some of us feel outside the human family."

"Is that the way you feel?"

Star pursed her lips.

"You're exceptional in how you can sense others' feelings—even animals."

Stella nudged up closer on the bed. Star gave a brief smile and rubbed behind Stella's floppy ears while staring off.

"I imagine there are times your sensitivity makes you feel different from other people. Most of us miss what you pick up on." Mariah joined in stroking Stella and vowed not to say another word. Long moments passed.

"I think you're right. Jen told the truth about her past because she could tell I was someone who would understand."

Mariah's heart swelled; she ached to embrace Star.

Star tilted her head into the crook between Mariah's neck and shoulder. "Mom," she whispered, "why don't I know about my past? About what happened to my father and . . ." Star lifted her head and looked at Mariah with a piercing intensity.

Numbness encased her. A familiar state that held her together. She opened her mouth, with no idea what to say. Star's penetrating gaze cut like a machete through her frozen detachment.

Star must have felt Mariah's arm go rigid, because she sat up straight, turned, and stared out the window. Mariah didn't remember pulling back her arm or lifting herself off the bed and walking around to Star's side. She did recall Star's face changing to one she scarcely recognized. Star's brow deeply furrowed. Her complexion splotched with red as if singed by heat. Mariah's own knees yearning to buckle. Her arms desiring to enfold this tormented version of her daughter while she remained locked in a standing position, safekeeping them both from an avalanche of emotion.

Chapter 34

Cocooned on the overstuffed couch, Mariah sipped her second glass of Riesling while surfing TV channels. Earlier she had delivered mac and cheese and a tofu sandwich to Star. Room service—a rare amenity to avoid Star's scorching eyes. Star's murmured thanks and her partial smile were an enormous relief.

As she returned her attention to some inane TV show, her phone sang in the kitchen. It was him—she had assigned a personal ringtone, a jazzy little piece. She hoisted herself up to catch the call. But she was in no mood to strike up a conversation. As his name paraded across the screen, her heart thumped. Guilt and embarrassment circled around her.

Two days had lapsed since the dinner with Candice. She cradled the phone in her palm and continued to stare at the display. Moments later a message emerged: "Hi. Miss you. Hope to connect soon."

She returned to the couch, hit the mute button on the TV, and listened again to Devin's voice. She took a long swallow of wine. The heat coursed through her tense muscles, and something inside her relaxed. One more sip, and she hit the call-back button.

"Hi," she said, recalling his concerned look as he had left his mother's living room after her accusations.

"Thanks for calling back. I... uh... want to apologize."

"But I'm the one who needs to apologize. It was a lovely dinner, and I shouldn't have spoiled it with my rampage about not being invited to your mother's talk." And then, before he could interject, "In the end, what does it matter that you didn't invite me? I heard the lecture."

"I'd say you were justified in being . . . uh . . . pissed off. I mean, I knew I would be there and I, well, just wasn't sure."

"You weren't sure?"

"My mother."

Relief washed over her. She held back from saying anything.

"You must have noticed she's changed. Okay, in all honesty, she's so different from what I grew up with, and her former colleagues . . . they see her as a wacko. It concerned me you would see her that way too."

"She most certainly has changed. Although she's as intense as ever." Mariah wanted to say she had a greater appreciation for what he had to have gone through as her only child. Except Candice's presence while Nicole was dying had healed the distance between them.

"True. She's always been intense. But now her intensity is unconventional in a big way, and I'm still trying to make sense of it."

"Adjusting to a new version of someone you think you know can be tough."

"Yeah. I had no expectation she'd come to New York. And"—his voice quaked—"be so in tune with Nicole."

"I'm glad she showed up." Mariah thought of her own mother who had literally saved her and Star in the aftermath of Charlie and Markus's death. Olivia had understood why Mariah couldn't live alone with Star in the small bungalow she and Charlie had bought.

Later, when Mariah tried to express in words how her view of the world had toppled, Olivia advanced her own narrative. A story about how lives are fraught with trials and opportunities to build faith. When this tale continued to repeat itself, Mariah knew she needed to find her own place, far away, to raise Star. Could she and her mother ever be close again?

The pause was long, and then he added, "She and Star sure hit it off."

"Yeah. Star's devouring the book she gave her. She's passionate about physics. It's kind of odd because, well, I lied the other night. Truth is, I've never even had a class in physics . . . and here she is, thirteen, knowing this is what she wants to study."

"Awesome."

"Yeah, not unlike you in high school."

"When we did that article together about gays and the prom, I knew there was something powerful in journalism. At the time, it felt so . . . renegade. Groundbreaking."

"It was. Unfamiliar territory. I couldn't say a thing to my mom about it. Couldn't even whisper the word *gay* around her. It was *sinful*." She pronounced *sinful* in a manner that mocked her mother's response. "Do you remember your mother's reaction?"

"Nope. I suspect, like most of my school experiences, she was too busy to read it. She's still rather self-absorbed."

"Hum. Sorry."

"So, by chance, would you be up for coffee at our old digs after UUCB?"

"Sure. Star has already asked if she can hang out with Jen. Why don't I meet you there?"

"Great. Thanks for calling back."

"Thanks for reaching out." Her phone clicked off, but his melodic voice continued to hum in her head.

Mariah entered the UUCB classroom to find Trudi, who typically only came to see how things were going, busy organizing the chairs around the rectangular table. Don stood off to the side of the room. Mariah sought Trudi's eyes and smiled. Merely focusing on Trudi grounded Mariah. If only she could navigate life with the same ease as Trudi.

The youth filled the classroom—loud and boisterous. Star and Jen migrated to a corner and appeared to fall into deep conversation. Mariah dodged groupings of teens and wound her way toward Trudi.

"Oh, Mariah," Trudi said. "I forgot to tell you. Each year I do a presentation. I'm sorry. I should have said something, because when I do my talk, no extra help is needed."

Mariah noticed that Don had left. "No problem. I'd like to stay if that's okay."

"Of course. My presentation can sometimes stir up feelings in our students—truth is, it might be helpful to have an extra pair of eyes. I'd love your help in noticing who might need some support."

Something inside her wobbled and then lifted. "Sure."

Aware of the change in format, the teens lingered longer with one another. Trudi bent down to ask Cal to scoot over, and Mariah squeezed in between Jen and Brittany, with Star sitting on the other side of Jen.

Positioning herself at the head of the table, Trudi captured the attention of all thirteen youths. "Last week I told you I would do my annual story talk." Trudi had a coy smile on her face. How had Mariah missed this announcement?

Trudi took a slow deep breath, vocalizing the exhale, providing a demonstration for what she wanted the students to do. Mariah's own breath went deep, her muscles loosened, and she felt a pulse of relaxation as she released. In her peripheral vision, she saw Star do the same. The room became still and quiet as they waited for Trudi to speak.

"When I was your age, something tragic and unimaginable happened in my family. My older sister, Lucinda, committed suicide."

Mariah's throat went dry.

"She overdosed on medication combined with alcohol." Trudi took another deep breath, prompting Mariah to do the same. "I loved my sister, and losing her was like losing a part of myself." Trudi's eyes dampened. "I will always miss her. But what made this especially painful was that I also lost my parents."

The room, wrapped in an awful, deferential silence, made it difficult for Mariah to breathe. Why hadn't she been warned about this? Star's eyes were no longer visible in their downward stare. At least six other youths opted to gaze down at the table, while others looked around the room as if they were in an unfamiliar environment.

"My parents changed that day. Suicide was not something that they were willing to discuss. They completely hid it. But I needed to know how and why my sister died. Once I knew, they insisted I not tell anyone. If I had kept the truth to myself, I wouldn't be here today telling my story to you."

The blanket of silence unnerved Mariah. The sound of her own beating heart fanned her anxiety. But then an entertaining rap tune from a cell phone spawned chuckles, and the rustling provided relief. When quiet returned, Trudi continued.

"I was fortunate. I had an aunt I trusted who I felt comfortable sharing my feelings with. And a teacher who hooked me up with a school counselor who listened. When our stories are heard, healing can take place."

In her peripheral vision, Mariah saw Jen reach for Star's hand.

Just then, a memory surfaced: a young woman with perfect bouncy curls and sunny, ruddy cheeks. Stacy, sporting a fourteen-karat diamond. Later Mariah had learned from her mother that Stacy had brought homemade meals following the funeral service. Mariah was barely eating, couldn't drag herself out of bed. And had no interest in doing so.

Weeks later, Stacy showed up, asking to take Milly in her stroller to the park. This had been helpful—a relief. Stacy continued to come multiple afternoons, and then one day Mariah found herself dressed and ready to go to the park with Milly and Stacy.

The air was pure, warm, with a vibrant blue sky—a jarring contradiction to Mariah's inner world. Seated on a park bench, watching Milly dip her hands in the fine sand, Mariah began to tell Stacy about her inability to step back into her own home. The emptiness had terrified her, knocked her senseless. In sharing, her body trembled. Her breathing became strained.

Turning to Stacy, thinking she might disclose more, Mariah was greeted by frightened saucer eyes. They darted all over the park but failed to meet Mariah's. Slowly exhaling, Mariah was left with her loneliness—outsized and immense.

Later, Stacy's reaction made complete sense. She had just been engaged. Mariah's very life was an existential threat in the most painful of ways to Stacy's fairy-tale vision of her future.

Mariah shook her head and returned her attention back to Trudi, who sat moving her gaze among students.

"My friends," Trudi said as she looked at each student in turn, "we all are traveling a path with no absolutes. No one imagines their loved one dying. Suicide is not what anyone expects. I'm sharing this because I want you to understand what saved me." Trudi's voice fell to a whisper. She took several steps toward the front and then met the eyes of her students. "I had two people I trusted to share my story. I told it until it no longer held power over me. My parents couldn't bring themselves to speak their story."

A light-headedness enveloped Mariah. She pinched her thigh to stay present.

"Each of you have had bumps in your life. Some of you have encountered cliffs. To remain alive and whole, you need to find someone you trust to share your story with. That someone may be your parents. But if not, maybe a relative or someone you trust at school."

Trudi's pose was relaxed, but Mariah squirmed, trying to shake her light-headedness, trying to stay focused. She didn't dare look in Star's direction, but in her mind she heard Star's hesitant voice, *What happened to my father* . . . and she felt a painful stab. Mariah's own mother had never shared a single thing about her father's departure. But then, she had never asked her mother what she'd experienced. She sensed this story was off-limits.

"Humans tell stories to heal," Trudi said. "My sister Lucinda wouldn't have taken her life if she had found someone to tell her story to." The silence was deafening. When she began again, her voice was a whisper. "Lucinda had become pregnant by her abusive boyfriend. She had an abortion. She was too ashamed to talk to anyone about it. And her shame grew within her." Trudi took a deep, centering breath. Mariah closed her eyes and allowed her lungs to fill and expand.

"Lucinda had no one she trusted to tell her story to. Without support, she could not face her life."

Mariah fixed her gaze on Trudi's colorful blouse, a combination of purple and orange. The orange was not random blots after all, but images of butterflies.

"This is a difficult story to share. And a hard one to hear. Thank you for listening." Trudi wiped her eyes with a single tissue and then circled the table, making contact.

As Trudi finished making her rounds, she said, "I want you to remember, if events weigh you down, seek someone you trust and share your story. We all need one another."

Mariah turned towards Jen and Star. Jen was now sobbing while Star was comforting her.

Chapter 35

Mariah stepped into Shiva with its all-is-well, laid-back atmosphere. She was still trying to regain her composure after Trudi's presentation. Why hadn't she texted Devin and canceled? She longed to be somewhere distant—a beach, a riverbank, some spring of happiness. A cuddle with Star. *What am I doing here?*

She turned to leave, but the aroma of caffeine drew her back to the counter, where she ordered a cappuccino and, hoping sugar would provide a lift, a double-chocolate brownie.

"Hey." Devin materialized in front of her. "Are you okay?" His familiar voice startled her.

She nodded. But wanted to cry. Her mouth was salty with tears. She took a quick breath and allowed herself to marvel at how he appeared out of nowhere in a church parking lot almost two months ago. Transported from the past into this disturbing present.

He pressed his hand to her upper arm and whispered, "I have a table towards the back."

Together, they moved through the café to a booth. She slid into the hard sculpted seat. The firmness pressing into her back created the same grounding as pinching her thigh during Trudi's story. But her face reddened as she placed the brick-like brownie alongside the frothy cappuccino. She sat in a daze.

"What's going on?" His voice soft.

She blinked and shook her head.

"You seem stressed."

Her lips parted. Where to begin? Images unfurled—Star consoling Jen. Star's contorted, angry face pleading to know her story. Her younger traumatized self, timidly opening to wide-eyed, frightened Stacy. She shut her eyes. The hum of a dated espresso machine, the symphony of voices surrounding her and Devin. She then met his eyes.

"I . . . Trudi . . ." She struggled to speak. "She . . . I wasn't prepared for what she shared." She squinted at the furthest corner of the cafe. And yet, she felt Devin's focus upon her. Unlike Stacy or her mother, or even herself, he could face the actuality of life unfolding in unimaginably painful ways.

How could she begin to put words to her new understanding, one so distressing she had hidden it from herself? She had used Star's sensitivities as an excuse to keep the story, which belonged to both of them, buried. Nursing a fictitious belief that starting over would give Star and her a path to a new beginning.

"Devin, have you ever wondered if it's possible to let go of the past and *truly* start over?" She only glanced at him.

Devin reached across the table with an open hand. She placed her hand in his. The clasp felt like a hug. She took a deep breath. Her throat was too constricted to say another word.

"You, my mother, and I have all started over in big ways," he said.

She sipped the foam from her cappuccino. A factually true statement. Except hers was an escape. Without license to let the past go.

"My mother decided a good ten years ago to leave her past. I'm not sure why. Everything she had worked for that meant so much for so long—tenure, scholarly reviews, keynote speeches." He paused, his face earnest. "She didn't run from her past. She simply walked away."

Mariah, in contrast, had driven eleven hundred miles without looking back. A familiar pang of guilt swept through her. She took a bite of brownie, yearning to be elevated, perhaps even transported, by the rich flavor. It tasted like cardboard.

"She chose a new life," Devin said.

"Any idea why?"

He sipped his coffee before answering. "Just an inkling. I suspect a love affair, but this is only a hunch. It's not something she's ever talked about." He took another sip. "So . . ." He paused, met her eyes, and then spoke with a tentativeness. "What did Trudi share?"

"When she was thirteen, her older sister committed suicide. She talked about telling one's story over and over to heal."

"That *is* intense."

"Yeah. I . . . I can't imagine. She goes over this every year. I don't know how she does it." She peered beyond his broad shoulders. Several of the students in that classroom had mirrored her own expression of the solitary deer caught in headlights. She had seen that look before, about a month prior to her decision to leave Daphne. While shopping with her mother and Milly at Harry's Market, Mariah had dashed one aisle over to grab some bread and came face-to-face with several church friends. The look in their eyes did not differ from the stunned faces in today's class. No one said a word, not even hello.

The lump in her throat migrated to a swell in her chest. Tears began streaming. Star holding Jen's hand as Jen sobbed; Trudi teary-eyed as she said her sister's name. Mariah grabbed a napkin and covered her face. The outpour, like a sneezing bout, came forceful and alarming. *This will pass. I can control this.* Devin slid into her side of the booth, leaned in, and wrapped his arm around her. The warmth of his body settled her breathing.

"Oh, Devin," she sputtered. "I have tried to bury a horrific past." How could she have ever thought it possible to make a fresh start?

Chapter 36

My Journal of Hidden Truths
November 11, 2012

For sure, Jen is the most real person I know. She tells the truth even if it makes her cry. She listens when I tell her about my dreams because she understands it's not just nighttime imagination. She believes me when I tell her I once had a brother and, even though he died, he still knows me. Mom can't listen when I talk about this. I don't need her to since I have Jen. And you, Journal.

Jen had to make her parents listen to her. She had no choice. She couldn't live being someone she wasn't. She would have ended her life if they had chosen not to listen. She had planned it out—an overdose of her mom's anxiety medication so it wouldn't be too dramatic.

She's so brave. Why doesn't everyone get this? Why is she not seen as a heroine for daring to be herself? It's because it scares them! To think about Jen's life means their life could also be turned upside down. I never questioned that I'm a girl and always will be. But Jen had a different experience.

I know Mom's life was turned upside down without warning. She tries to hide it, even from herself. Some truths can't be ignored. That's what Jen figured out for herself. And that's why Mom continues to suffer horrible headaches.

Who knows what else is not the way it starts out seeming to be. We all like to think we know ourselves, or at least where we're heading. Trudi's right, it can all change. Like my brother and father. And Mom.

I know she didn't plan on being alone with me, I catch it in her sadness. And it makes me sad even though I don't mind being alone, because I visit other people online, in books, and in dreams. But Mom is lonely.

It was hard for her to listen to Trudi's talk. I saw her squeeze her eyes shut, holding back tears. I've never seen her cry. She was all shaky when she stood up. I was listening to Jen and then Trudi came over, but I heard the shakiness in Mom's voice when she dismissed the class. It didn't sound at all like her. I sort of wanted to not stay with Jen and to be with Mom, but Jen needed me and I'm not sure how to help Mom.

Mom tried talking with me on the way home about what Trudi shared, but I knew she didn't really want to talk about it. She spoke in her rushed get-it-over-with voice, as if filling out the blanks in a form, verifying she's a good parent. What she really wanted was to hear more about what Jen was going through. But not really.

Chapter 37

Mariah raced back to the church to meet Star as planned, her pathetic sputtering voice replaying itself: "Oh, Devin, I've tried to bury a horrific past." He had remained rock solid. Long enough for her to regain a normal breathing pattern. And then he murmured, "It's okay."

But no, it wasn't okay. She had failed to give Star what she needed most—her story.

She walked into Trudi's office, still not fully recovered from the crumpled mess of explosive tears. Crying was so unlike her. Trudi seemed to grasp the fullness of her turmoil, taking Mariah in with the same unwavering manner as Devin had.

Mariah forced herself to speak. "I admire you for sharing your story. I . . . I can't fathom disclosing a tragedy such as you experienced. I . . ." Her voice faltered. She glanced around the office, decided to change course. "Jen seemed quite upset. Is she doing okay?"

Trudi merely smiled before saying what Mariah already knew. "Jen had a rough time coming out to her family. Since transitioning, it's been a challenge. Star is a blessing in her life." She fixed a knowing gaze on Mariah, allowing a few seconds' pause. "I'm not worried about Jen. She has at least two skilled listeners. I wonder, though . . . I saw in your face a terrible fright, a panic of sorts. If you need a friend to listen, I'm here for you."

"Thanks, Trudi. It's . . . it's hard to imagine such a tragedy."

"I'm sure you know, as a mental health professional, that when it's difficult to talk about a loss or trauma, an intermediary step is to write about it."

That evening, the landline rang, splintering her thoughts. It had to be her mother—solicitors didn't call this late. She leapt up and grabbed the phone, imagining an emergency.

"Sweetheart," Olivia said.

"Mom, what's up?"

"We missed our Saturday call. So I thought maybe I could catch you at home this evening."

"I'm caught. What's so urgent?"

"Urgent? Like I said, we haven't spoken for a couple of weeks. And here we are, into November."

Oh God, she wished it were still September. "So . . ."

"So I'm asking: Thanksgiving or Christmas?"

"You know we don't do a lot of celebrating."

"That's okay. I do. And I want to see my only granddaughter."

"Maybe we'll come out in the summer, or Star can come on her own—"

"You said this last year. Is it too much to ask to spend a holiday with my family?"

"No." Mariah caught her breath. "Let's do Thanksgiving. We're snowed in by Christmas." There was a hush across the telephone line, seconds unfolding. Putting the visit off until December might have been easier.

"Darling, I miss you. I know it's been hard . . ." Olivia's voice broke midsentence, catching Mariah off guard. She both wanted her mother—the one who had shown up to comfort her when she skinned her knee—and rejected the mother who failed to grasp why she needed to give Star a fresh start.

"Mom . . . I'm glad you're coming." Her heart throbbed with a heaviness. She leaned against the kitchen entryway and stared at the TV, now muted.

"You and Star. You're all I have. We used to sing together in the church choir. Star doesn't even know me."

"That's ridiculous. Of course she knows you. It's just—I know you don't understand—I had to raise her my own way. Star and I both needed a fresh start. She was just a baby . . ." Mariah clutched the thick phone handle and leaned her head against the cool of the wall. "She's super sensitive and nothing like me. Sometimes . . . well, there are times when I hardly recognize her." Mariah returned her gaze to the mute TV screen and held her breath, relieved there was no immediate response.

"All parents go through this. Not recognizing their children. Believe me."

Mariah could hear her mother's breathing; she considered how alien she had to have appeared all those years ago while involved with Devin. Not only then, but the past thirteen years as well.

"Mariah. Your father. He passed."

"What do you mean?"

"His sister sent me an obituary. I know I've never shared much with you, and that was a mistake."

Mariah nodded yes to no one. Admitting to a mistake was rare for her mother. A heavy lump migrated down from her throat to her chest. She wished it were possible to reach across the thousand-mile span and touch her mother's soft arm.

Olivia said, "His death doesn't surprise me. He drank like a fish, and it ruined his liver." She sighed. A long, tired exhale, like a moan.

"I thought he became sober—that time I saw him in seventh grade."

"He did. But it was too late. Years ago, the damage was done."

Mariah's body swayed at the ease in which her mother proclaimed the unforgiving impact of past behaviors on the present. Of time marching forward, never to undo transgressions.

"It got me thinking. God only knows when it's our time. I want to make things right with you and Star."

"Mom, I understand. Schedule the flight. I can get the Wednesday before Thanksgiving off."

"Mariah. Star deserves to know the truth about her father and brother."

"Mom." Mariah muffled her groan and gripped the phone tightly, her knuckles whitening. "I'm trying. I'm in the process of telling her. Please, I don't need you to do this for me."

Alone in her bedroom, Mariah stared at the empty page of an unused notebook. The light-blue lines mocked her. Beginning in elementary school and continuing through college with the horrible blue-book experience, facing a blank page had always been pure torment. And here she was, voluntarily inflicting the misery on herself!

When she was nine, her mother had given her a gold-lined diary with a small lock that worked. It had caused her great anguish. Unlike Star, she hadn't known what to write worthy of such a beautiful journal. Or any journal. Back then, she didn't have secrets that needed to be revealed in the privacy of a journal.

My God, she thought. At this very moment, Star was likely writing in her own journal about Trudi's story and her time with Jen.

Star had remained quiet on the way home. Hoping she could get Star to talk about her experience of the class, Mariah had said, "Trudi is so brave to share such a tragic story." But Star continued to look out her window in silence.

When Mariah was in seventh grade, her mother had told her that her father wanted to see her. She could not ask the questions that meant the most to her. *Why did he leave? Why see me now? Is he still my father?* The only questions that arose were the superficial ones. When, where, and how. Difficult topics like those that Trudi brought up—suicide, abortion, the need to find someone to talk to—were beyond anything she could have ever imagined discussing with her own mother.

After driving in silence for a bit, Mariah again tried to open the possibility of discussion with Star. "Honestly, I wasn't at all prepared to hear her story. It was so heart-wrenching."

Star gave her an odd look, as if puzzling over something. Mariah then switched gears and checked in about the visit with Jen.

"Jen's okay," Star said. "Since we're best friends, we went to the bead store and made friendship bracelets."

"That's nice. I noticed she was having a hard time in class."

"Mom. Duh! It made her remember when she almost committed suicide." Star turned and looked directly at her. Eyes, full of accusation, burrowed into Mariah's face. "Her parents didn't want to hear her tell the truth about who she is. They kept denying it."

Now Star's bitter words . . . *her parents . . . kept denying it . . .* played over and over. A mounting pressure surged in Mariah's chest. She tossed the empty notebook aside and fixed her eyes to the far corner of her bedroom closet. The sealed box. Pictures Star deserved to see. Pictures tucked away from herself. In the remote reaches of her mind, she heard the plaintive cries of baby Milly. Cries that foretold the events forever leaving her hollow.

Chapter 38

The following evening, Mariah gazed longingly at the intricately layered slice of tiramisu placed between her and Devin. Two forks graced the flowery petite blue plate. When she hastily reached for one, a trace of a smile showed at the corners of his mouth. Her face reddened.

Each savored bite of the decadent dessert shaped a quiet intimacy. She dabbed the corners of her mouth with the creased white linen napkin. "The tiramisu is wonderful."

Devin leaned back and folded his arms. "So was everything else." His eyes twinkled in the ambient lighting.

There was a brief flutter of anticipation in Mariah's rib cage. She glanced around the upscale bistro—couples engaged in conversation, servers exchanging pleasantries. His face so earnest.

She breathed deeply, swallowing a rising tide of anxiety. "I'm . . . in the process of facing a painful chapter in my life. C*hapter* is a way too diminutive description. *Epic* is more like it. Large and . . . devastating. I'm not ready to talk about it. But for the first time, I can imagine doing so."

Devin's gaze was open, void of panic or inquiry.

"I agree with what you said yesterday. There's no leaving the past. It must be brought into the present. Trudi's story made this clear." She took a sip of water. "I need to start by talking with Star about the past." She shifted her focus away from Devin, steadied her breath. Returning to him, she felt reassured by his gaze.

"My experience with Nicole would have been easy to bury. The pain, guilt, and depression seemed to last forever." Devin sighed. "Finally, acceptance surfaced." His voice remained calm, solid. "No matter how painful this epic experience, I am here for you."

Sincerity filled his face, and yet the thought of opening up tied a knot at the base of her spine. "I . . . I need more time before I can go into it."

As she reached for another sip of water, Beethoven erupted from Devin's pocket. He frowned. The ringtone pleased her ears, and she wondered if she might like classical music after all. He had lit up when she revealed this possibility several weeks ago; he confided that it was Nicole who had introduced him to the symphony.

"It's my mother," he grumbled. "Would you mind?"

She gave him the go-ahead. He stepped away to a private corner. She captured the crumbs on the tiramisu plate with her fork and smiled to herself. She was on a *date*! When he'd called, she hadn't realized at first that he was asking her out. She still could hardly believe it. Earlier today, she put fresh sheets on her bed and tidied up the house. Star was spending the night at Jen's.

Devin returned, pulling his credit card out from his billfold before sitting down.

"Are things okay?" she asked.

"Overall, absolutely. She has a new computer and is in a tizzy over getting Skype set up. Evidently there's someone pretty special she's expecting to connect with first thing in the morning. Would you mind if we swung by on our way to your house?"

"Of course not."

When they pulled up, Candice was pacing across the front porch, projecting her usual intensity, reminding Mariah of when they'd first met twenty-three years ago. She greeted them as if they had come for tea and then, as they walked inside, quickly pivoted the conversation to her consternation with technology, to which Mariah could relate. She had to rely on Star to access online banking and to navigate the world of malware.

Within moments, Devin plugged in some wires, clicked on various settings, and announced, "It's set to go, Mom."

Candice radiated as she brought her hands together in a slow-motion clap. "I'm expecting a very important Skype date—five a.m. tomorrow."

A long pause followed. Mariah expected, waited, for Devin to say, *We need to get going.* Instead, he said, "Wow, Mom, this must be important. Who do you plan to talk with at five a.m.?"

"Well, are you two in a hurry? It's a rather long story. Can I entice you with either tea or"—she looked at Mariah—"wine?"

Devin shot Mariah a look of concern. Yet she found herself intrigued by this brilliant woman who spoke her mind and had undergone some sort of transformation.

"A glass of wine would be lovely," Mariah said.

They sat in the Buddha room, and with wine, the room became ever more accessible. She and Devin on the futon, Candice kitty-corner in the floral wingback chair.

"I've renewed my connection with a close friend," Candice said. "She lives in India, in an ashram in Tamil Nadu. She suggested we Skype. Five a.m. is the only time that works for both of us."

Devin looked thoroughly puzzled. "So, who's this friend of yours?" he asked.

Candice took a long sip of tea before answering. "About fifteen years ago I had a frozen shoulder. A miserable imposition. No amount of physical therapy made a difference. I could hardly undo my own bra—the pain was excruciating." Candice slowly shook her head. "At the urging of a colleague, I relented and saw an acupuncturist." A furtive smile arose on her face as Devin raised his brows and tilted his head. "Believe me, I had to be quite desperate to consider such an archaic method of relief. Yet it seemed *so* much easier than facing surgery."

Mariah found herself nodding, though she wasn't sure why. Devin's hands intertwined on his lap while he watched his mother.

"Hmm," Candice murmured, gazing somewhere distant. "It's so interesting how easily we can dismiss an idea only to have it re-emerge later as plausible." She took a deep breath. "In fact, I found myself wishing the very practice I had disparaged would be my salvation."

With the wine loosening her thoughts, Mariah added, "Like me, desperate to find community for Star, considering a *church*, of all places." And then she realized neither Candice nor Devin would appreciate this—they had known her only as a church person. They had no idea that when she left Daphne, church was the last thing she wanted.

Mariah couldn't tell if the smile on Candice's face was genuine until she declared, "Within the spectrum of churches, you chose well."

"Mom, what does this have to do with your Skype call tomorrow?"

"The acupuncturist, Tori, is the person I'm meeting with tomorrow. She healed my shoulder." Candice paused, glancing upward, and lightly touched her heart with her right hand. "And something much deeper."

Devin's face seemed pained, or distressed.

Candice continued with a new softness to her voice, "Tori was truly . . . masterful. I, I fell in love with her."

Mariah's mouth fell open. She clamped it shut and tried not to react. Devin stared blankly for a moment before an understanding traveled across his face.

"I too was shocked." Candice then gave an unabashed smile. "I had given up on ever having a romantic relationship, and certainly not with a woman."

Did Candice blush? Mariah looked away to give her some privacy. Devin also lowered his eyes.

"I'm convinced falling in love with Tori was fated. The affair was brief, but it irrevocably changed my life. She reconnected me with parts of myself I was longing to heal."

"Is she why you started meditating?" Devin asked.

Candice nodded. "She opened all kinds of doors. Doors I had shut during the endurance race to gain tenure at UCLA."

"So," Devin asked, "what happened?"

"She had a calling to study with her spiritual teacher. That was ten years ago. She's now ready to reconnect. I must admit, I'm thrilled to hear from her."

Mariah wondered what a spiritual teacher was.

"Can I get you more wine? Tea?"

Mariah waited for Devin's response. When he signaled no, she asked for half a glass, and Candice scurried off.

Mariah placed her hand on Devin's upper arm. He continued to stare straight ahead. She moved her hand down his arm and gave his hand a gentle squeeze. He responded in kind, quickly and dismissively.

"This must be . . . totally overwhelming." She kept her voice light so that he wouldn't detect her shock and amazement.

"Yep. My mother is full of surprises," he said with a biting tone. She pulled her hand back.

Candice returned with a chilled bottle of white wine. "Meeting Tori was such an unlikely, beyond-belief connection." Candice punctuated these words, and then continued in a measured tone, "As you know, I've been a committed atheist my entire life—and raised Devin to be similar."

Mariah nodded.

"Which makes it rather interesting that the two of you had any kind of connection, not to mention that you reconnected in a church of all places." Candice gave a sly smile and sipped her tea.

Mariah blushed and took a healthy swig of wine. She reached over and clasped Devin's hand. The warmth of his palm comforted her.

"Being with Tori imparted a profound realization. In my pursuit of science, I had dismissed a range of alternative accounts—equally valid interpretations of reality. The discovery that Western medicine could not heal me and that a love I had not believed possible bloomed made me reevaluate the core of who I am." Candice gazed directly at Devin and stated in a voice solid and unwavering, "What I felt for Tori is something I tried to feel for your father." She took a deep breath. Her tone shifted to soft and hesitant. "I hope you can forgive me."

Devin's face stayed set like stone. But Mariah saw his eyes thicken with moisture.

"Mom, when did you meet Tori?"

"Right after you shared Nicole's diagnosis."

"Why didn't you tell me?" His accusing tone was chilling.

Red blotches formed on Candice's face. Mariah looked away.

"By the time I came to New York," Candice said, "my relationship with Tori had ended. I . . . I had no frame for it."

Mariah stopped herself from proclaiming how magical it had felt to fall in love with Devin in tenth grade. She, a straitlaced, plain-looking girl. It was so long ago. And yet here she was with him at his mother's house. She snatched a glance at him and came to her senses. This was not the time to celebrate unexpected reunions. That was a wine-infused sentiment.

"I was so *honored* you had reached out to me." Candice met Devin's eyes, which seemed to have softened. "Had I not known Tori, I would have responded differently."

Devin's face had lightened. A wave of hope lifted Mariah.

Finally, Devin spoke. "I loved that you came."

A ripple of energy passed through Mariah. She almost pinched herself. *Is this real? Can parents really talk to their grown children so honestly?*

"Tori taught me it doesn't matter what we call it, so long as we recognize within us a life-affirming presence."

Life-affirming? There was nothing affirming in Mariah's life.

"This presence is the piece science can never grasp—just as the eyes can't see themselves without the use of a mirror. She reawakened everything I let go of in pursuit of success. What I've sought we're all seeking. A lasting inner peace." Candice paused, taking a deep breath and gazing upward. Mariah found herself also taking a deep breath. "I've heard it said that the soul is homesick and cannot recover until it finds union with its source. Finally, this makes sense to me."

Was it the wine that created the sense of serenity? Squinting her eyes, Mariah glimpsed Candice, Devin, and even herself glowing.

Chapter 39

My Journal of Hidden Truths
November 13, 2012

Here's the thing, Journal, maybe Tilly and her friends are right—I am a crazy psycho. I should have kept the craziness to myself. Except what I saw today looked real, which is freaky.

I started out minding my own business. As always, I slipped out of the cafeteria before anyone knew I was even there. I scanned the area for teachers and tattlers, like jerky Shawn. Once I knew the coast was clear, I darted across the asphalt parking lot toward the thickets, where squirrels, spiders, and Steller's jays hang out. But something had changed. The welcome was gone. I noticed right away.

As I moved farther away from the schoolhouse prison and into the forest, something totally bizarre happened. I saw blood splattered across a smooth surface, a man drenched in sweat running through the forest with a loaded gun in his hand. My heart pounded so hard I truly thought I might be having a heart attack. I shut my eyes, opened them again, and was wobbly. I couldn't move.

Then I heard Tilly's high-pitched voice and the fakey laughs of her friends heading for their part of the forest—the section with a small forbidden path. I must have looked totally wacko weird. I closed my eyes and felt them stare at me. Tilly asked, "What's wrong?"

I couldn't tell if she really wanted to know. I shook my head, opened my mouth to say something, but the words were crushed in my throat. I took a step toward the school. And then it happened again. I saw this crazy dude with a gun. He began shooting, and blood splattered everywhere. Tilly and her friends started moving toward the forest, and I couldn't stop myself from yelling, "Don't go!"

Then I was in a tunnel, hearing echoing sounds—"Why?" "What's wrong?" I forced the words out, "Not safe." They circled around me with teasing questions. I saw the blood again and yelled, "You'll be shot!" I heard laughing. Someone asked me, "How do you know?" And then Tilly's voice called out, "She listens to the devil."

Ms. Donners's whistle shrieked in my ears, as deafening as a train in a tunnel blasting its horn. She was about to bust us, and then the bell rang. But I couldn't move. They were mumbling "weirdo," "psycho," "crazy"—I was too dizzy to know if Tilly said those things. Someone, maybe Ms. Donners, placed a hand on my shoulder and nudged me toward the building.

Once inside, I knew I couldn't face social studies and everyone else I'd pass in the hall. I needed to be alone. I made my way to the restroom and hid in a stall until the bell rang. That's when I decided to skip school.

It was easy. I slipped out and was home in fifteen minutes, ten minutes quicker than my walk to school. Later, when making a cup of soup, the school called, and the computer voice reported my absence. I erased it. I had no idea how easy it is to skip. I might do it again tomorrow.

Whatever happened today was super scary. If You are reading my journal, it's because whatever happened to me totally took me down. It was worse than a nightmare. At least you can wake up from a bad dream and you don't embarrass yourself during it. If I were to tell Mom about this, for sure she would suspect that I'm sick in the head. I wonder if Candice would understand.

Chapter 40

Georgie's disclosure the previous week had set a new bar for the hoarder/clutter sessions. With minimal facilitation, Angela and Thelma both grasped an unspoken connection between what they chose to collect and the many losses they had endured. Mariah took heart in seeing Kelly and Georgie reach out. But even with positive steps forward, the session drained her.

When the end arrived and Georgie spouted out, "Messies, be gone," Mariah sprang to attention, ready to leave, pining for a quiet evening.

On the drive home, when she spotted the red-and-yellow sign for Papa Sander's Take-and-Bake, she pulled over. The tuna casserole sitting in the fridge since Sunday held no appeal. Stella, however, would relish it. Once parked, she gave Star a quick call, even though she could have ordered Star's favorite.

"Hi, sweetie. I'm at Papa Sander's. Do you want the usual?"

"Okay." The damp tone in Star's response signaled something was off. Star loved it when she arrived home with ready-to-bake pizza—and it wasn't even Friday.

"Is everything okay?"

"Yeah."

"You sound kind of down."

Star said nothing.

"Star, what's wrong?"

"I'm fine," she said in a muffled tone.

"All right, see you in fifteen minutes."

Back in the car with the pizza, Mariah took a breath before turning the key. Something was clearly going on with Star. She made a vow not to say a single critical comment to Star. To simply be present—like Trudi—and make space for Star to share.

Then there was Devin. She owed him a call. More so, an apology. He too deserved her to be present without all her damn judgment. They had driven home from Candice's house in silence. He, upset and confused about his mother. She, at a loss for what to say. It didn't help that she had chimed in with a supportive response to Candice about the difficulty in revealing the past.

But how could he, or anyone, understand? Mariah had had no choice but to start over.

Her heart went out to Devin. What he must be going through.

Had her own mother ever been attracted to someone else? After all, Mariah's father had left two years after she was born, which meant her mother had been only twenty-eight years old. Olivia had hurled herself into the activities of the Jesus the Savior Church. She sought Reverend Eddie's approval endlessly. Maybe she'd had a crush on him?

But to discover one's mother had had a lesbian relationship—unfathomable. Devin, having lived in New York, had to have known gay and lesbian people. She, on the other hand, had been raised with a rigid sense of what was acceptable, what was "normal." Could it be she'd passively absorbed the ideas she was continually exposed to without question?

Mariah started the car and pulled out of Papa Sander's. As she turned onto the road, a wormy resentment twisted in her stomach. The dinner with Devin had been romantic. And it was completely lost in his mother's story.

That night, when they had reached Mariah's house, she'd asked,

"Would you like to come in?" The way he looked at her made her wonder if she had slurred her words. She should have declined that glass of wine Candice had offered.

"I would," he said. "But not tonight."

All she could say was "I understand." But she didn't.

The house was quiet when Mariah walked in with the pizza. She turned the oven on and called out, "Star?"

Stella preceded Star into the kitchen, angling first left, then right, her wagging tail taking charge of her movements. Star sauntered in behind, a mirror opposite, moving as if roused from a deep sleep. Mariah poured herself a full glass of chardonnay, and then turned to Star. Star's eyes, red-rimmed, her skin a pasty pale. Mariah set down the glass and circled her arm around Star's waist. Star shifted away.

"You look upset. What's bothering you?"

Star's face fell, and some unreadable emotion passed across. She turned her back on Mariah and poured herself a glass of orange juice.

"Sweetheart, what's going on?"

"School's boring. And I'm tired." She moved toward her bedroom.

"Wait a minute."

Star stopped and looked at her.

"Are you sure you don't want to talk about it?"

"I've already told you. I don't like Aspen Creek. I want to do online school like Jen so I don't have to deal with stupid rules and crazy people."

Mariah stopped herself from further probing. Besides, she had no argument for "stupid rules." The oven buzzed. She shoved the pizza in, grabbed a handful of rice crackers and made her way into the living room.

Star would do better with a small school. Gretchen had also complained about how difficult the transition was for Tilly.

At Star's age, Mariah had been bussed from the outskirts of

Pasadena to a building in the city five times the size of her elementary school. Lost in a wave of unfamiliar faces, she chose to quietly observe. With time, she figured out how to fit in. Later, she began to blend in. This came naturally. Star, who put comfort before style, couldn't be more opposite. Mariah had to trust that she would find her way.

She took a strong sip of chardonnay and grabbed the remote. The TV blared about Tide laundry detergent and the new Honda CR-V. She half listened while shuffling through the pile of junk mail scattered on the end table. When the music softened to a calm, melodic tone, the words *security* and *future* captured her attention. "State Farm Life Insurance" paraded across a serene scene of mountains and river, and the dreaded question wormed inside her. The unthinkable. *What would happen to Star if* . . .

But she couldn't pursue that line of inquiry right now. Instead, she returned to the unopened pile of mail until the familiar, paternal voice of anchorman Tom Watts announced, "Breaking news."

"Police are looking for the suspect in a shooting that took place two miles north of Aspen Creek Junior High, just prior to noon. The suspect, believed to be a male between the ages of twenty and twenty-five, took off on foot. He has a handgun and is dangerous. Aspen Creek was locked down for forty-five minutes while police combed Farland Park, the wooded area next to the school."

"The forest," Mariah hissed and then hurried to Star's door. She gave an obligatory knock but didn't wait for an answer. She walked into the bedroom. Star jerked her head up from the open journal resting against her thighs as she sat with her back against the bed's headboard.

"Sweetie, no wonder you're so quiet this evening. I could tell something was wrong. It must have been very frightening having a lockdown."

The startled look on Star's face confirmed Mariah's suspicion; Star didn't want to worry her. Star slapped her journal shut and stood up.

"Come here, let me give you a hug." Mariah wrapped her arms around Star. "I'm your mother. No need to hide your worry from me.

Lockdowns can be scary, but the school just wanted to make sure everyone was safe." Mariah pulled back, trying to read Star's face. She couldn't tell if the slight tremble in her daughter's jaw was due to worry or sadness.

"It's okay, Mom. It wasn't a big deal."

"Well, it was. I just heard it on the news. I'm sure there are plenty of police looking for this suspect, but . . ." She peered into Star's face; this was the child who sensed the death of Candice's dog. "So you *weren't* upset when they announced a lockdown?"

"I knew everything would be okay."

"But, sweetheart, you seem upset."

"Mom. Life itself can be a grand upset. I'm just trying to figure things out, and, like I said, school at Aspen makes it difficult. Too much drama."

"Such as?"

"Please, Mom, I don't feel like talking about it."

The oven timer blared. The pizza was done.

They sat together at the dining room table eating in silence. Mariah looked up between bites, offering a smile with each catch of Star's eyes. Star, unresponsive, appeared deep in thought and only nibbled on her favorite meal: thin-crust pizza with peppers, onions, and tomatoes.

"Looks like you're not hungry tonight," Mariah said.

"I had Top Ramen for a snack when I got home."

Mariah took a second piece. Just as she bit into it, Star set aside the slice she was working on and looked up. "When can we see Dr. Quinn again?"

Mariah chewed and swallowed the bite of pizza before responding. Candice had asked for a date with Star as they said their goodbyes the other night. And even though she felt something of an alliance with Candice that night, for the fact that they both held their experiences close and were careful about sharing, Mariah did everything she could to divert Candice's request. She'd said, "Oh, Star is quite busy now that she's in junior high. She has a new dog and a new friend. I'll get back to you once I check her schedule." But she had hoped Candice would let it go.

She smiled at Star. "I'm not sure."

"I'm almost finished with *The Holographic Universe*, and I want to discuss it with her."

"It's my impression she keeps herself rather busy. Next time I talk to Devin, I'll ask him what her schedule looks like."

"If I knew her phone number, I could text her and find out myself."

"Well, not everyone's into texting."

Star stared at her. She tore a congealed piece of cheese off her slice of pizza and mumbled, "It must be cool to have a mom who's a scientist."

"I remember thinking that too."

Star looked up and arched her eyebrows.

"It's normal to think your own mother is not as glamorous as someone else's," Mariah said.

Star shifted her eyes back to the pizza.

"But if you were to ask Devin, I think he'd say the downside is that his mother was very busy while he was growing up. She had little time to do special things with him. And now that I'm grown up, I realize I did lots of things with my mom. In fact, I spent more time with her than Devin ever did with his."

Star rolled her eyes and picked bits of onion off her pizza and tossed them aside.

"Do you remember third and fourth grade when I went on field trips with you?"

"Sort of. I mean, it was nice you came, but no one else had their mom with them."

"That's because most parents are busy, and I made sure I could be available to help," Mariah said. "Which reminds me, Grandma wants to come spend Thanksgiving with us."

"Okay," Star said in a muted tone.

"You don't seem very excited."

"Well, last time I saw her, all she did was talk about her church and try to get me to go clothes shopping with her. I like Grandma, but I don't like the way she thinks I should dress, and I'm not interested in her church."

"Maybe now that you're older, it'll be easier to tell her that. She feels a little left out. You're her only grandchild, and she wants to get to know you better."

Mariah was loading the last of the dishes into the dishwasher when her phone began to play a jazz tune.

"Hi. Thought I'd check in to see how Star's doing."

"Fine, I think. Why?"

"The lockdown. I know she's super sensitive to things, and today's event seemed rather intense."

"You're right. But oddly, she seems okay. She didn't say a thing about it—I think she didn't want to worry me." Mariah moved to the living room and plopped onto the couch. "So, do you know more than what's been reported?"

"I'm afraid not. He's still on the loose. This dude had me rattled when I realized how close he was to Star's school. I could imagine her freaking out about it. I mean, anyone who'd pick up on Hafiz—"

"For sure! I expected her to be upset. But she's not. She's more focused on wanting to do school online. Truth is . . ." Mariah weighed whether to say more. She replayed Star's startled response as she entered her bedroom to talk about the lockdown, her evasiveness. "I'm worried she's withdrawing from me. At Star's age, I was sick of sharing dinners alone with my mother. And now, here I am, unable to control myself from doing the very thing I hated—grilling her with questions."

"Hum. Makes sense. Not wanting to repeat your childhood history with her. My experience was the opposite—most evenings I'd pull out a TV dinner and work on my homework. I never imagined feeling close to my mother." He sighed. "I'm not a parent, so I may be wrong, but perhaps it's a phase?"

Mariah groaned. "I sure hope so."

"You know my mother's crazy about Star and would welcome time spent with her. Perhaps we can arrange for an evening visit while we have our own date."

She tried to force an enthusiastic response—*Fantastic* or *Great idea.* Their date was fun. Even romantic. Until Candice interrupted. "To be honest, Star alone with your mother makes me a little nervous." Mariah gave a laugh. Devin's silence was palpable. "I mean, Star can be so intense, and she's impressionable."

"So you're nervous about the impression my mother may make on Star?"

"Oh no, I didn't mean it like that. She has already impressed Star as an ideal mother." Mariah rolled her eyes and caught her breath. "Really, Devin, *The Holographic Universe*? She's only thirteen."

"Evidently she began reading David Bohm when she was twelve. My mother views her as exceptional."

"That's what concerns me. She is, and she isn't. There are so many things she doesn't pay attention to that typical thirteen-year-olds do. Besides," she said, "it's no secret your mother doesn't see me as credible to raise a child like Star."

"My mother's full of judgment. It's her nature. Blessed are those she judges to be special, brilliant, and wise. Which is how she views Star."

"I get it. I'm in the category of slow learner."

"I doubt that. I've never been intuitive, scientific, or bright enough to meet her expectations. But I must admit—okay, for the last decade or so—she has softened. You know what? She has taught me that people can change even after they're supposedly grown up."

"Her experience with Tori sure seems to have had a lasting impact." The abrupt silence had a bitter edge. "I'm sorry it took her so long to share it with you."

"Yeah. It hurt. Felt like a betrayal." His voice sounded sharp. "I mean, this was clearly the most important change in my mother's life, and she says nothing until, well, she needs computer assistance, and then all at once spills it out—fifteen years after the fact."

An uncomfortable emotion swelled inside her. "Devin, this must have been terribly painful to hear." She paused. "It can take years to process big changes . . . I've been through a devastating change myself and . . . well . . . as I've told you, I'm still struggling with the sharing. Your mother came clean—sure it wasn't as fresh as you wanted, but she did it."

"No. You don't understand. I'm her only one. She has no siblings or other children. She came to be with me while the woman I almost married was dying. I felt close to her. And to think she wouldn't share the most significant life-changing experience of her life? Well, it sucks." She heard his loud sigh.

The sour tone of Devin's voice saying *betrayal* echoed in her head.

Chapter 41

Mariah awoke with a start. She squinted at her alarm clock. *Ugh.* Two hours before her wake-up time. She sat up. Had Star slipped beyond her grasp?

Why wouldn't Star share what had happened at school?

Before they'd gone to bed, she had offered to give Star a ride to school this morning, allowing her an extra forty minutes of sleep. Yet Star insisted on walking. "Mom, you don't understand. This is how I clear my head in the morning. Besides, my crow friends expect me." Mariah made Star promise again to stay out of the forest.

Unable to sleep, Mariah shuffled into the kitchen, encountering dark mirrors of windowpanes and the clicking of the wall clock against a foreboding silence. Her body felt wooden and thick, as if she had taken a sleeping pill. Had it been two or three in the morning, she would have done so; but it was four thirty.

How unusual she'd slept at all, given the disarray of circling thoughts. Candice's confession, Devin's disappointment, Star's distance, and in what way she might keep her close. She clutched her cup of coffee, comforted by the smell. How odd to be living with her daughter and feeling so alone. Star was so sensitive, assertive with her needs. So very different from herself.

A deep pain swelled within her. When Markus was six months old, Charlie had arrived home from a music festival two hours later than expected. She met him as he entered, smelled the alcohol, and turned away in a fury. He fell to his knees. Promised to never again drink while away at work. He honored that promise.

My God, why have I kept him from her?

She shook, gripped her hand over her mouth, but her shaking was so violent a snort shot between her fingertips. Her heart hammered in her chest. She took a long breath, trying to find some steadiness.

Star had never insisted, or even expressed bold curiosity. She had appeared satisfied with Mariah's simple answers. Explanations that were lies—not directly, but by omission. Did Star *know* what happened, the same way she knew Hafiz had died? Just the other night she had asked, "Why don't I know about my past?"

Mariah stepped into the kitchen and poured another cup of coffee. Peering out the window, the dark trunks of trees blurred into one as fresh tears swelled in her eyes. She withdrew a piece of ice from the plastic tray in the freezer, dropped it in her cup, and watched it dissolve. Taking big swallows of the cooled coffee, she anticipated a caffeine lift. After emptying the cup, she tiptoed toward Star's room.

Cracking the door ever so slightly, she could make out Star's form sprawled under the covers. Mariah slipped in and heard her daughter's peaceful, rhythmic breathing, with a light moaning sound. She brought her lips to the exposed forehead, free from the loose curls that typically shielded her round high-cheek-boned face, and stopped short of contact. Her legs gave way, and she was on her knees, her fourteen-year-old self praying for forgiveness.

Except it was from Star, not God, she needed forgiveness.

As she drove to work, Mariah convinced herself Star would be fine. She left a sweet note reminding her of the leftover pizza, a rare treat for lunch. She held back from mentioning the lockdown. Star had enough on her plate—she needn't concern herself with Mariah's worries. And given the morning news report, no different from last night's, there wasn't a reason to be worried. There *wasn't* a reason to be worried!

Inside BHP, the gleam from the fluorescent lights bouncing off the lime-green hall panels jarred her. Up ahead, Gretchen was moving toward Mariah. Her face set in a way that stirred panic. There was no avoiding her.

"Good morning," Mariah called out.

"Can you believe Thanksgiving is just a week away?"

Mariah reeled. Her mother. "Oh my goodness, no."

"Exactly. Jim's entire family plans on coming. It's my turn to host." Gretchen slowed. Her office was to the right; Mariah's another ten paces ahead. "I guess you heard about the lockdown yesterday afternoon."

Mariah braced herself.

"Is Star okay?"

"Well, of course it was upsetting, but she seems to be handling it okay."

"Tilly was quite upset."

Mariah took a slow deep breath.

"Not so much with the lockdown, but with how Star was acting."

"How was she acting?" She kept her voice steady so Gretchen wouldn't detect how violently her heart was beating.

"Tilly said . . ." Gretchen peered downward, as if about to divulge a secret.

Mariah wanted to yank at her shoulders and shake her head back up. "Tell me."

"She saw Star before the lockdown. Noon. She said Star acted as if she knew what was going on."

Mariah's face heated up. The anxiety that had aroused her early in the morning entered full force; her knees began to buckle.

"It could be nothing . . . just thought I'd let you know Tilly was worried for her." Gretchen now stared directly at her. Mariah quickly looked away, desperate, as if it were possible to discern the truth from the very air surrounding them.

"This makes no sense," Mariah said. "Star had no idea what was going on." Her lips trembled. She couldn't tell if she had shouted the words.

"I'm not sure what Tilly meant. Likely she was reacting to whatever Star's response was."

"Star's fine. She was hardly bothered by it."

"Well, it's disturbing that he's still on the loose."

Mariah checked her watch as she walked toward her office. Star would be in the shower; there was no good reason to text and check in. Her morning group work thankfully drew her attention elsewhere.

On her way to the cafeteria at lunchtime, Mariah revisited Star peacefully at rest in bed. *Star is all right.*

But then, splayed out in pieces across the Formica table lay the *Boulder News*. Before swiping it from view, she caught the front-page headline: "Manhunt Underway for Dangerous Murderer." Richard entered as she read deeper.

"Scary son of a bitch."

She looked up, and he gave her a quick smile before adjusting the chair and plopping down with his sack lunch.

He then continued, "He was pissed off at his ex for daring to date another dude."

"Adding to the statistics that a spurned male is the most dangerous animal on the loose," Mariah said.

"Sadly, she had a restraining order."

"They never seem to work in this situation."

"How'd Star handle the lockdown?"

"She didn't say much about it . . ." Mariah paused as she flashed on her interaction with Gretchen. "But I noticed she was upset about something. Oddly, she didn't even tell me about the lockdown."

He cocked his head.

"Okay, I'm worried. I mean, if she is psychic, she would have sensed this. Why wouldn't she tell me? The only thing I can figure is that she didn't want me to worry."

Richard nodded. "Makes sense."

"This morning, Gretchen told me that Tilly said Star was acting strange, like she knew what was going on just prior to the lockdown."

"Wow. That must have given you a jolt."

"Yeah. I can't wrap my thoughts around this psychic stuff. And . . ." She choked down tears, leaving the rest of her sentence unsaid: *I want a closer relationship with my daughter.* Only a parent would understand. "I worry about what she knows and doesn't share."

After lunch, as her client settled into the sofa-like chair, kitty-corner from where she sat on the rolling desk chair, Mariah's cell phone rang. She prepared to shut it off but saw "Aspen Creek" parading across the front. Her heart sped up.

"Oh, so sorry. I need to take this. I'll only be a moment." She stepped outside the small office and shut the door behind her. "Hello?"

"Ms. Palmer?"

"Yes." She placed a hand on the door, bracing herself.

"This is Mr. Petersen."

Oh God.

"Star is not at school today, and I'm checking in to see if everything is all right."

"Are you sure? Did you check with attendance?" Mariah began pacing up and down the hall.

"We're sure."

"She leaves after me. It's possible that she wasn't feeling well. Can I get back to you?"

"We were hoping you could come in and meet with us."

"I have clients scheduled. I'm not sure when I can get away—"

"Ms. Palmer, this is important. Some students seem to think Star had some knowledge of yesterday's event."

"What do you mean?"

"Our records show she skipped her afternoon classes."

A sudden gasp came up in her throat. "I'll be there as soon as I can." Her head spun; she placed the flat of her right hand against the wall behind her while she speed-dialed Star with her left. It rang once before going to voice mail. She pushed off the wall and swayed as she considered whether to rush to Gretchen and demand to know the rumor Tilly had spread or race out of this place and get home.

At her front door, her hands shook so hard she struggled to maneuver the key into the lock. Stella's barking welcomed her like a death knell. She called out to Star but heard only the clicking of the kitchen wall clock and Stella's whimpers.

Mariah swung open Star's bedroom door to see her empty bed with a rumple of covers. She dashed out of the room, checking the back door, the windows, for any sign of a break-in. Apparently her daughter had walked out and locked the door behind her.

Back in Star's bedroom, Mariah found her cell phone on a pile of books without a charge. Unlike any other teen, Star needed constant prompting to keep the phone charged. Mariah scanned the room, landing on the nightstand drawer. She strode forward. Star left her with no choice; she had to check the journal.

But the cork-covered journal was not there. Nor was it tucked under her bed or among the pile of books.

Chapter 42

The school bell blared as Mariah walked toward the entrance of Aspen Creek. No wonder Star complained that the sound "shatters" her thoughts. Inside, Mariah took small steps to avoid the crush of students, assailed by the cacophonous wave of laughter, scowling faces, and looks of suspicion at her forty-year-old face. These were the students Star said pierced her "bubble space."

Her legs had their own agenda, and she moved toward the office with an increasing sense of urgency. Until a familiar face brought her to a halt. There was no mistaking that round, pasty white face, thin strands of blond hair pulled back. A good six months had passed since she had last seen Tilly with Gretchen—the resemblance continued to amaze her. Tilly stood just five feet away, wide eyes watching Mariah.

"Tilly, I need to talk with you."

Tilly's white cheeks flushed. As Mariah stepped toward her, Tilly turned and disappeared into the sea of fresh teenage faces.

Mariah pushed through the kids to reach the main office counter. "Excuse me," she called in a voice meant to disrupt. "Mr. Petersen is expecting me—can you please let him know Mariah Palmer is here?" A bead of sweat formed above her upper lip; her heartbeat quickened.

Mr. Petersen met her with a somber face. "Thanks for coming," he said, and motioned for her to follow him down the narrow corridor. In the office, she chose the stiff-backed chair facing away from bright light pouring in the window. Another man walked in then, who looked familiar.

Mr. Petersen turned to Mariah. "You remember Mr. Nolen—our vice principal."

She forced a smile, stood and shook his hand, and went numb inside. The three of them took their seats, and Mr. Petersen's gaze drilled into her. She said, "Star's at home with a headache. She should've called me, but she forgot to charge her phone." The lie singed her cheeks, and her leg bounced. "When she didn't answer my call, I had no choice but to go home and check on her."

Mr. Petersen said, "I didn't mean to alarm you. Several students came to me this morning, upset. Apparently, Star's behavior before the lockdown troubled them." His brow creased, and he and Mr. Nolen nodded at one another. "I was hoping to catch up with Star this morning. When she didn't show up at school and it appeared to be an unexcused absence, and given her absence yesterday afternoon, I became concerned."

"What were the students' concerns?"

"Evidently, before the lockdown, she became quite upset when several of the students walked towards Farland Park," Mr. Petersen explained. "She said something to convince them she knew the suspect."

"That's ridiculous! There's no way Star knows who this person is." Her mind flashed to Tilly with her look of guilt.

"Ms. Palmer," Mr. Nolen said, "I understand that Mr. Petersen has met with you before and that the counseling team recommended your daughter have a mental health evaluation."

Mariah peered into his droopy blue eyes and imagined he was childless, making his role of managing other people's children easy.

"We're not saying she knew who or what was going on, only that she behaved in ways that were upsetting to other students."

"I haven't talked with Star about leaving school early yesterday—if that's what she did. The lockdown upset her. More so, whatever the others said to her made her feel uncomfortable." Both Petersen's and Nolen's eyes roamed over her as if she were an unfit parent. Just as they viewed Star to be an unsuitable student. She shook her head, gave them both a hard, determined look. "It takes a lot of nerve to imply that Star has anything at all to do with some crazy man who killed his ex-girlfriend. Star is afraid to step on a bug for fear of harming it."

Mr. Nolen stiffened in his chair. "Hold on, Ms. Palmer, no one is accusing Star of having any kind of relationship with the perpetrator. We are trying to sort the origin of some of the students' concerns. When we realized Star left just *prior* to the lockdown, and she is absent today, it raised alarms. You must admit, leaving the school grounds is out of character for her."

Mariah shuddered. *My God, Star walked home while everyone else was in lockdown?* She *had* to find Star. She should have refused to meet with them. She should have called and said Star was at home sick and she couldn't leave.

Her lips tightened, and she felt her cheeks grow hot. "All I can say is that she knows nothing about the man who caused the lockdown. She's at home with a headache. She's sensitive. The damn passing bell drives her crazy." She stood up. "I'm not sure this school is the right environment for her."

Back at the house, she yelled out Star's name before her first step inside. Her shrill voice echoed off the walls. She dashed into Star's bedroom, and the emptiness drained the blood from her head. Dizzy, she stumbled to Star's bed and briefly collapsed on the heap of covers.

Forcing herself up, she went to the kitchen—nothing had changed, except the clock. It was one fifteen, time for her afternoon hoarding group. Fear slammed inside her and for a lingering moment she imagined calling her mother.

She paced between Star's bedroom and the living room and then called BHP, requesting to be connected to Richard. She thought it unlikely he'd answer at this hour.

"This is Richard Stevens."

"Hi, it's me."

"Mariah?"

"I'm at home."

"What's going on?"

"It's Star," she sputtered out. "She didn't show up at school today."

"Mariah, what is it?"

She gulped back a tide of tears. "Star freaked out Tilly and her friends." Her voice was high pitched and strained. "She must have sensed the shooter; she was warning them, I guess, but they took it wrong and started a rumor, telling the school counselors that Star knew the guy that shot his girlfriend."

"Oh my God," Richard murmured. "How is she?"

"Don't know. I came home to check on her . . . she's not here."

"You have no idea where she is?"

"No," she whimpered.

"Was there any sign . . . uh . . . of a . . ."

"No. The doors were locked. She took her journal and her key," she said. "Yesterday upset her. She skipped her afternoon classes. This isn't at all like her."

"Have you called the police?"

"God no. They'd never understand. Richard, I finally get it. Star *is* psychic, that's what this is about. She's misunderstood. She knew someone dangerous was approaching her school."

"That may be. But you don't know where she is."

"I'm terrified. The school counselors think she's crazy. They want her evaluated. The police will also think she's crazy or see her as an accomplice."

"Mariah, listen. You and I both know she's not crazy. She's intuitive, sensitive, but . . . she may very well be confused. You *need* to call the police—especially if other kids think there might be some sort of connection with the shooter."

"Star knows nothing about him. It was a rumor Tilly started—I saw her at school with guilt written all over her face. She avoided me. She's lying, Richard. I know my daughter. She would freak out if I called the police."

"But she not only skipped school, she's also not at home." Richard's voice, calm and methodical, unleashed a new torrent of fear through her veins.

"*If* she skipped school." Mariah gripped her leg and told herself, *That must be what she did. Star hates school and wanted a break.* "She wouldn't expect me home until four thirty at the earliest."

"Let's compromise. If she doesn't come home by four thirty, promise me you'll call the police. In the meantime, does she have friends you can get in touch with?"

Of course, Jen. They talked all the time. Maybe they were together. "Yes. Jen. Thanks, Richard."

Why had it never occurred to her to get Jen's number or her parents'? She started toward Star's cell phone and then remembered it was dead. She called Trudi and left a message.

Mariah strode between the kitchen, Star's bedroom, and her own room, holding her cell phone tight, sure it would ring at any moment. A good ten minutes passed. She turned on the TV to see if there was any news regarding the gunman. All she found were talk shows. This led her back to the kitchen, where a small radio sat next to the dishwasher. She tuned it, moving from station to station. And then she heard: "Breaking news. Just after the noon hour, a woman left her car running in front of Video Et Cetera. When she returned, someone had slipped into the car and sped off with her three-year-old son asleep in the back."

Mariah winced at the thought of leaving Markus alone in a

running car, even for a minute. A description of the car followed, and Mariah switched to another station, trying to learn more about yesterday's event. The woman with the hijacked car was front and center on all the news stations. She paced around the room before collapsing into a chair, feeling the edge of a headache develop.

And then her phone rang.

"This is Jen. Trudi asked me to call you."

"Is Star with you?"

"No."

"Do you have any idea where she might be?" There was silence. "Please, she was upset yesterday, and now she's not at school or at home."

"Uh, we talked yesterday. She was totally pissed off by the jerky response some kids gave her."

"Yes. I figured this much. They don't understand her."

"Yeah. They get freaked out when she talks about hearing voices. She's so brave."

"By brave, you mean being honest about what she hears?"

"Yeah. Star always tells the truth. That's why she's my best friend."

"Does she know the man who shot his ex?"

"No! Why would she?"

"I'm not always sure who she connects to online."

"First off, she's never herself when she's online. She has an avatar. And second, she only talks with nerdy people who are cosmologists and crazy stuff like that. Not murderers."

"Do you have any idea where she went?"

"Well, my best guess is that she went to school." Jen giggled, infuriating Mariah. "Her old school, where the famous Mr. Seng is. She misses him."

Her whole heart welled up. Why hadn't she reached out to him?

"Actually," Jen said, "she told me she wanted to see him soon. So for sure, that's my guess."

"Thanks so much, Jen."

Chapter 43

Mariah approached the familiar faux-granite countertop at Mountain View, desperately trying to recall the name of the woman with the rosy cheeks and loose brunette curls sitting on the other side of the counter.

"Ms. Palmer. What a surprise. How's Star doing?" Before Mariah could say a thing, she added, "We miss her. Mr. Seng has not had another helper of the same caliber as Star. She was fastidious about emptying our recycling bins." She pulled up a bright-green plastic wastebasket full of paper and grinned. Mariah forced a smile, but her chest dropped like an anchor. She had failed to appreciate Star's impact in sixth grade.

Just in time, the name came back to her. "Thanks, Deena. Star's adjusting, but she misses everyone here. Especially Mr. Seng. In fact, that's why I came by. I promised Star I'd drop in and say hi to Mr. Seng for her."

"How sweet. I'm sure he'd appreciate hearing from you. Let's see. I bet you can find him in his office, room 124. Here's a visitor's badge."

Five paces down the hall, her thoughts ricocheted back to the empty house, to Richard's suggestion of Star in a state of confusion, and she completely forgot the room number. She slowed her pace; surely there'd be a door labeled "Janitor."

At the end of the hall, she encountered the label "Custodian." She knocked and was soon face-to-face with a gentleman who was close to her own height, five four. He had a serene smile, a broad, smooth forehead, and a balding head, and he wore small round wire-rimmed spectacles.

An ease enveloped her, and she wondered why she had never made time to meet this man her daughter had talked so enthusiastically about.

"You must be Star's mother."

"How can you tell?"

"You share the same hazel-colored eyes. This is a very special attribute to have in common. It means, someday, you will see the world the same way." His face broke into an impish grin. He winked and said, "Star came for an unexpected visit. Come in." He motioned to an overstuffed chair in the corner across from a desk.

Her chest heaved, and she collapsed with relief, mentally thanking a God she no longer believed in. She swallowed the lump forming in her throat, afraid she would burst into tears.

"When did she leave?" Mariah asked.

"About an hour ago."

If home was Star's destination, she would be there by now. In fact, even before Mariah had left. Mountain View Elementary was only a few miles away from their house.

"Did she say what her plan was?"

"No," he said. "I just listened. She shared that junior high was stressful, and she misses Mountain View. We talked about the illusion of time and the importance of staying in the present."

"I'm so glad she saw you. I, well . . ."

"You discovered she wasn't at school."

Mariah nodded. "The attendance office alerted me. So, did she seem okay to you?"

"This is the first I've seen her in at least four months. My experience of Star is that she's always wrestling with some inner demon."

Mariah flinched. The word *demon* triggered images of the devil.

"I'm sorry. What I mean is that she's tuned in and recognizes the discord within herself that we all experience."

Mariah leaned forward.

"I'm impressed with her confidence," he said. "She's maturing in a wonderful way."

"Except for skipping school and not telling me."

"Star has an incredible sense of who she is and what she needs."

Mariah's heart stirred; this wise man understood Star. "I doubt she'd have survived sixth grade without you. You have meant so much to her. I wish I'd made time to visit well before this." She scanned his desk, hoping to see a family photo or some clue as to who he was. Beyond, a tidy closet space was filled with assorted wrenches, tubes, vacuum cleaners, a ladder, and various piping. "I'll let you get back to your work. She must be on her way home."

"I'm sure you're right, she's on her way home. But some of us take the long route home."

Mariah nodded and wondered how someone as insightful as Mr. Seng could settle for a job fixing broken pieces and cleaning other people's messes.

Mariah slid into her car and pulled out her phone. Star's smiling face filled the screen. Her eyes teared up. She had no messages, no missed calls. She tucked the phone away, started the car, and pulled out of the parking lot.

There was no direct route between the house and the school. The vast expanse of old growth—*the forest*—diverted any straight path. Her breath quickened. Star loved walking through the forest. Mariah considered driving the perimeter—stopping every twenty to fifty feet, stepping into the dense trees, and calling out for her. No one suspected the killer was still lurking in the forest. Even so, it was a dangerous place for a young girl to be. But Star was likely home by now.

She clicked on KPWO, hoping for an update. The latest report suggested that the hijacked car had been spotted in the Denver area.

She turned off the radio as she pulled into her driveway.

Stella rushed to greet her, an ominous confirmation of Star's absence. Mariah fell to the floor, massaging her hands through the thick, bristly hair. "Where is she, Stella?"

She reminded herself that Star still wouldn't have expected her to be home. She had to have taken the long way home, as Mr. Seng had suggested. But the waiting was agonizing.

In the kitchen, Mariah began to scrub the stubborn stains on the stove top where Top Ramen had boiled over, leaving a pasty residue. There was a beating inside her chest, like something trapped inside. She moved on to the cabinet faces, focusing on the ring of brown around the knobs. At three thirty, the landline rang. Mariah grabbed it after the first ring only to hear an automated call from school reporting what she already knew: Star had been absent that day.

Fifteen minutes later, she could wait no longer. She grabbed her phone. Her heart galloped. A horrific déjà vu buckled her knees, and she curled on the floor, screaming to a God she had long ago rejected—"No! You cannot take her! She's all I have! No, no, no!" She sobbed and gasped for breath.

"I'm calling to report a missing person. My daughter. Thirteen. What do you mean? But you see, there's a possibility that she may know the man who shot his girlfriend. I met with the school this morning, and they were concerned . . . Yes . . . 2200 Forest Street, Ash Grove."

She hung up the phone and stared out her kitchen window at the boughs of the fir tree tossing about in the wind. As she stood motionless, she entered a trancelike state reminding her of earlier days when she had flirted with the magical notion that if she didn't move, she could somehow step out of her life and simply evaporate.

She blinked hard. Had she truly called the police? Waiting until four thirty had become unbearable. She shook her head and refocused her attention on the kitchen appliances. The fridge, it too could use a cleaning. As she took her first steps toward it with a wet dishcloth, the cold, distant voice on the phone filled her mind. They no longer look for missing teens—they'll only take a run report. Star obviously had no association with whoever this crazy, violent person was. The only way to grab their attention was to state the remote possibility of a connection.

By four fifteen, Mariah's regret over suggesting a possible link between Star and the gunman grew so heavy she needed to sit. But where was Star? Almost three hours had passed since Star had met with Mr. Seng. Mariah sat herself down in the easy chair, but her mind refused to settle. Pouring herself a glass of wine occurred to her. She dismissed this at once. It wasn't at all like her to drink before five.

A firm knock at the front door brought her to her feet. Stella broke into frenzied barking. She reverted to her younger self, beseeching God to answer her prayers. *Please let Star be safe.*

Her heart racing, Mariah opened the door to find two clean-cut men in navy-blue uniforms. Her eyes fell on the guns hanging in their holsters, and her knees began to fold.

"Ms. Palmer? We're from the Boulder Police Department . . . are you okay? Do you need to sit down?"

She placed a hand on the door frame. "I'm fine." She motioned them in and then asked, "Where's Star?"

"We understand there's reason to believe your daughter may have a connection to the suspect in Tuesday's shooting."

She caught her breath. She wanted to retreat into the living room and collapse into her chair. "I . . . I'm sorry, I was mistaken." Her voice shook violently. She took a deep breath, conjuring the counselor within her. "Star has nothing to do with the suspect. Nothing at all. She skipped school, and I expected her home by now. I . . . I just panicked."

They exchanged glances.

The thrumming in her chest swelled. "I found out she visited friends from her grade school. Mountain View. It's been a difficult transition to seventh grade."

"When was she last seen?"

For a moment, Mariah's mind went blank.

"Around one," Mariah said. "Or maybe before that."

One of the officers wrote something in a small notepad. "Your daughter's school told us that some of her friends believed she knew something about Mr. Walls, the suspect."

Mariah's stomach dropped. "But they aren't her friends. She has no friends at Aspen Creek." Mariah hesitated. "My daughter reacts to the level of energy in a situation."

The cop with the notepad looked up and squinted at her. The other one raised his brows ever so slightly—the same expression she would give to her confabulating clients.

"What I mean is that Star responds to events even though she doesn't know a thing about them."

"That may be, Ms. Palmer. But we need to make sure there isn't a connection." They proceeded to pepper her with questions she could not answer. The social media sites Star visits, how late she stays up, her online friends.

Twenty minutes later, the uniformed men left with Star's drained cell phone, her sixth-grade school picture, and her computer, despite Mariah's protesting. On their way out, they confirmed that an internal bulletin would alert other police to keep an eye out for Star.

Mariah's head throbbed, as though the mass inside her skull had swollen. She made her way to her medicine drawer and took one small pill for the pain. She then collapsed into the overstuffed living room chair.

It was nearly five now, getting dark, and still no sign of Star. When her phone rang, she answered it without even glancing at the screen.

"Mariah." Her mind raced to identify the familiar voice. Gretchen.

"How's Star?"

She almost said *It's none of your damn business*, but Gretchen's voice carried a conciliatory tone, and she heard herself responding in kind.

"I'm not sure. She's not talking to me right now."

In the silence that followed, it occurred to her that Gretchen had something important to say—she rarely called after hours.

"Tilly's worried. She said that some of her friends got the wrong idea."

"Tilly as well."

"She wants to apologize. When Star warned her and her friends not to go into the forest, they took it to mean she knew about this guy."

"She had no way of knowing—"

"I believe you. So does Tilly. When she saw you at school, she realized that her friends, or I should say her ex-friends, had gone too far."

"Gretchen, listen. Even though Star knows nothing about the shooter, she picked up on the danger. This isn't the first time Star has known something without being in the know." Mariah was astonished to hear herself speaking these words . . . maybe it was the pill making her more candid than she'd ordinarily be.

"I see." Gretchen's clinical voice rang through her ears.

"Star refused to go to school today. She gets teased daily. I may need to take tomorrow off just to settle things down."

"I don't blame you. Take as much time as you need. You rarely take leave."

"I'm thinking I need to explore other school options. No one seems to understand her. Teachers included."

"I'm so sorry. I know how challenging she's been. You're right, she's very sensitive. But the voices..."

Mariah felt herself swaying; the medication had brought on a gauzy light-headedness. Through this fog, she realized it was true: *Star does hear voices, but we all do to some extent.*

"No. It's not what you think it is. I need to go."

Chapter 44

When bright headlights streamed through the picture window, Mariah's heart raced. Again she beseeched a no-longer-believed-in God for Star's safe return. She rushed to the door and opened it.

"Ma'am, is this your daughter?" Two uniformed men flanked Star, who stood with head bowed, hair falling forward, hiding her face.

Stella yipped, and Mariah nodded, too stunned to immediately wrap her arms around Star.

"She is refusing to answer our questions," said the older officer with a worn face, hair thinning. "She just mumbles, seems to be confused. Perhaps in a delusional state. There's no sign of alcohol or drugs. Although she reported hearing voices."

Mariah advanced and threw her arms around an unresponsive Star. She then turned to the officers. "Please. Come in." She reached for Star's hand. "Sweetie. I was worried. What's going on? Where have you been?"

Star pulled away, stammering, "I have the right to remain silent." She took several steps into the living room and crumpled to the floor, where Stella nuzzled her, tail wagging.

"Ms. Palmer," said the younger officer, "we picked her up at the corner of Elm and Mountain View. She seemed puzzled as to her whereabouts." He lowered his voice, averting his eyes from Star. "Does she have a history of . . . uh, mental illness?"

Mariah shook her head. Her knees almost buckled.

He turned toward Star. "Some students suggested you know the gunman. You're right, without representation, you can remain silent. But we may book you if there is a reason to believe you are hiding something."

Mariah gasped. And then moved between the officer and Star. "Wait a minute. You're wrong! I spoke to the mother of the student who started the rumor. Star only *acted* like she knew the gunman, but she knows nothing. Right, Star?"

Star continued to bury her head in Stella's wiry fur.

Mariah turned back to the cops. "The woman said her daughter overreacted to something Star said, and her friends blew it all out of proportion. I can give you her number if you want to verify this."

They all gazed at Star sitting on the floor, rocking Stella in her arms. The older one spoke up. "If I were you, I'd keep a closer watch on her whereabouts. She shouldn't be left alone. In fact, I highly recommend she be evaluated. There's a clinic in Boulder."

After Mariah locked the door, she turned to see Star rise from the floor, hollow and weary. She stepped toward her, yearning to swaddle her as she had infant Milly. But Star stepped back, rebellion in her move, frustration etched in her face.

"Sweetheart, what's going on?"

Star's eyes blazed with an intensity that made Mariah quake. "I had planned on being back before you got home. I took the day off. All I wanted was a break."

"Sweetie. I was worried. I didn't know where you were, and the school didn't know."

"Mom!" Her tone declared Mariah insufferable. "All I did was take a break. You have no idea how crazy school is!"

"But you didn't leave a note. Your cell phone was dead. I had no way of reaching you or finding out where you were. I was terrified."

"If you hadn't called the cops on me, I would have been home before you."

"But you weren't home. You left me no choice. I was out of my mind worried for you."

"You created this mess! You don't trust me. You think I'm crazy. I hate you!"

Star's words skewered Mariah. In a flash she imagined her hand slapping Star's face the way her own mother had the day Mariah's cigarettes tumbled from her purse. *How dare she put me through this.*

Upon finishing the second glass of merlot, along with another pill, Mariah could finally relax, the evening's drama mercifully dampened. Star was right. Why had she called the police? She'd been on her way home. Mariah too had skipped school—not at age thirteen, but times had changed. She had lived in fear of being caught and grounded. And here she was, in her daughter's eyes, overreacting.

Mariah had despised her mother's constant monitoring. At sixteen, she had wanted to yell out to her mother, "I hate you." But the words stuck in her throat.

That was the year her friend Suzann had encouraged her to go to the Sadie Hawkins dance. They wore the same size dress, and Suzann had the perfect one for Mariah. But her mother refused to let her go. Olivia went on and on about how Reverend Eddie would view it as sinful. Besides, it just wasn't proper for a girl to ask a boy out.

Mariah had retreated to her bedroom and prayed for forgiveness for, at that moment, hating her mother. To have said it aloud would have been an unforgiveable sin. At least she had raised Star without that guilt.

Chapter 45

My Journal of Hidden Truths
November 14, 2012

Well, Journal, and You—whoever You are—I was right. My life has taken a terrible turn, and You are reading what may be my last entry. Mom called the cops on me. They came and took my computer and phone. Good thing I'm old-school and kept you safe with me. I can't trust anyone.

I had to tell her "I hate you" because in that moment it was the absolute truth, and it might be true tomorrow too. My words made her flinch, which stabbed my heart.

Whatever pathetic excuse she had for calling the cops to chase me down totally sucks. She has no idea how degrading it was to ride home in their cop mobile. They almost handcuffed me. I'm tired of the way she makes me feel crazy. Why would Mom tell them I knew who this deranged person was? Now for sure I won't go back to Aspen Creek. And since they took my phone, I can't call Jen.

This morning, I knew I couldn't go to school. Yesterday, I acted like a full-blown freak—playing the role of the psycho they see me as. Tilly's right, I do hear voices. But it's not the devil. I can still see Tilly and her friends laughing at me. Why couldn't I keep it to myself? It's not like she's a best friend and I was uber worried. I seem to have no choice but to react, which is creepy.

Here's the totally weird or amazing part. There was a lockdown, and it had to do with what I saw. I was right! Tilly could have been hurt if I hadn't made a fool of myself. Does this make me a freak because, somehow, I knew what was happening?

It felt crummy lying to Mom about the lockdown, even though she's rarely honest with me. Besides, she wouldn't have understood if I told her the truth. And she'd be flipped out big-time to know I go into the forest every day.

I almost always do as I'm told. The only thing I cheat on is going to the forest. All I did was skip one frickin' day of school—big whup! And Mom freaks out. I know kids who skip all the time.

Okay, whoever You are, here's what has my mind blazing with worry. On my way home from seeing Mr. Seng (which I wish I'd done weeks ago—he was so great to see!), I began to hear the same child voice from my dreams.

Except the voice seemed like it was coming somewhere from within the forest. A voice breaking into sobs. And it's possible I am making this up cuz I'm totally obsessed with my brother.

If he were alive, he'd be my older brother, which is weird to think about, because I've seen him in my dreams for years and he's always 3 years old. Maybe the world outside of this one doesn't run on time, and without time there's no growing older. If I were to die soon, would I be stuck at age 13 forever? But maybe I just act like I'm 13 because my body's stuck in time, and without this body I would be 1 and 100 years old and everything in between, making me ageless. I wonder what Jen would think about this.

What if the crying I heard in the forest is as real as the shooter? I should have tried harder to make the cops understand what I was hearing. When they pulled up, I stupidly thought they were looking for the missing child and wanted to ask me if I heard or saw anything. Instead, they peppered me with a bunch of lame questions about the shooter. When I tried to tell them about the crying, their blue uniforms became shields, and my words crumbled to the ground, like a bird trying to fly through a picture window.

I can't believe Mom sent the police after me. I would have kept looking for the child if I hadn't been worried about getting home before Mom to keep her from freaking out. So I gave up looking. She freaked out anyway. Even without my phone to tell time, I knew when I had to leave, and I did, and I would have made it home in time if she hadn't left work early.

Here I am putting this in writing—I made a big mistake. I should have followed the voice I was hearing instead of turning away to get home before Mom.

I hate that I need Mom. And now this. I wanted to tell her how scared I am about hearing voices that sometimes come from my dreams, sometimes come to me like dreams while I'm awake, and sometimes, like today, seem to be outside of me. The stupid cops made her think for sure I'm crazy. And maybe I am. I don't care. This world is crazy, and I don't have to keep participating.

Jen understands—she knows what it's like to choose to leave. I'm not sure I want to keep living. I used to think being a grown-up would solve all my problems. But why suffer through all of this without a guarantee that being a grown-up will be any different? Mom has plenty of pills in her medicine cabinet. It would be easy to leave this world. Who knows, I may end up wherever my brother and maybe my dad and Jeffrey are.

Chapter 46

Mariah washed down a second piece of toast with her third cup of coffee when Star entered the kitchen, looking clown-like with her untamed curly hair, striped pj's, and neon-pink slippers. But there was no smile or frown, only a look of fortitude as she made her way to the pantry. Stella marched behind.

"Good morning," Mariah said, doing her best to sound cheerful. Star mumbled "Humph," and Mariah imagined responding, *After all, it is ten a.m. on a school day.* Instead, she brought the nearly empty coffee cup to her mouth and took the last sip. "So, a day off from work for me and day off from school for you. I'm hoping we can find time to talk."

Star filled her bowl with shredded wheat, poured in some milk, and took a spoon from the silverware drawer. Mariah watched. *Is this a silent protest left over from last night?*

"Perhaps we could have lunch in Boulder . . ."

Star turned to leave with the cereal bowl, her face set in its immovable manner.

"I don't plan to talk to anyone today. I want to be by myself."

"Wait a minute." Mariah's voice shook with anger. "I stayed home from work so we can sort things out. And that's why you also got a free pass from school. We need to have a meaningful conversation about what's going on."

"Since when do you want to have *meaningful* conversations about anything?"

"Excuse me?"

Star scowled. "Like I said, I'm not in the mood to talk to anyone. I want to be left alone."

Mariah suppressed the urge to demand an apology.

"You're angry with me. Perhaps I overreacted. I know it's hard for you to understand, but I did what I did because I love you and I was worried."

"You don't trust me; you think I'm crazy, just like everyone else does." Star's face crumpled into a familiar pained expression, the beginnings of a meltdown. She turned to leave, and Mariah heard her own reedy-voice plea.

"I didn't say I don't trust you. I was worried—you left me no other choice."

Star faced Mariah and shouted, "How was I to know you came home early?"

"Sweetie, your school called me. They *grilled* me, wanting to know your whereabouts. And I had no idea you weren't at school. And then I found out you weren't at home. I was terrified." Her heart raced. She sucked in a deep lungful of air and let it out slowly, willing herself to be calm. "The lockdown, the shooter, you acting as though you knew something about it, and me being clueless. Can you imagine how frightening it was to discover you were gone?"

"I *needed* a break. You don't understand anything." Star's face flushed. She set her cereal bowl on the counter and collapsed to the floor, where Stella eagerly joined her. Mariah envied that dog, her ease in displaying unconditional affection. What was it that kept her from taking in the fullness of her precious, irreplaceable, unique daughter?

"But . . ." Mariah's voice cracked. "You don't know him, do you?"

"Are you kidding? Some deranged, violent freak? I have no idea who he is or where he is."

Mariah watched as Star released herself from Stella. She knew it was the wrong question to ask. Before she could utter the right question, Star swept past and slammed her bedroom door shut.

Mariah moved to the easy chair by the living room window and watched the crows foraging in the soft mounds of dirt with nimble pecking motions, always alert to danger. Star routinely sprinkled bread crumbs or bits of cereal on her way to school—something Mariah had learned only recently—but today there was little to scavenge for. Star once told her that the birds mated for life. Mariah mused . . . even with slim pickings, at least they had each other.

At midday, Mariah knocked on Star's door. She didn't expect Star to respond. Her stomach rumbled as she stood there, hesitating, and yet she had no urge to eat. She finally cracked the door open and found Star huddled under her blankets.

What kind of parent drove her daughter into a state of hibernation in the middle of the day? Mariah tiptoed in, lowered herself onto the edge of the bed, and was seized by the desire to crawl under the covers, wrap her arms around Star, and join her in the undefined world between sleep and wakefulness.

"Star, sweetie. I'm so sorry." Her voice faltered upon the word *sorry*, and she held her breath to prevent the undamming of a bottomless reservoir of remorse. Star remained motionless. Mariah placed the palm of her hand firmly on the curve of Star's back and felt the movement of her breath. "I overreacted. It's just. I, I worried."

Her mind circled around her new view on Star's uniqueness. How could she begin to share her recent insights with Star? She cleared her throat to begin, but the words dried up. What came out was, "I know you've been teased. I'm willing to work with you to figure out some alternative if this is what you want—I mean to school."

The covers raised up and down; Star repositioned herself toward Mariah but kept her head hidden. The lump of Stella under the blankets migrated from the foot of the bed to nestle between Star's torso and Mariah's hip.

"Maybe together we can find a different option to Aspen Creek. My worry is you being isolated. That is, if you were to not go to school."

A muffled voice from beneath layered blankets responded. "Maybe I can go part-time. Like just to science." After a pause, Star's face emerged. She stared up at the ceiling. "My friend Jasper's in my science class, and I'd like to keep seeing him. But otherwise, it's boring."

Stella now popped her head out from under the covers too. Mariah reached out to rub the soft spot behind Stella's floppy ears.

Star said, "I can quickly get through junior high and on to high school if . . ."

"If?"

"If you'd trust me."

"It's not about lacking trust. It's about safety, about . . . about caution in making the right choices. Like I said, I worry about you becoming too isolated."

"Too isolated—*this* is isolation! Letting the cops take my phone and computer. I can't even call my best friend."

"I had no idea they would do this. I'm a first-time parent. I panicked when you didn't come home."

Star yanked the blankets back over her head. Stella circled around, looking for an entry point, and then dug in under the covers.

Tension rose in Mariah's neck. She continued to sit in an uncomfortable twist on the side of Star's bed. Waiting. Finally, Star's muffled voice emerged.

"You think I'm crazy."

"I don't think you're crazy," Mariah snapped. As she opened her mouth to further deny Star's accusation, she thought back to Gretchen's and the police officers' warnings, or admonitions, that this child needed an evaluation. She took a breath. "Star," she began, "you and I are so different. I'm still learning about your unique ways of sensing things." Mariah was unsure what to say next and felt a flutter of panic. And then, as if she had engaged in a prayer, an answer surfaced. "I finally met with Mr. Seng. I now understand why you respect and like him. He's a wonderful person."

Star shifted and then lowered the covers to reveal a somber face. "I love Mr. Seng. He made it possible for me to survive losing Jeffrey."

"He's a wise man. I'm glad you got to see him yesterday." She stopped herself from adding *I only wish you would have told me.*

But she also knew, had Star asked permission, she likely would have responded with her own mother's voice filled with suspicion and refusal.

Chapter 47

An hour later, after tidying up the living room, Mariah still wasn't hungry, but she definitely wanted to get out of the house. She called Devin.

"Mariah?"

"Hi. I was wondering, are you by chance free to meet for coffee?" Her stomach growled again. "Or a late lunch?"

"Aren't you at work? I mean, I could travel on down to Behavioral Health's cafeteria—"

"No need. I took the day off."

"Okay . . . what'd you have in mind?"

"Perhaps the Big and Easy?" She glanced at her watch. "Two o'clock?"

"Will be there."

After ending the call, Mariah approached Star's bedroom, and her chest constricted as she eased the door open. Much to her relief, she found Star propped up in bed writing in her journal. Mariah stood immobilized, unsure whether to take a step in or stay put. Star's glare made it clear. She stayed.

"Just wanted to let you know I've decided to go to Boulder for lunch. You're welcome to join me."

"Mom, I told you. I want to be alone today. Why didn't you knock?"

"I'm sorry. You're right, I should have. Are you sure you don't want to get out?"

"No. I need alone time."

"Well, there's plenty of Top Ramen and mac and cheese. I should be back a little after three."

Entering the breezy space of the café was like landing in another universe. Subdued hip-hop music, the walls sporting an unusual lineup of black-and-white prints featuring crows. Star would have enjoyed it.

Mariah glanced at her watch, five minutes early. Her thoughts shifted from Star to Devin. She missed him. And what, only a week had passed? It seemed like months. So much had transpired. As she turned back to the door, thinking she'd wait for Devin outside, he walked in.

"What a nice surprise," he said.

She held out her hand. He took it and then embraced her in a full-body hug. Perhaps he wasn't angry with her after all.

"I'm home today to be with Star," she said. "Although, clearly, I'm not with her at this moment. I'm taking a break." Her voice trembled. "It's been an intense couple of days."

Her stomach twisted. Where to begin? And then a host arrived to seat them. They glanced at the menu and ordered the sandwich-and-soup special. His face, bursting with questions, remained poised.

Time shifted to a standstill, as if she had entered a serene bubble. Taking a deep breath, she studied the details of his face. If only she didn't have an agenda and could swim in this inviting state and quite possibly know him again for the first time.

She took a sip of ice water and then whispered, "Thank you."

He blinked as if he too made a transition. "For . . ."

"Being here."

"So, what's going on with Star?"

Mariah's voice quivered. "Remember when we talked the other night and I said that Star didn't seem too disturbed by the lockdown?

Well, that's because she didn't *know* about it. She skipped school that afternoon."

"Oh God. She must have known something."

"Right! She knew there was danger in the forest. So much so she tried to warn a group of girls during lunchtime. They teased her . . ." Tears pressed forth before she could stop them. She dabbed at her eyes with a tissue, took a breath, and continued. "That's why she skipped her afternoon classes. I just found out yesterday."

"So she picked up on Walls's nasty energy," Devin said. "Just like she knew my mother's dog had died."

Mariah nodded. "I'm trying to wrap my brain around this. I've always known something was unusual about her. That she's extremely sensitive." She paused. "Your mother totally picked up on this. She understands."

He nodded. "I must admit," Devin said, "I too am trying to make sense of this."

Her head spun. Did *this* have to do with reconciling the old Candice—Dr. Quinn—with the "new" Candice who now believed in a science that was not taught?

My God, how had Candice pried herself from the canon of truth to examine an alternate reality?

Yet Mariah too had all but tossed the *scientific method* out the door.

"Devin!"

He jerked and met her eyes.

"Remember when I asked you what caused Candice to change so dramatically? You suspected it was an affair."

He tilted his head and raised his brows.

"You were right! Tori changed her." She paused. "Just like Star has changed me. She's crushing so much of what I grew up believing."

His face tensed. Did this have to do with her bringing up Tori? She hadn't intended to poke at a wound. His slow nod was a relief.

He glanced away briefly. "Damn. I still don't get why she took so long to tell me." The pain in his voice led Mariah to move her hand across the table. She rested it on his forearm.

"Devin, I have ghosts in my past too. I'm ashamed of what I've kept from you." She pressed her eyes shut, yearning to erase the hidden scorched parts of her life. "Sharing the past can be terrifying." She kept her hand on his arm and felt a twitch.

"You don't owe me your secrets. I left you twenty years ago. You're entitled—"

"Not now," she whispered.

In the silence that followed, as casually as an inhale of breath, both leaned forward, their lips met. She prayed forgiveness was possible.

"So, Star's at home?" he asked.

She shared the meeting at school, the police, and the most disturbing element. "Kids and the school counselors view her as crazy." A lump formed in her throat. "She accused me of thinking she's crazy." She held her breath, trying to resist the flow of tears. Devin's hand brushed hers.

"I can't imagine what you both have been going through."

She dabbed her eyes with a tissue. "To make matters worse, my supervisor —Gretchen—is the mother of Star's classmate Tilly." She shook her head. "Tilly told Gretchen that Star reports hearing voices. Gretchen advised me to have Star evaluated."

"Whoa. That would freak any parent out."

"The voices or the recommendation?" She regretted her sharp tone, as if quizzing him.

"Both."

She looked down at the plate in front of her, food uneaten. "My training is in mental health. I know zippo about so-called psychic phenomena. In fact, the whole concept freaks me out."

She thought of Candice glowing, proclaiming that physics had proven some undefined interconnectedness between all things, and her penetrating gaze as she murmured, "I sense it's been a horrific decade."

"Your mother understands . . . ," Mariah said. "And she's a brilliant scientist."

Devin's face relaxed. "Yeah. And yet, I totally don't know her. It's hard to wrap my mind around this . . . weird reality."

"No one in my world talks about this," Mariah said.

"Not in mine either." He gave her an amused look, as though he had winked at her. She refrained from saying, *Except your mother.*

"I need a better understanding of what's going on with my daughter. She's a wreck. She's teased at school, and I don't know how to help her." Mariah held her breath, letting it out slow; letting it out too fast, she'd cry. "Your mother spoke of ideas I wasn't open to hearing. But now I want to know more."

"Mom has taken a lot of flak from colleagues here and abroad." He hesitated and scanned the café. "I've come to admire her. I doubt she ever imagined ending up here in Boulder working with psychics."

"Me either. I mean, to live outside of Boulder."

He smiled and bit into his BLT. "I guess you can say all three of us didn't expect this."

Mariah flushed and took a sip of water.

"You know my mother adores Star. She could help—she'd welcome the opportunity."

Mariah nodded vigorously. This was, after all, why she had reached out to him. "Actually, yes . . ."

Devin's cell rang. He scanned the caller ID and then gave her an apologetic look. "I'm sorry. I need to take this." He slid out and disappeared.

Mariah glanced at her watch; forty minutes had lapsed. Was Star still holed up in her room?

When Devin returned, his face was flushed and serious. He slid back into his seat, but she could tell he was about to leave.

"What is it?"

"They found the shooter just outside Denver." Devin still gripped his phone. "It turns out he was the one who hijacked that car. Don't know if you've been aware, given the stress with Star, but a three-year-old kid was in the car. When they spotted Walls in the car, there was a shoot-out and . . . damn." Devin's face fell.

"What happened?" Mariah's hands trembled. The urge to get home almost overtook her.

"They botched it. They ended up killing him. The three-year-old was not in the car, and now they have no fucking idea where he is. Why do they aim for the heart when it should be the legs?"

Mariah's hand flew to her mouth, muffling a gasp. "My God, this is so sad. They have no idea where—"

"Zero. Total inane stupidity." He shoved his plate away and looked at his phone again.

"You need to return to your computer."

"Yeah. I'm afraid so."

"Go ahead. Let me take care of this—I told Star I'd be back at three." She stood up, and they embraced.

Chapter 48

Mariah rushed through the café's doors to her car. Her hand trembled so hard she struggled to get the key into the ignition. *Stop it. There's nothing to worry about.* Star was in bed wrapped around Stella with an empty bowl of mac and cheese on her nightstand. Throughout the five-mile drive home, her heart beat ferociously.

Once parked, she forced herself to stay put and take three deep breaths, declaring her fears irrational. She then sprinted to the front door. While Mariah fumbled for her key, Stella's high-pitched, frenzied bark on the other side assaulted her.

She tossed her coat on the couch, ignoring Stella swirling around her legs, and went straight to Star's bedroom. There was no need to knock; the door was open. Star was not in her room.

She rushed to the kitchen. She found an empty box of mac and cheese, half a glass of milk, and a countertop full of drips and spills. Next to her coffee cup was a piece of torn paper with Star's uneven lettering. Her heart went staccato as she grabbed the note. "Mom, I'm going to a place where I can find the truth. Don't send the police after me or I'll never come home."

Panicked, she weighed her options. And then she remembered. She now had Jen's number.

"Yeah?" Jen answered.

"It's Star's mother, Mariah."

"What's up?"

"Do you have any idea where she is?"

"We haven't talked for about two days. Sorry."

Of course, without her cell, Star had no way to get in touch with anyone.

Mariah returned to Star's bedroom. She eyed the nightstand, the place Mariah typically restrained herself from probing. She opened the drawer and stared in stunned recognition at the cork-covered journal.

She grabbed its stiff borders, and a swell of emotion swirled within her—relief and a foreboding to be on the cusp of breaking trust with her daughter. Her pulse quickened as she parted the cover and opened to the most recent entry. November 15, this morning. "Finding the truth." She braced herself and read. When she reached the last sentence of the brief paragraph, "I've had enough of this craziness, I need to find the truth," tears streamed down her cheeks.

She mumbled "I'm so sorry" and raced to her medicine cabinet. The pill bottles appeared untouched. Yet she had no way of tracking how many pills there were. They were tiny. Three at a time in a thirteen-year-old body would be enough to stop a heart from beating.

She moved to the living room and collapsed on the couch, clutching her cell phone. Her fingers trembled as she attempted to navigate the keys.

"Devin, it's me. Star's gone. She's hearing voices—she … oh my God … I'm terrified. I have no idea where she is."

"I'm on my way."

Mariah held Star's scrawled note and journal tight as she opened the door to Devin. Her body felt so stiff she wasn't sure how to take a step forward. Tears of fear hardened in her throat.

Devin circled her waist with his arm, guiding her to the worn plaid couch in the living room. She wasn't sure she could speak, but then her words tumbled out in a breathless blur. "She's gone. There's no way to reach her. The police took her phone. She was furious with me for calling them. I wouldn't have left if I didn't have the sense that she had calmed down about yesterday."

Devin had his arm around her shoulders now, and he squeezed her close. When she looked at him, she saw he was eyeing the journal.

"It's her journal. I was hoping to find some clue where she went." He'd never understand what it was like to read your child's disparaging words about yourself. Star's bitter, true accusations had captured the utter failure of her life. "And I found this in the kitchen." She handed him Star's note. He read it out loud.

"What do you think she means by going to find the truth?"

Mariah clutched the journal at her side. "When I was freaking out because she skipped school and wasn't at home, Star apparently heard the voice of a young child crying."

Devin's eyes widened.

"Now I understand why she was so upset with me. She was trying to find a lost and crying child. She stopped looking so she could get home before me. She didn't know I left work early. But I panicked and called the police. They picked her up on her way home." She cringed, remembering the way the beefy officer in blue had looked at Star, as if she were an object to be identified, and then labeled her a sick child.

"My God, Mariah. Who knows? It could be the child Walls abducted."

Her head spun. Another mother had also lost her child. "Here's the thing. I know we're both thinking Star's psychic. How else to explain Hafiz and picking up on Walls? But, *she's* not sure. She's questioning if what she's hearing is real or imagined. That's what she means by needing to find the truth." Her voice trembled. She dabbed at the tears pushing their way forward.

My God, what is *real?* She had tried to deny—brush off—her panic in getting home. Was this some sort of sixth sense? She shook her head.

"Devin, I'm terrified."

"We need help in finding her. She's vulnerable. We may need to get the police involved."

"Oh my God, no. They demoralized her. Told me right in front of her that she's crazy and needs a mental health evaluation."

"But they delivered. They brought her home."

"At a steep cost." Her sharp voice made him recoil. "She no longer trusts me. I won't call the police. You saw what she wrote in that note." She pointed at the piece of paper in his hand.

He read it again and tightened his lips. "You're right." He handed the note back to Mariah and eyed the journal she firmly held.

"You have no idea how guilty I feel reading this. She'd never forgive me. I can't share it." Star's words played over in her mind. She opened the journal and skimmed. "It's the forest." She then read, "'The forbidden area of my life. Why is Mom so afraid of beautiful, messy, natural things? My crows love coming here. Maybe they will help me find . . .'" Her voice cracked. She couldn't read this part out loud. She closed the journal and said, "She hears the cries of . . . of a little boy." Mariah trembled and couldn't contain the tears any longer. "Can Candice help?" Mariah asked. "She works with psychics. Maybe they can help without involving the police."

Devin had already pulled out his cell, and with one tap, she could hear it ringing. She held her breath. There was no answer. "Mom. Call me back. It's urgent." He rose to his feet and began pacing.

The sweat from Mariah's palm dampened Star's note. What if Candice didn't have her phone with her? Or what if the battery was dead because she'd forgotten to charge it, like Star often did?

Mariah joined him in pacing the room, but soon she fell onto the couch, alert and fatigued at the same time. Devin stopped pacing and sat next to her. His right leg bobbed up and down.

The feeling inside her head, airy and light, seemed no different from the sensation of consuming several glasses of chardonnay. She closed her eyes and noticed a steady erosion taking place. The crumbling of a partition.

She turned to Devin, experiencing herself in an intoxicated state, where filters had faded and the ever-present wall within her diminished. Clarity entered.

As easily as she could second-guess this clarity, she followed its promise. Because saying what she intended, however brief this moment of lucidness, made absolute sense.

"Devin." Her tone captured him. He turned to face her.

A million thoughts swirled in her head, including changing the subject. But she gave herself over to the part of her that knew, regardless of pain, she needed to move beyond the barrier that kept her separate from Star and from herself.

"I've not been honest. With you or Star. This is all my fault. It has to do with . . . my lack of courage." Her hand holding the journal began to shake. "I suffered a tremendous loss. And I tried to move on without telling the truth." She placed her hand on her rapidly beating heart. And breathed deeply. "A drunk driver killed Star's father." She shuddered, hearing the words spoken aloud. "Charlie. My husband. A musician. An amazing dad." She took another deep breath. "And . . . and . . . my son." Something caught in her throat. "Beautiful three-year-old Markus." She didn't try to stop the tears this time. "Star was only four months old."

Devin's arm wrapped around her. "My God, Mariah," he whispered.

Chapter 49

"After the accident, I could no longer set foot in our house. Charlie and Markus were gone. And yet, they were everywhere. A million agonizing reminders. The sticky countertop, the smell of shaving lotion. Closets and drawers full of clothing. My God, I stumbled over a sprawling Lego display in the middle of our living room. The entire place assaulted me with an empty presence. I had to leave."

The squeeze of Devin's hand brought her back to the couch.

"Star and I moved in with my mother. But I couldn't live with her, not for long. I took my baby and left." Her voice cracked. "I wanted Star to have a fresh start. I . . ." She shook her head. "She was just a baby. I . . . I somehow thought if I removed her from all the reminders of the past, maybe she could go forward without carrying the weight of living life as a trauma victim." Mariah swiped at her damp cheeks. Her body trembled. "It was a terrible, cruel mistake for me to assume it was possible."

The familiar scolding voice screamed out, *How could you be so selfish?* And then a prayer rose: *Please, God, forgive me.*

She turned to Devin. "I'm too late. Star knows she has a brother. She may believe this child she's after is her brother." Mariah stood up. "We need to look for her. I can't wait another minute." Stella began circling Mariah's legs. "Maybe Stella can help."

She rifled through the coat closet for the leash. Devin checked his phone and then tried calling his mother again. "Damn, where is she?" He shoved the phone in his pocket and grabbed his jacket.

Mariah left the door unlocked. Perhaps Star would come home and didn't have her key. Stella bounded ahead as they moved toward Devin's car. As he clicked open the doors, a green Land Rover came barreling down the driveway.

"It's Mom," Devin called out and ran to the driver's side. Mariah stood back, holding Stella's leash. She heard Devin asking about his call and saw Candice shake her head.

Mariah bent down, snapped Stella's leash on, and moved closer.

Devin turned in her direction and called out, "Mom needs to see Star's journal." She stared. *Candice wants to read Star's journal?* Stella began pulling, jumping up and down. The only clue to Star's whereabouts in her journal was the forest.

Candice got out of her car and approached. Mariah stood fixed. *Where are the psychics—hadn't Devin asked for this?* Candice knelt and massaged Stella behind her ears. When she stood up and met Mariah's eyes, Mariah suddenly had the sense that Candice knew her story. Maybe not the details, but the contours. The shape.

"You want to read Star's journal?"

"No," Candice said. "I only want to hold it."

Mariah turned to Devin. His eyes were wide.

Candice continued, "Trust me. Your daughter and I have a lot in common. The big difference being that she has a parent who supports her ways of being in this world." She turned to Devin. "Devin, my dear, I owe you a long-overdue frank conversation. Now is not the time." Candice sighed. "Mariah, sweetheart, blaming yourself will do no one any good." Candice turned back to Devin. "No parent is perfect. It's the nature of the job. We're all in school."

Was this Candice's attempt at a confession, or an apology, to Devin? But Mariah knew the words were directed at her too.

Candice turned back to Mariah. "Please, trust me. Allow me to hold Star's journal. I'm . . ." Her voice faltered. "I'm learning to trust myself with this. In fact, it took a fair amount of courage to follow whatever brought me here."

"Devin's phone call?" Mariah asked as she held out the journal.

"No. I forgot to charge my phone. I knew, somehow, to come here."

Candice wrapped her hands around the journal with a reverence, like a churchgoer choosing to take communion. She appeared to relax into an almost worshipful posture. The journal rested in her left hand while her right lifted, fingertips spread across the cover.

Mariah strained to keep her anxiety in check. All that mattered was to find Star. Find her safe.

Candice opened her eyes and confirmed, with an air of assuredness, what Mariah already knew—Star was in the forest looking for a three-year-old boy.

They piled into the Land Rover, Mariah taking the back seat with Stella. Candice drove with confidence, appearing to operate on a unique GPS signal. There were numerous access points to the forest.

When they pulled onto a narrow unmarked street that soon turned into a dirt road, Devin said, "This makes sense, it's the first turnout past Video Et Cetera. He at first didn't know he had a kid in the back seat." As Candice drove down the narrow path, Devin murmured, "Of course, who would look here. My God, I hope he's alive."

Mariah glanced upward and inwardly begged, *Please, dear God, help us find Star.*

The road dwindled to nothing more than a small footpath. Candice brought the Land Rover to a stop, and they all slid out. The sky was overcast now, and there was a chill in the air. Mariah's breath was visible. Her hands shook as she fumbled with her jacket zipper.

Stella had her head down, nose anchored to the ground, pulling Mariah toward the tangled trail. Devin was at her side. Mariah turned back to see Candice standing still, as if in a state of meditation. Then she stiffened and announced, "We need to hurry."

Stella lunged ahead on the leash, making small yipping sounds. Devin took Mariah's hand as they followed Stella.

Deeper into the forest, she heard Candice call out, "Let her go! Unleash her!"

Mariah unhooked the leash, and Stella veered off the barely discernible trail, plunging deep into the thicket. Within minutes, she was back, barking at Mariah to come and follow.

Mariah let go of Devin's hand and burst forward with unexpected energy. Devin's voice calling out faded behind her as she scrambled over fallen logs, limbs, and navigated dried creek beds. Small branches and bushes tore at her clothing, but she ripped herself free to keep up with the mutt, who crawled under and leapt over branches with ease. When she heard her daughter's wails, her pace doubled.

A dense tangle of underbrush, grasses, and red-berried elder shielded Star. She was hunched over, rocking back and forth, moaning and crying.

Mariah collapsed to the ground, where Stella lay pressed against Star's thigh. She wrapped her arms around Star. *Thank you, God.*

Cocooned to Star's chest, beneath her overcoat, were wisps of milky hair.

"Mom," she sobbed, gulping a lungful of air, "he's dying. I didn't come soon enough."

Mariah stood up and yelled to Devin, "Call 911!"

Chapter 50

Mariah crouched next to Star and placed her hand on the child's cheek. Cold. His eyes were closed. She moved her hand under his shirt, searching for a beating heart, and felt the rise and fall of his chest.

Unzipping her jacket, she said, "Star, sweetie, it's going to be fine. Sweetheart, you saved him." She wrapped her jacket around the small, quaking body.

Star sniffled, her breathing returning to normal. Cradling the child on her right side, Star reached her left hand over to touch Stella.

Mariah eased the bundle from Star's lap into hers. She had forgotten the faultless heft of a three-year-old. She touched the child's cool, damp forehead, clearing the loose cream-colored twists of hair from his remarkably small eyelashes. His resemblance to Markus was uncanny. An agonizing pain gripped her heart.

But the boy's skin was much too cold. Her jacket wrapped around him was insufficient. Her fingers went to work unbuttoning her flannel shirt. She unwrapped her coat from his trembling body.

"Star, take this!"

In one smooth motion, she untucked her undershirt, peeled off the child's thin damp outer jacket, and nestled him against her warm torso. The bite of his cold body faded with his moist breath upon her breast; her eyes prickled, and she blinked hard, resisting the urge to break out in sobs.

"Mom." Star inched over and placed a trembling hand upon the swell of the child tucked against Mariah's chest. They both watched the rise and fall of breath. "You saved him."

"Sweetheart, you found him."

"And you found me."

The shrill sound of sirens crushed the silence of the forest. For an instant she was transported into the past. These were the same sirens racing to save her son and husband before she even learned the futility of their attempt. She tightened her grip on the tender bundle and soothed herself with the warm puffs of his breath.

Devin appeared, ahead of a passel of medics. The sight of him and the medics brought her to her senses. She looked toward Star and saw Candice kneeling next to her and Stella, and her heart lifted.

"Ma'am." A young man in a navy-blue shirt strained to make eye contact. He held a blanket draped over his arm, ready to take the child. Behind him, another medic stood poised with a stethoscope. She didn't know how to let this child go—her baby.

Devin knelt beside her and touched her upper arm. "It's okay. He's going to make it." He moved in front of her.

Mariah shifted her hands under her shirt, resting her palms on the now warm, breathing body. A deep ache rose within her, and trembling began again.

Devin whispered, "Mariah. His name is Noah. He needs to go to the hospital to get help. His mother will be so happy to know he's alive."

Tenderly she eased the child from his warm perch to Devin's waiting arms. She planted a kiss upon his forehead and murmured, "Markus." Devin transferred the toddler to the medics.

Mariah, Star, and Stella rode in the back seat of the Land Rover, Star resting her head against Mariah's shoulder. Candice drove in silence while Devin responded to texts from news outlets, the clicking and beeping of returned communication creating a calming rhythm of its own. A mere five minutes and they returned to where they had started. A place that now seemed a lifetime away.

Candice parked next to Devin's Subaru. For a long moment no one moved. And then, Devin unlocked his seat belt and stepped out. He opened the back door on Star's side, and Stella tumbled to the ground ahead of Star.

Candice got out of the car just as Mariah exited her own door, bringing them face-to-face.

Unable to grasp the different ways Candice and Star navigated their worlds, Mariah had held this woman at bay, in a cocoon of judgment. Peering into Candice's eyes, Mariah felt exposed and supported. Her heart swelled.

"You understand my daughter."

"No more than you do." Candice gave a soft smile. "She's perfect."

Warm tears moistened Mariah's cheeks. An assuredness rose within. She opened her mouth to speak, but all she could do was nod.

Candice stepped forward, and Mariah held out her hands. As they clasped hands, a well of warmth flowed through them.

They turned from one another and met on the other side of the Rover, where Devin stood absorbed with his phone, and Star crouched down, murmuring to Stella.

Star sprang to attention as Candice approached. They looped arms and Candice called out, "We'll be back shortly."

Mariah caught the glow of a rising full moon hanging over the trees, set against the opaque blue of the darkened hills and soft indigo of the sky. It was five thirty, and the day waned.

Now she found the chill in the air refreshing, so she held the coat she had wrapped around the little boy, Noah, rather than putting it on. Devin tucked his phone into his pocket and looked up at her.

"Your mother is amazing," she said.

He smiled while gazing at the tree-lined horizon. "So different from the mother who raised me." He turned to her. "I'm liking the difference."

Mariah took his hand and gave it a squeeze. With each bracing breath of cold air, her senses became more alert, and she experienced herself starting anew. His smile, with its slant and folds, and the creases around his eyes, were just like his mother's.

His phone pinged with a text. He released Mariah's hand and pulled out his phone.

"Have they confirmed?" Mariah asked. "Is he the missing boy? Do his parents know?"

"Yes, it's Noah Millbury."

Relief washed over her. She murmured his name several times.

"His parents, as you can imagine . . ." He paused.

It had been only a few hours since she had shared losing her baby boy. Her body quaked.

"His parents are ecstatic." He nestled her hand in his. "Walls had no idea Noah was in the car. Until he did. So, he ditched him in the forest. Noah was alone for forty-eight hours. Star saved him." He brought her hand to his lips.

She nodded, chanting *Thank you, God.* Enduring the devastation of this child's death was unimaginable.

"He's distressed. Dehydrated. But he's going to survive." Devin brushed a loose strand of her hair away from her cheek and then kissed her. "Everyone wants to know who the young woman is that discovered and saved him." They both looked to the far corner of the yard, where Candice and Star were deep in conversation. Star perked up as though she had heard their conversation. She strode toward them. Devin and Mariah grinned at one another.

"Can we see him? I really want to see him again."

"Well," Devin said, "turns out I need to snag a few interviews at the hospital . . . and I'm certain reporters want to hear from you."

Candice had made her way to the Land Rover and was poised to get in.

"Mom," Devin said. Candice gave a soft smile. "Thank you."

Candice clasped her hands together and partially bowed.

"We're heading to the hospital to see Noah."

"Fabulous," Candice pronounced. "I have work waiting for me." She paused and met each of their eyes before proclaiming, "All is well!"

Mariah turned to Star. "Star, sweetie, are you sure you want to be part of this?"

"Of course! I'll just tell them the truth. I want to see him one last time. Can we, Mom?"

At the entrance to Boulder City Hospital, Devin reminded Star, "You don't need to talk to anyone—that's your choice. Say only what you want."

"No worries. I'm good at that."

"I'll join you both later," he said. He had caught sight of a news reporter just prior to entering.

Mariah hadn't stepped into a hospital since she and Charlie had taken baby Milly home for the first time. The gleaming fluorescent lights, big open spaces, elevators, signs, all were foreign and familiar at the same time.

Devin had told them where to go: third floor, west wing. When they reached the third floor, Star seemed to know the direction to take without scrutinizing the numbers and arrows on the wall. As they passed the nurses' station, a heavyset nurse greeted them with suspicion.

"Which room are you headed for?"

"Number 336."

"Are you family?"

"No—"

"Reporters and interested onlookers have swamped us. Until the family arrives, we're restricting visitors. Up ahead is a space where you can wait if you'd like." A few steps from the station was an alcove with chairs set up next to a cushioned bench. Several people looking official with cameras and lights milled around.

Mariah leaned in and whispered to Star, "This makes sense. It's only been thirty minutes since we left the forest."

"Mom, here they come."

Mariah turned to see a tall, awkward man moving at a fast clip, holding the hand of a woman who appeared to be in her late twenties with bleached-blond hair pulled back. Her makeup streaked by tears. An older version of the young woman, probably her mother, trailed behind. The reporters keyed in at once and followed. For a split second the young woman made eye contact with Star as they passed. Star's face was hard to read.

Mariah flashed to the forest, feeling the weight and innocence of Noah, his velvety breath upon her breast. *Markus.* She profoundly missed him. Her mouth was salty with tears. Her nails dug into the heels of her hands. She shifted closer to Star. She wrapped an arm around Star's shoulders and wished she could tuck the two of them into a corner far from this fray.

"Excuse me." A woman who looked to be about her age but half her weight, wearing heels and a fitted jacket, stood before them. "My name is Arielle. Are you the girl who found Noah?" she said to Star.

Star's face brightened and she nodded. Mariah wished Devin were with them; she would read his face and know what to say.

"I'm from KMCI. Would you mind if I asked you a few questions?"

"Will I be on TV?"

A young man with a video camera approached, trailed by another with lights.

"Yes. Everyone wants to know your story," the reporter said. She motioned to the cameraman. "Can you tell us your name?"

Mariah caught her breath.

"My name is Star, and sometimes I hear voices. This doesn't make me crazy. But . . . at times I feel confused. I heard Noah crying."

"You were in the forest close to where Noah was, and you heard him cry?"

Star shot Mariah a look that beckoned for understanding—Mariah nodded with encouragement.

"Sort of like that. When I first heard his voice, I thought no one would believe me—that was yesterday. I knew my mother would worry. I forgot to charge my cell phone, so I couldn't be in touch, so I decided instead to go home. But then this afternoon, I kept thinking about what I had heard, and I knew I had to find him."

"Why didn't you tell your mother about hearing him last night?"

Mariah's face burned red; she forced her eyes to stay fixed on Star, keeping the attention off herself.

"Well, I only *thought* I heard his voice. Sometimes I hear things that other people don't, so I wasn't sure. And besides, I skipped school, and my mom was upset."

"But you followed the voice you heard, and you found Noah."

"Yes! I knew I needed to follow his voice. I'd like to see him one more time."

When the reporter began to ask another question, Star interrupted with Devin's advice.

"That's all I have to say."

The reporter turned to Mariah with a look of incredulity. Mariah shook her head and glanced away. She wouldn't speak for Star.

Mariah imagined Gretchen and Tilly watching Star validated on TV for hearing voices. And then she pictured herself championing the rights and understanding of those who heard voices that most people either could not or refused to tune in to.

Once the reporter and her entourage left, Mariah reached for Star's hand and detected a fresh layer of closeness. Perhaps a whisper of what was to come. Star leaned her head on Mariah's shoulder.

They sat that way for several minutes, and then Noah's mother appeared. She seemed fragile; a sneeze would erase her. Mariah held back from jumping up and asking, *Are you okay? Is there anything I can do for you? Your baby boy is beautiful. So soft. I had a three-year-old too.*

The woman zeroed in on Star, who stood up. "You are the one who heard my son crying," she said, and Star nodded. "You saved his life." Tears began streaming down her face. "Is there any way, anything I can do in return?"

"I'd really like to see him one more time."

"Yes, of course, come with me." She motioned down the hall and then turned to Mariah. "Your daughter is amazing. I just saw her on the news."

Mariah smiled and stood up to join them. Noah's mother led them into the room where a little body lay hooked up to a variety of tubing, including an IV for hydration. Star made her way to the three-year-old. Mariah held back, as did his mother.

Star smiled at the child. "Hi, Noah. My name is Star." She reached over and touched the IV. "Wow, looks like you are receiving superpowers through these tubes. Can you feel them?"

Noah nodded and called out, "Vitaminsss!"

"Vitamins," his mother confirmed. "That's what I told him. Liquid vitamins to make him strong."

Mariah clung to the wall next to the bed. This child was different from the one she had held and not wanted to release. This was a little boy with parents waiting to bring him home.

Star took the boy's small hand and mimicked a handshake. "So glad to meet you, Noah. You have a wonderful voice, and I'm happy to have heard you."

Chapter 51

Mariah, Star, and Devin reveled in watching the news clip, all of ten seconds, with Star explaining that hearing voices didn't make her crazy. They ordered a pizza, but by the time it arrived, Devin was pacing about, eager to get to work on his column. He devoured a slice while standing in the kitchen and left with a promise to call in the morning.

Star ate several slices as she fretted over getting in touch with Jen. "She must be out of her mind trying to reach me."

"You can use my phone," Mariah said.

"You know her number?"

"When I was in a state of panic, I called Trudi, and Trudi asked her to call me," Mariah said as she handed her phone over.

When Mariah added that she could use it tomorrow as well, Star stood up and wrapped her arms around her mother. Mariah's heart lifted, even with one sealed chamber that still sought forgiveness.

"I promise I'll go to the police station tomorrow to get your phone and computer," she said. She also gave Star a free pass for another day at home. After all, her grades were good.

While Star was in her room talking with Jen, Mariah poured herself a second glass of wine. Within several sips she felt warm and indistinct at the edges, allowing her to ease into dwelling on the staggering amazement of the day. She allowed the cacophony of feelings to rise and inhabit her evening. A flood of appreciation washed over her for the ways miraculous events had drawn her closer to Star, Devin, Candice, and her dear Markus.

The landline rang. It was Olivia. Thank goodness her mother had never adjusted to the cell phone. Olivia was due to arrive at two o'clock, Wednesday, the day before Thanksgiving.

Mariah ached to share, with someone who had known her from her earliest beginnings, what had transpired in the past two days. But it was too much to get into over the phone, and the chasm between Mariah and her mother was too wide.

"I'm so glad you're coming," Mariah said. "I miss you."

A long pause followed and then, the sound of Olivia sniffling.

"I miss you too."

She saw Olivia alone in the small three-bedroom Craftsman. Her mother, now a grandmother with a single grandchild, a teenager, who didn't know the name of her father or her brother. This controlling mother of hers had remained on the sidelines longing to be invited in. Why had she shut her mother out all these years?

The day flashed before her as a cartoon flip-book. Beginning with terror, ending with promise.

Mariah took a deep breath and asked the question Olivia had waited years to hear.

"Can you bring pictures?" The lengthy silence prompted her to wonder if her mother had heard her.

"Pictures?" Olivia said. "Really?"

"Yes. Not only the ones you keep on the mantel, but all of them. We have a lot of catching up to do."

"Are you sure? I mean, this is what I want, but, sweetcakes, are you ready?" It had been decades since Mariah had heard this pet name—catapulting her back to the needy ten-year-old in her Sunday school dress traipsing after her mother. Emotion swelled within her.

"It's . . . I may have waited too long, but I'm ready, and so is Star."

A lump formed in her throat at the sound of Olivia's sobs. Mariah squeezed her eyes to lose the haunting image of her mother cradling a distraught, screaming Milly, while coaxing Mariah, huddled under her quilt, to wake from the insidious fog that had enveloped her. She would have lost her daughter had Olivia not been there.

Her mother had tried her best within the framework of a rigid belief system. Mariah had pushed into the unknown in adulthood, rejecting the God of her childhood. A God that, in desperate times, she continued to court.

After the phone call, Olivia's question returned: "Are you ready?" She flashed on Trudi, proclaiming the necessity of telling one's story. The terrifying heaviness that had lodged in her chest while her arms wrapped around the shivering child, no older than Markus.

Mariah swallowed a large swig of wine and considered topping it off. She stood up, went to the kitchen, and poured the remaining half glass down the drain. *Am I ready?*

She went to her bedroom, peered at the upper corner of her closet. Her body quaked. But no, now was not the time to visit the raw remnants of cherished items. It was, however, time to take the next step.

She walked to Star's bedroom and knocked. Star lay propped up in bed, writing in her journal, with Stella nestled against her hip. Once Star put her pen down and made eye contact, Mariah moved from the doorway and slid onto the opposite side of the bed from Stella. A cool breeze billowed in from Star's cracked window, creating a cloudlike formation with the chiffon curtains.

"After today, I imagine you have a lot to catch up on."

Star nodded, closed the journal, and held it to her chest. "This is my most important journal ever. I've named it My Journal of Hidden Truths."

A shiver rippled down Mariah's back. "That's an interesting title."

"It's been my life."

A sharp, stabbing pain entered Mariah's upper chest, followed by a familiar leaden weight at the pit of her stomach—the stirring of shame.

"I'm so sorry . . . ," Mariah said. "I sense you know . . . the hidden truth I've kept from you."

"Mom, I'm finally understanding why."

"Why . . . ?"

"Why I can know things that are hidden. Dr. Quinn helped me to understand," Star said. "She's like me, and her parents didn't understand."

"The same way I've struggled to understand." Mariah recalled Candice linking arms with Star and walking over to the tall cedar.

"No, Mom. She said she wished her parents were more like you. Her parents made me think of Mr. Haze. He had already made his mind up about what's real and what isn't—without even reading David Bohm."

"I'm only beginning to grasp . . . Star, you are so very special, and it's not been easy—"

"Did you know that Dr. Quinn works with psychics?"

"Yes, Devin told me. I can see how she is like you. I somehow knew she could help find you—"

"Mom, don't you get it? You knew Dr. Quinn not only worked with psychics but *was* a psychic! That's why you let her hold my journal."

"And that's how she knew where to take us," Mariah said. She flashed back to Candice tearing up after the dinner at her house, revealing knowledge of the devastation Mariah had suffered. "You're right, Star. I sort of knew but didn't."

"Remember those six shattered test tubes? I told Dr. Quinn about them because it made me think I was crazy. She told me about something I had never heard of—psychokinesis."

"What's that?"

Star grinned. Shifted herself up to a full sitting position. "It's a form of mental energy that can cause physical objects to move."

Mariah thought of the dish that had fallen as Star walked by, just prior to starting junior high.

"She said it's not all that unusual for a sensitive teenager like me to lose control of their energy."

"That's interesting." Choosing not to say *That's nonsense.*

Star gazed up at her ceiling, as if trying to recall more of the conversation. "Dr. Quinn was impressed I could hear Noah's voice."

Mariah nodded. "So am I." But her mind wrestled with these new concepts.

Star looked at her. "I know you know why I heard his voice and needed to follow it."

Mariah's hands shook. She grasped her thighs. "You were looking for Markus."

"That's my brother's name?"

Mariah nodded.

"Why didn't you tell me?" Star peered into Mariah's eyes with an intensity that almost made her come undone.

"You were only a baby when he left us. There was no way to explain then. Later, I was so afraid of upsetting you. Foolishly I thought I could carry the pain for both of us. It was a terrible mistake. I'm so sorry."

"I asked you about him."

She moved her head up and down and whispered, "I had buried him."

"Without saying goodbye."

A piercing pain cut through Mariah. Star was right; it had been a superficial goodbye at a church she no longer accepted.

"Meeting Noah . . . I, I . . ." The memory of Markus's delicate body molded against her chest and shoulder choked her response. She grabbed a tissue.

Star lay down with shoulders and head propped up by her pillow. She turned toward Mariah and patted her arm.

"Mom, he wanted you to see him. To not keep him secret."

"Star," Mariah started, and wiped a tear from the corner of her eye. "You finding Noah, saving his life . . . you brought me back to Markus. Oh my goodness. Sweetie. He, he was three when he left us. He loved having a baby sister—you were only four months old. And yet, you knew."

They met one another's eyes, and Mariah recalled with splintering tenderness those predawn mornings when she had swaddled her shrieking daughter, drawing upon an unexpected calm within, bringing forth one song after another, settling her colicky child.

"Mom," Star said. "He found me. In my dreams. But he wanted you." Star repositioned herself and rested her head in the crook of Mariah's shoulder. "What about my father?"

Mariah pulled out another tissue to catch the tears streaming down her cheek.

"His name was Charlie. He was a wonderful man. When you were just a baby . . ." Her throat constricted. *I can do this.* Star needs to know.

Star sat up and placed her hand on Mariah's arm. Mariah touched Star lightly and faced her.

"He was a good father. And a musician. We both wanted a daughter so bad. He was over the top when you were born." She trembled, reached out, and ran her fingers through Star's hair.

"You have his hair color, beautiful, thick chestnut brown. You also have his height—tall and slender." She took a deep breath. "I have pictures to show you. But not now. I promise I'll share them all. And Grandma's coming for Thanksgiving—she'll bring more pictures."

"Mom," Star said. "Tell me what happened."

Nausea roiled within Mariah. She regretted having had the pizza and the wine. She covered her mouth and dashed to bathroom.

When she returned, her face moist from a cold washcloth and the drenching of tears, she sat on the edge of the bed, steadied herself, and looked directly into Star's eyes. She told Star everything she knew about the accident; the four-way stop, the drunk driver, the truck traveling too fast.

"Hiding the truth about your father and brother was wrong. I hope someday you can forgive me." Mariah exhaled and the dense tension inside loosened. "Sweetheart, you are the center of my life. I promise to do my best to be honest with you. I sincerely hope this is your last journal of hidden truths."

"Me too."

Mariah glanced up at the solar system pinned to Star's ceiling. "I'm remembering something Candice said. A quote from Einstein. She told me he may have been right when he said that the most important decision one can make is whether the universe is a friendly place."

With her head against her pillow, Star stared upward.

"I have no idea why I'm recalling that now."

Star turned toward her. "Maybe because you've made your decision."

Star held her gaze, and as she began to smile, Mariah's own mouth and heart responded in kind. They wrapped their arms around each other. Tears drenched Mariah's face.

Holding Star tight, she heard her daughter murmur, "I love you, Mom."

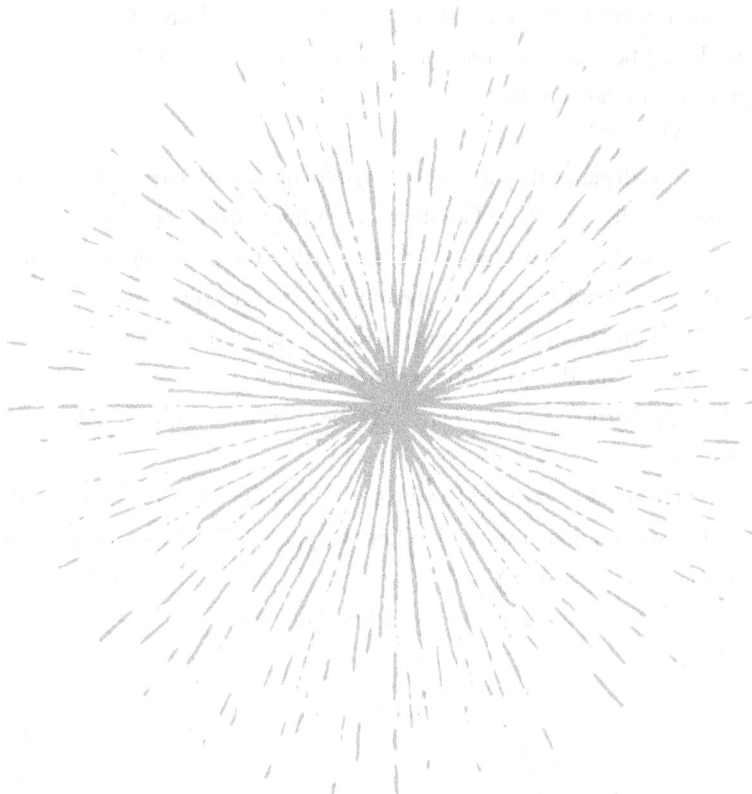

Epilogue

Journal of New Hope
June 6, 2022

In less than two weeks, I'll be Dr. Mildred Palmer. This is what I've wanted my entire life. A few friends have made a big deal of me getting my PhD at age 23. The truth is, this graduation would not be happening, at least at my age, and at this university, were it not for a set of events that took place when I was 13 years old. Once Mom let go of the reins and allowed me to move through junior and high school online, the school part was easy.

When I made this realization, I decided to revisit my journal from that year—the most intense school year of my life—at Aspen Creek Junior High. I've written in journals forever but never go back and read them. I made an exception, though, because if Mom had continued to hide her past, I wouldn't be here today. In honor of Mom's bravery, I opened the cork-bound journal she gave me for my thirteenth birthday, right when I started seventh grade. Such a crazy time. Jeffrey knew it would be rough; his soul greeted me the first day of school.

Back then, I called myself Star. After the big "breakthrough" with Mom, Grandma visited and revealed who had named me and who I was named after.

I was sitting at the kitchen table, excited for Devin and Candice to arrive. As Mom chopped carrots and Grandma peeled potatoes, Grandma looked at me, cocked her head, and said, "I think Mildred is a beautiful name." I replied, "Ugh." Mom, who, back then, never shared anything that might have been upsetting, hadn't told me they named me after my father's sister who had died of brain cancer at 16.

Grandma gave Mom "the look" when she realized Mom hadn't told me. The same one Mom had given me many times over—her eyes narrowed, and their razor-sharp focus diced the atmosphere. Mom stopped chopping carrots. She grabbed the damp hand towel and wadded it up, as if she were drying her hands, and pulled up a chair next to me. I looked away, wanting to get back to anticipating a Thanksgiving with more than just Mom, me, and takeout.

And then I remembered. She was different now. I turned to this new version of Mom who shares her life. She told me how important Mildred had been to my dad, how she tried calling me Milly, but Dad loved the name Mildred. She said that Mildred means "gentle strength," and this meant a lot to my dad. By the time she finished, I liked the name Mildred. It was a name as unique as Star. Except my father had chosen the name for me. As soon as I chose this name for myself, warmth brushed across my upper neck with the lightness of breath. I felt my father's closeness.

That morning, alone with Mom and Grandma, I also found out my brother's full name, Markus *Henry* Palmer. When I saw his picture, I recognized him at once. It was like meeting someone from your faraway past who looks different, but familiar.

That Thanksgiving was the first one I remember feeling thankful. I had at last learned the truth about my brother and father. Henry, Markus's middle name, was my father's favorite uncle, who gave him his first guitar. I love knowing this because now I have an 8-year-old brother named Henry. Mom and Devin chose the name. He has my curly, untamed hair. And Devin's big blue eyes and wiry body. I got to pick his middle name. I chose Jeffrey. Even though Stella is so dear to me, Jeffrey was my first love. He was a dog with amazing intuition, devotion, and totally comforting.

Anyway, reading My Journal of Hidden Truths made me realize just how confused I had been. I knew my brother was lost because he kept showing up in my dreams. I half thought the lost child I found in the forest was my brother. I wanted to connect with Markus so desperately. And I felt lost too. Mom was the one who needed to find him. She had stepped out of his life. Grandma coming with a stack of pictures and Mom opening the mystery box buried in her closet made it possible for Markus to be seen. Since then, he no longer visits me in dreams.

I now understand better why my mom kept her past to herself for so long. It's why I waited ten years to look at this journal. And I get it. She wanted me to go forward without carrying the burden of a tragic past. How could she have known that I'm a person who sees beyond the visible? Secrets poison me. Even well-intended ones.

Even so, it was painful revisiting seventh grade. I'm so relieved to be done with that chapter of my life. As soon as I started reading and reliving the anguish, I remembered what Trudi at UUCB had shared that year. Telling and retelling a story is how we heal. Most important—I never want to be sealed off from the pain of the past. It only intensifies.

So here I am, putting this in writing. I hated that year of seventh grade. But Mom reconnected with Devin, and Candice and I grew closer. She saw me as special, not crazy. She also helped me get into UCLA. And I now have a brother—Henry Jeffrey—who loves dogs. Stella is close to 15 years old, and Henry takes such good care of her I don't feel quite so bad being away. They all, including Stella, show up at Grandma's once a month to visit me.

Reading the journal also made me realize the importance of having a close friend. I called Jen as soon as I finished reading because she's still the one who I can tell anything to. Everyone needs at least one Jen in their lives. I used to think crows, dogs, and books like *The Holographic Universe* would suffice. But then Mom made me go to this cool church that made it clear everyone is okay as they are regardless of what they believe.

Jen just started her first year of a master's program in social work. She lives in Seattle, which is not too far away. She plans to be a therapist specializing in transgender issues. I know she'll be great. She's coming to my graduation, and I can hardly wait.

Reading the journal made me ache. It reminded me that even now, any sense I have of incompleteness is an illusion. The fact that I can know the end even before it happens—when I trust myself—confirms my deepest philosophical convictions, aligned with David Bohm's: there is an implicit wholeness to the universe.

This is further confirmed by the brokenness Mom and I experienced when separating ourselves from our past. I want to go forward with my eyes wide open in both directions. Past and future. In the end, I know they come together as one unbroken whole.

Acknowledgements

Writing a novel is a long, lonely experience. I am deeply grateful to the on-going support of my editor, Erin Cusick. From the earliest draft, she saw the promise of a successful story and inspired me to continue. As the years passed and I completed multiple revisions, Erin's support never wavered.

Erin introduced me to Jennifer Hager whose expertise lay in the arc of character development and themes. Her excitement about the manuscript and detailed feedback re-ignited my enthusiasm building my capacity to deeply revise yet again.

Many, many, thanks to my writing partners Dorothy Van Soest and Roger Roffman who listened to multiple iterations of scenes and chapters and always responded gently, with honesty and precision. Thank you for continuing to urge me forward while providing new ideas and inspiration.

Early in the developmental process, a group of trusted friends took time away from their obligations to read a draft of *The Journal of Hidden Truths.* Thank you, Janet Brinkman, Becky Jasper, Sue Lerner, Kay Beisse, and Lina Morrison. I am grateful for your feedback. I also want to acknowledge some specialized editing from my good friend Brooke Griener.

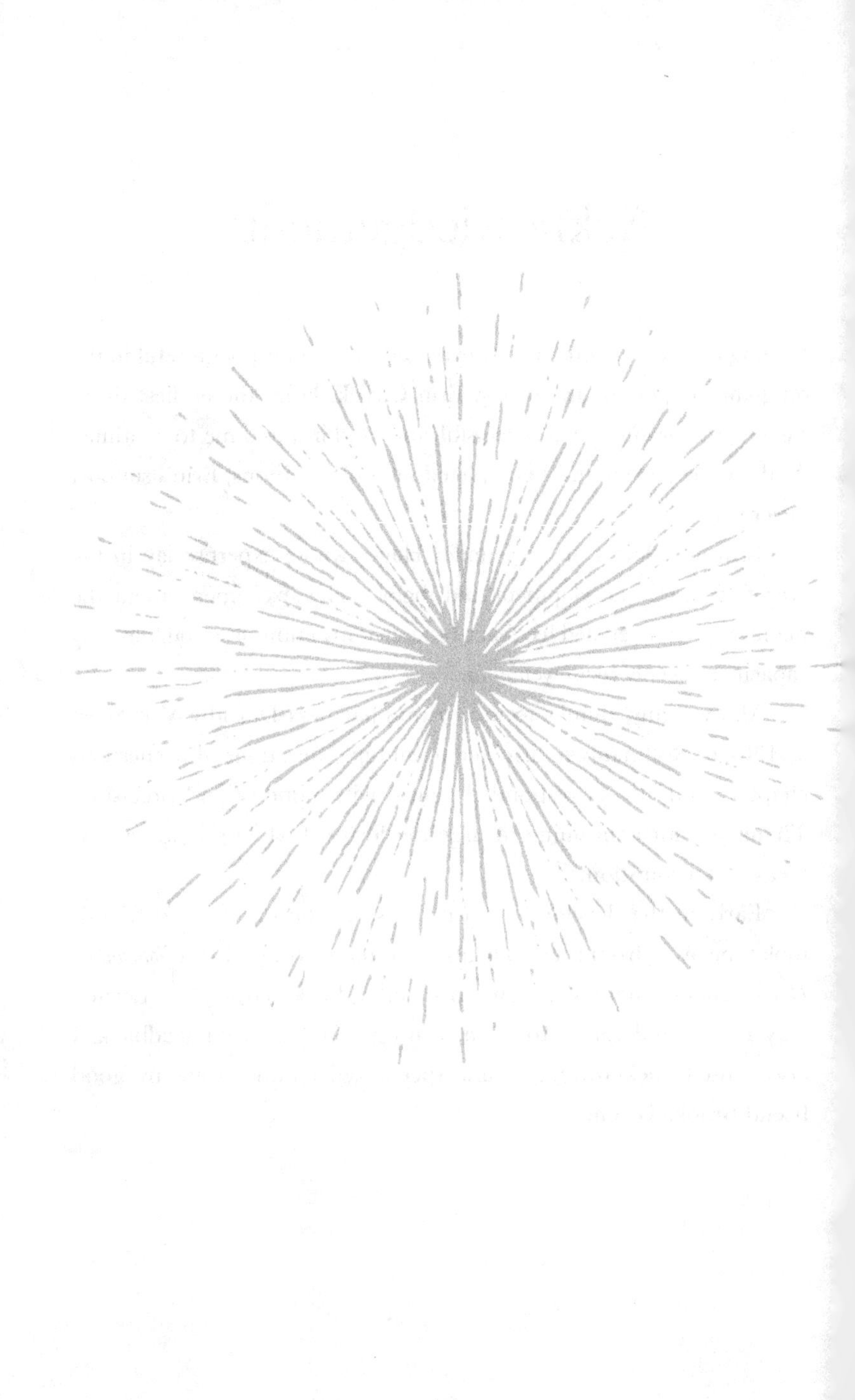

Questions and Topics for Discussion

1. What do you regard as the primary theme(s) in The Journal of Hidden Truths?
2. Which characters did you find most compelling? Who and why?
3. How would you advise Mariah to address her dilemma about when to tell Star about her brother and father's death? Given Star's apparent sensitivity, would you wait as long as Mariah did?
4. Dreams are important to Star. Have you ever experienced a dream that stood out as especially meaningful? Did the dream inspire action?
5. What do you think about the possibility that highly sensitive, reactive, emotional children (and adults) may be more sensitive to energy patterns? Have you experienced another person's energy?
6. Have you ever experienced what Star would call 'synchronicity'? If so, how do you conceptualize it?
7. Do you believe in psychic phenomena? Have your beliefs changed over time? If so, why?
8. What influences on Candice would you credit in shifting her perspective from a materialist viewpoint to a spiritual perspective? Did you find her changes credible?
9. How have your perspectives on spirituality or religion changed over time? Do you have safe places to share your thoughts and beliefs?
10. Why do you think Einstein's quote, shared by Candice, surfaces in the last page of the novel?

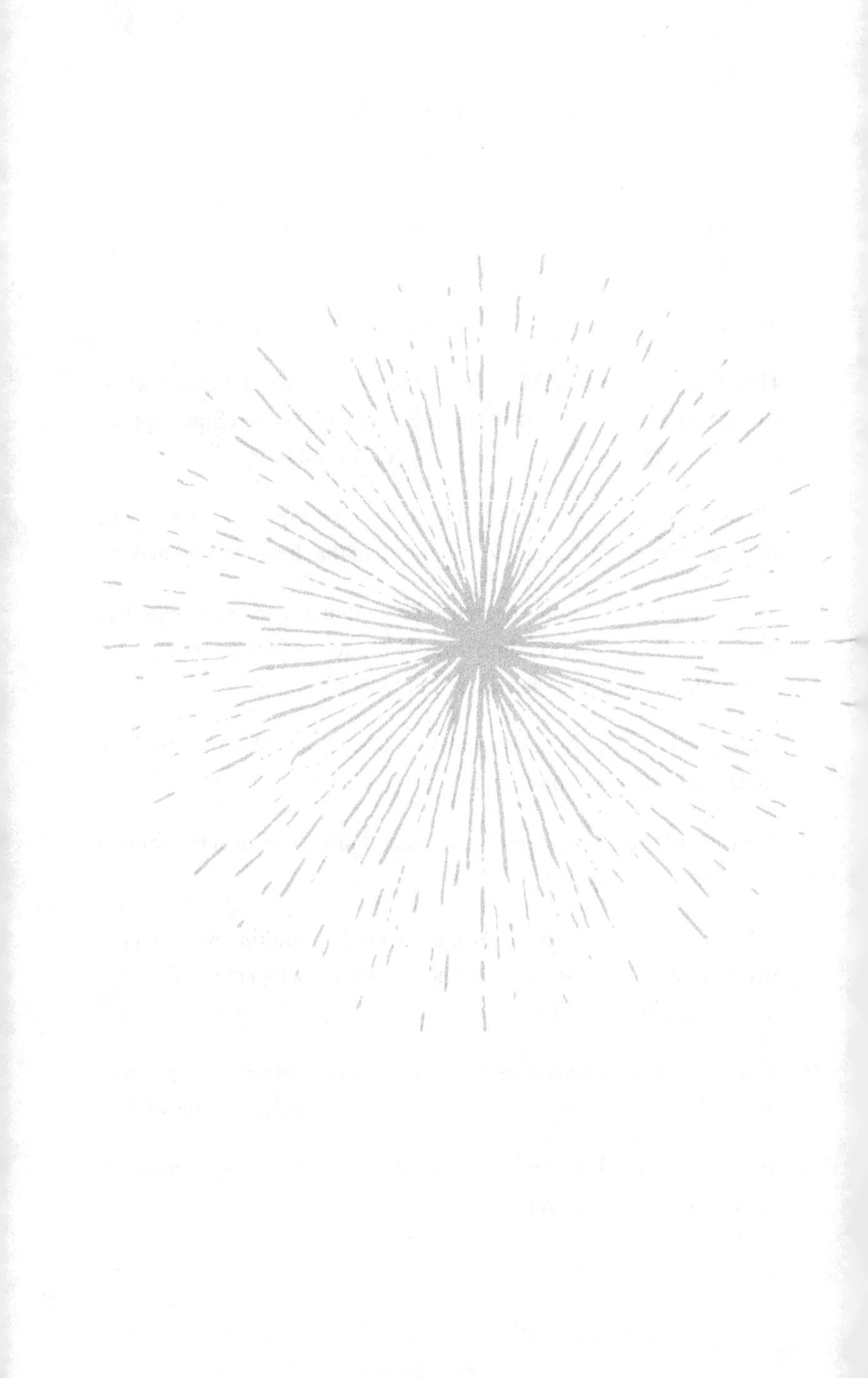

Made in United States
Troutdale, OR
11/14/2023